Wingmann

Wingmann

Denny Anderson

WINGMANN

iUniverse books may be ordered through booksellers or by contacting:

iUniverse
1663 Liberty Drive
Bloomington, IN 47403
www.iuniverse.com
844-349-9409

Because of the dynamic nature of the Internet, any web addresses or links contained in this book may have changed since publication and may no longer be valid. The views expressed in this work are solely those of the author and do not necessarily reflect the views of the publisher, and the publisher hereby disclaims any responsibility for them.

Any people depicted in stock imagery provided by Getty Images are models, and such images are being used for illustrative purposes only.
Certain stock imagery © Getty Images.

ISBN: 978-1-6632-1732-5 (sc)
ISBN: 978-1-6632-1731-8 (e)

Library of Congress Control Number: 2022906061

Print information available on the last page.

iUniverse rev. date: 03/31/2022

Prologue

In February 1985, the snow pounded Hackamore, Montana, like it did every winter. The small rural town was nestled between two mountain ranges and was built along a river that was fed its icy waters from Canada. The residents were prepared and hunkered down in their houses with woodburning stoves and plenty of supplies to last for the next few weeks.

Those who had cattle or crops had unloaded them before the frost even covered the ground, and their only chores were preparing for next year and finishing the never-ending "honey do" lists that went ignored throughout the productive season. The rest of the town operated in a business-as-usual fashion as long as they could drive on the icy, snow-packed roads. The city snowplows ran constantly, trying to keep up with the onslaught to little avail. It had been like this for the last few weeks, the town operating on the good days and shut down when the cold and snow overtook the city's best efforts. The county did its best to keep the two-lane highway open so that small town wouldn't be isolated, but their efforts in this storm were futile.

Soon one of the town's old power poles could no longer stand up to the snow, the wind, and the cold, and the weight of the snow-covered wires snapped it in two. When it went down, it took four of its companions with it, and the town of Hackamore went dark.

The blackout lasted for ten days. During that time, the residents of Hackamore had little to do, being confined to their houses. Neither the city nor any of the businesses had opened up during that time, leaving the residents to rely on their own resources for food, warmth, and entertainment.

Nine months later, the largest baby boom that the Hackamore hospital had ever seen began. Fourteen babies in all were delivered in less than six days toward the end of October. The small hospital was overwhelmed with all the activity, but they endured, sending all fourteen out the door with smiling parents.

Brandy "Dusty" Mann and Justin Walker were born on the same day, less than an hour apart; they grew up more as siblings than anything else. They were always together, roaming the small town, inseparable. Even when one or the other was in trouble, they would be either getting into to it or helping the other get out of it.

Dusty had more than a little to drink after one heartbreaking home football game and found herself walking back to her house after she had gotten her brand-new Camaro stuck in a hay field. One opportunistic would-be suitor had offered to pull her out or give her a ride to the local motel where she could show him her gratitude for being so gallant. Dusty wasn't feeling like a roll in the sheets, and after he made many attempts to sway her, he abruptly left, leaving her with no options. The year was 2002, and cell phones were starting to be all the rage, but her father had told her that if she had wanted one, she was going to have to pay for it herself. Dusty did not like the idea of having to spend her own money on such a lavish accessory that she really didn't need to have. Besides, she preferred the personal touch.

The moon was casting some light on the old asphalt road as she ambled along, slowly sobering up. The words coming out of her mouth were not pleasant as she cursed the boy that had left her stranded to walk alone. She looked down, and her hopes sunk as the world behind her started to cast a light on her and she could clearly see her shadow starting to form.

Damn it, she thought. *My dad is going to kill me for staying out all night.*

She had lost track of time and had just noticed the sun starting to rise when she paused and heard a sound—not the sunrise; that would be stupid. No, this was a vehicle also making its way down the road. She smiled broadly; she knew that motor. It was Justin in his '88 Chevy pickup. She straightened her hair, put one leg out and gave him her best impression of a lowly hitchhiker asking, not begging, for a ride.

The truck slowed but then revved up and blew past her.

"Dumbass!" she yelled at the taillights.

The brake lights lit up, and then the reverse lights came on.

"I am going to kill you," Dusty told Justin when she hopped in the cab.

"Rough night?" he asked her.

"Got stuck. Everyone left, so here I am."

"Wow, everyone?"

"Well, everyone except Jason, the douchebag."

"Oh?"

"Yeah, he offered me a ride—you know … grass, cash, or ass?"

"You don't have any money?"

"He didn't want money."

"Gotcha."

"How you doing? That was a hell of a game."

"Yeah, it was."

"Don't feel so bad; you had a great game."

"I know," he replied glumly.

"What the hell is wrong with you?" Dusty asked impatiently.

"I, um, well … it's really nothing."

"Struck out with Suzie Green again?"

"Yup."

"I don't know why you keep going after her. She has always told you she never thought of you as anything but a friend."

"I know, but aren't you supposed to marry your best friend?"

"Give it a rest, cowboy. She is more concerned about getting into college. She probably doesn't want to start something that won't last long."

"Why wouldn't it last long?"

"Because she is going to go to college somewhere out of state. She's really smart, so I am guessing an Ivy League school."

"I could move to wherever she is going."

"If you did, you would be an idiot."

"What? Why?"

"Just stop. Any who, can I spend the night at your place? I reek of alcohol, and I am sure Mr. Bank President wouldn't approve."

"Sure thing," Justin said as he pulled into his driveway, and he and Dusty headed up to his room.

They didn't spend too much time together after that, as Dusty, too, was trying to get into college. After they graduated high school, Dusty went off to college and Justin settled down with a girl from a nearby town.

Chapter

One

The Walker ranch sat nestled in a valley were they raised Black Angus beef and a few Holsteins for milk. They also farmed part of their property for hay, corn, and soybeans. There were a few rolling hills on the western side of the property, a river that passed through the northern edge, and a couple of small ponds that Justin and his dad had stocked with fish. The ranch boasted almost fifteen hundred acres that also included a small forest on the far eastern side, which Justin and his friends frequented for hunting. Justin and his family, with the help of team of seasonal workers, worked the ranch diligently each year and made a somewhat-better-than-modest living doing it. Justin's mom, Doreen, had been very careful with the family's business expenses and was the main reason for the successes they had each year. When down times had come, she had prepared for that, and with occasional help from the local bank they never had to suffer through the lean times.

Doreen kept chickens and a couple of pigs to go in the freezer along with deer, fish, squirrels, and whatever Justin brough back from his hunting or fishing expeditions. Her garden and small orchard were meticulously kept and always produced enough to feed her and some less fortunate families throughout the year.

Justin Walker sat on his horse he had playfully named "Dusty" as they were perched on a small knoll overlooking his family's ranch. He watched thoughtfully; some deer had wandered onto their piece of dirt and were foraging for food. There was a pile of apples he had left for them to help get them through the winter. He loved hunting deer but would never hunt them near his property, because his mom loved watching them as they ventured over to the pile that gathered under the apple tree his dad had planted near their back porch.

His dad had planted that tree right after they bought the property, and when he was alive the three of them would sit out there for hours, drinking coffee or cocoa and snapping pictures. His mom would keep an album of the deer and would name each one and keep track of their progress from youth to adulthood.

The sound of hooves padding the snow and dirt made both his horse and him twitch their ears. Justin patted her neck reassuringly.

"Easy, Dusty," he said without turning to see who was approaching.

"She's all right," came the voice behind him.

"I was talking to you," he said sarcastically.

Brandy "Dusty" Mann pulled her horse up beside him.

Brandy's five-foot-seven, 136-pound frame sat adeptly on her steed. She was beautiful, with dirty blonde hair, big blue eyes, and a smile that kept the boys coming around. She was wearing a straw hat, a blue plaid shirt, light brown leather gloves, Wrangler blue jeans, and brown cowgirl boots that rounded out her ensemble quite perfectly for the occasion.

"I hate that you named that horse after me," she said after quietly taking in the view for a minute.

He grinned and shrugged.

"Her name is Dusty; yours is Brandy."

"I go by Dusty; you know that, and you knew it when you named her, ass."

He shrugged again and fell back into watching the deer.

"You okay?" she asked him.

He fought hard to hold back a tear, but the cold weather attacking his eyes help one slip out. He didn't move to wipe it away as it slid down his cheek and landed on his gloved hand.

"I will be," he replied when he composed himself.

"She's a bitch."

He shook his head slowly.

"She is just confused."

"No, dude, she is a royal bitch to just up and leave with no explanation."

The deer had caught their scent or had heard their talking and started looking around nervously. They took stock of what was happening and decided the better part of valor was to seek shelter and work out the details later. As if one of them had given the word, they all took off in the way they had come.

Justin was contemplating Dusty's words as he let them roll around in his head for a minute. He shrugged and replied, "she did say she had to go find herself."

"That's girl talk for 'Screw you, I am done.'" Dusty fired back.

"Really?" Justin asked as he slightly twitched.

"Or it could mean 'I found someone else,' or 'I want someone else,' or 'I have some wild oats to sow,' or even 'I just want to be single,'" Dusty replied in a softer voice, seeing her friend's pain.

Justin sat in silence, processing her words. Dusty reached out and grabbed his forearm.

"Come on; let's get some coffee. It's hella cold out here."

He cast a sideways glance at her.

"Okay, okay, I will get a coffee and you can get a hot cocoa," she said sarcastically as she rolled her eyes, trying to make light of the situation.

They turned their steeds around and headed to the barn. They rode in silence as the made their way back just listening to snow crunching under the hooves and watching clouds of steam from four noses and mouths.

They reached the barn in silence and dismounted.

"You know what I can't understand?" Dusty asked as she pulled the saddle off of her horse.

"No telling," Justin groaned.

"No, I am serious."

"Okay, what?"

"Why now? Was there a catalyst?"

"A what?"

"Catalyst. It means—"

"I know what a catalyst is," he said as he cut her off. "I just don't know what you mean."

"I mean, was there anything that happened? Did she meet someone new? Did she reconnect with an old flame? Were there any issues you two were having?"

Justin pulled his saddle off, put it in its place, and then led his horse over to its stall and locked it in. He did the same with Dusty's horse as she leaned against her borrowed saddle on its cradle.

"Issues? You mean, like, were we fighting a lot?" he asked, returning to the conversation.

"I didn't mean it like that; I was just wondering what happened to make her leave."

"That makes two of us, and if I ever find out, you will be the first to know. She just said—"

Dusty cut him off. "I know, she just had to find herself."

Two

T he red 2002 Camaro Z28 with white racing stripes on the hood came to life as Dusty turned the key.

"You sure you don't want to drive?" she asked Justin as he pulled off his Stetson and sat awkwardly in the car.

"Naw, I am good," he said as he buckled in.

"If we took your truck, you could wear your hat."

He shook his head and looked out the window. Justin was tearing up again but was careful not to show it.

They rumbled down the long driveway and headed toward the old road that passed in front of the Walkers' ranch. She looked in her rearview mirror and saw Doreen Walker peeking out the window with a look of concern and relief on her face.

"Your mom is watching us; does she need something?" Dusty asked Justin as she saw the elderly woman peeking through the curtains.

He shook his head. "No, she has been worried about me. I think she is glad you are here."

"Of course, I am always happy to help."

"You think this coffee run is going to help?"

"Coffee does solve a lot of problems," Dusty said with a large smile.

He shook his head.

"Besides, Suzie Ferguson is working, and I hear she is now recovered from her divorce," Dusty added.

"I will pass."

"Why? She is a little cutie."

"I am still not over Joleen."

"Fuck that bitch," she replied as she put the petal to the metal and hit the speed limit quickly.

Justin looked at her in surprise. He had heard Dusty curse before, but not like this. He could tell she was pissed but wasn't sure why. He was the one hurting; this didn't happen to her. Dusty always did have trouble keeping a man, but not finding one. Her tall five-foot-seven-inch frame with dirty blonde hair and very curvy attributes made her a target for many men to chase. She was not only very beautiful outside, but she had a heart of gold. She was one of those women you could always count on if you needed someone to help you out. Justin could never figure out why she was always single; she had told him in the barn that over the last five years she hadn't had a relationship that lasted over six months, and before that only one that had lasted over a year.

Dusty turned up the volume on her radio, but Justin quickly reached over and turned it off. She looked at him but only shrugged and turned her attention back to the road.

The Camaro pulled up into the parking spot directly in front of the coffee shop's door. They exited the car and headed into the shop.

"Welcome to the Caffeine Addiction," Suzie said sweetly when they entered.

Dusty bumped Justin's arm and winked when he looked at her.

"Dusty, will you be having your usual?"

She nodded.

"And for you, tall and handsome?"

Dusty smiled impishly at Justin. "Yes, Tall and Handsome, what will you be having?" she repeated in a seductive tone.

"Just a hot chocolate," he replied doing his best to ignore his counterpart.

He pulled out a twenty and told Suzie to keep the change.

She quickly made both of their drinks and handed them to him. Justin handed Dusty hers and retuned to Suzie. Justin thought she pushed out her chest a bit, but he resisted the temptation to look down and made the mistake of keeping eye contact for a moment longer than he felt comfortable with.

"Thank you, Suzie," he said after a long, awkward silence, and he tipped his hat.

They chose the table farthest from the counter near a window so they could see the street and the bank across the street that Dusty's dad owned.

"He is still driving that old truck?" Justin asked, breaking the silence.

"What?" Dusty asked, sounding confused.

"Your dad—I see he is still driving the old Chevy. He could afford a BMW or even a Ferrari, but he still drives that old truck."

Dusty shrugged. "He grew up on a ranch, like you. He is old fashioned that way."

"I respect him. Not just for that, but he is a good man, helped us out a few times when he knew we couldn't afford to pay him back right away."

Dusty nodded and smiled. Her dad was a good man, and smart; he made his money by investing in the community. Every time a big franchise bank had come in to offer to buy him out, he always refused. He told her after one large proposal that they would not take care of the people in this town and that that was more important to him than the large check they were dangling in front of him.

She looked up and saw Suzie watching them. She smiled, and Dusty smiled back; then Suzie went back to cleaning.

"You know you are in," Dusty remarked impishly.

"In what?" Now it was Justin's turn to be confused.

Dusty rolled her eyes.

"With Suzie. She wants you."

"Wants me for what, exactly?"

"Men are so dumb. She wants you to ask her out. Then she wants to show you her lady parts."

"What? You mean like have sex with me?"

"I love you so much, but you really are a dumbass."

"I am not over Jo."

"Don't say her name around me, ever!" Dusty said, interrupting him. "Call her 'Bitch' so I know who you are talking about."

"I am not going to call her that."

"Well, she is."

"I am not over her."

"How long is that going to take? I mean, it's been like a year now, hasn't it?"

I don't know; I never been hurt like this before. They say I am supposed to go through some kind of process, like the ten steps."

"That's twelve steps."

"Oh, sorry."

"Do you even know what the steps are to get over a broken heart?" Dusty asked, her tone more serious.

"Not really; I was using the interweb to do some research."

"Its internet, dummy, or World Wide Web. Dude, it's 2020; you really need to get with the times."

"Whatever. Anyways, it doesn't seem like anyone really knows what the steps are or in what order."

"What do you mean?" Dusty asked curiously.

"Well, some say there are five steps, others seven, some even ten," Justin informed her.

"They all are different, but anger, confusion, sadness, pain, acceptance, and coping seem to be the theme running through all of them. I am not sure in which order or how long each is supposed to last."

"Where are you at?"

"Can I do more than one at a time?"

"Of course. What are you feeling."

"Sometimes I feel betrayed, other times angry, but most of the time I am just confused and sad. I just can't get my mind wrapped around it."

"What are you doing to try to get over it?"

Justin stared at his half-empty cup. He started processing his answer and trying to figure out what he really was doing and the things he wanted to do. Dusty watched him intently as he formed his answer.

"I cannot listen to the radio; there are just too many heartbreaking songs that make me want to …" He paused as he cleared his throat. "Well, they remind me of Jo—er, her."

"Duh, it's country music, maybe you should switch to rap," she said jokingly.

He shook his head.

Justin felt a hand resting on his shoulder and looked up to see Suzie.

"How is everything over here?" she asked them. "Any refills? It's on the house." She leaned on her perch—Justin's shoulder.

Justin just shook his head, and Dusty smiled.

"Yes, please," Dusty responded brightly, holding up her cup.

Suzie looked at Justin, who hid his eyes under the brim of his hat and kept them locked on Dusty.

"Okay, then," she said, sounding a little discouraged, and she walked back to prepare Dusty's coffee.

"You are so in!" Dusty reiterated, but she saw the look on his face and added, "When you are ready, I would hit her up if I were you."

Justin shrugged and looked up at Suzie as she returned.

"Thank you, Suzie. I appreciate you," Justin told her when she gave Dusty her drink.

Suzie smiled and pushed her long red hair back behind her ear. A few strands stayed behind and fell across her cheek. Suzie was definitely a looker; she always had been, and that is why Justin had tried so hard in high school to get with her. She had definitely filled out her five-foot-five body in all the right places. Even now, fifteen years later, she still took his breath away. Her green eyes were always bright, and they had captured him every time he looked at them when they were in high school.

Suzie resumed her perch on Justin's shoulder and looked at Dusty.

"When did you get back in town?"

"Yesterday; I am moving back," Dusty informed Suzie.

"Oh?"

"Yeah, the big-city life isn't for me," Dusty added.

"Where are you going to live?" asked Suzie.

"Daddy said there is a place he had to foreclose on that I can purchase from the bank."

"That's good. Whose house is it?"

Dusty and Justin smiled knowing smiles. She wasn't asking because she was completely interested in where Dusty was going to live, but rather because she was curious who had run into financial difficulties. Small-town gossip.

"It belonged to the Kinders a long time ago, then they died, and the kids rented it out to a few families, but no one really took care of it. A couple from Seattle bought it thinking they would fix it up and sell it quick—flipping, I think they call it. Anyways, they came out a few times but then lost interest, I guess. Daddy said they made payments on it for two years then just stopped. He tried to contact them, but they just disappeared. He went through all the right channels, and now he owns it outright."

"He is going to make you pay for it?" Suzie asked incredulously.

"Yes. You would have to know Daddy; he is a nice guy, but he is still a businessman."

"But you are his daughter; shouldn't he just give it to you outright?"

"That's exactly the argument I gave him, but no, at least he is selling it to me at cost, plus all the expenses he paid."

"Well, that seems fair. I am sure he would do the same for anyone," Suzie remarked.

"I am sure he would," Dusty agreed.

"No, really, he did that for me after the divorce. I bought my house a year ago when the Millers filed for bankruptcy and moved back to Oklahoma."

"He is a good man," Justin interjected.

"Well, I will leave you back to your conversation. If you need anything, don't hesitate to holler." With that, Suzie turned and went back to behind the counter.

"Well, she just can't keep her hands off of you," Dusty said with an impish smile when Suzie was out of earshot.

They went back to the ranch in silence, and it almost killed Dusty to drive without her Garth, Shania, and Hill singing their sweet melodies singing in her ears.

She pulled up, and Justin jumped out and started heading up to the front door.

"Hey!" she called out to him.

He turned and looked at her.

"You okay?" But she knew the answer when she saw he still had his hat in his hand.

"I am going to go take a nap," Justin informed her.

She reached in and killed the motor on her car, and she then ran up to him and put her hand on his waist. He tried to object, but she wasn't having any of that. She tugged on his belt loop and dragged him up the porch and pushed him through the door and into the front room. Doreen looked at them in surprise and concern when they burst in. Dusty just shook her head and continued to push the broken man up the stairs and into his bedroom. She grabbed his hat and chucked it on his dresser; then she threw him on the bed. She leaned over and, grabbing his boot by the heel and toe, gently pulled it off. She then repeated the process with the other one.

He started sobbing as he lay defeated on his bed, covering his face. She rolled him onto his side and spooned him from the rear. He squirmed a bit, but she gripped him tighter until he finally gave in and let her have her way. Justin had learned the hard lesson many times not to stop her when she had her mind set on something.

He started squirming again, but she realized immediately he wasn't trying to get away but was fully crying. She snuggled into his back tighter and waited patiently till he finished.

She lost track of time as she lay there letting him spill out his emotions, not daring to move or say anything.

Eventually she felt his body stop shaking, and then it went limp.

He started snoring and then farted.

"Dumbass," she muttered under her breath. She kissed his neck and then got up. The door squeaked as Dusty left his room and almost ran into Doreen, who had taken up station on the railing that overlooked the front room on the first floor.

"He good?" Doreen asked her softly.

"He will be." Dusty replied.

"When?"

"When he is ready."

Three

T he next day after lunch, Justin was sitting in his old room in front of his new computer when he heard familiar footsteps hitting the steps leading to the second floor and toward his room.

"Hello," Dusty greeted.

"Come on in, Dusty," he called out.

She came in and sat on his unmade bed. It was the same one he'd had in high school and still looked pitiful sitting in the middle of the room. She surveyed her surroundings with anguish. The room hadn't changed much since she had visited here in high school. There were quite a few trophies for football and rodeo sitting in a large display case he had made in shop class. The same dresser he'd had forever still sat near the corner with the same old blue lamp with no shade covering it. Dusty noticed the closet doors had been replaced from sliding glass to wooden ones. The old desk was still in the corner, but there was a new addition sitting on it. Other than that, the room looked pretty much t it had the last time she had been there in high school.

"This is a change," she remarked.

"What is?" he said, not looking up from his computer on his desk.

"Your room. It's a mess, and your bed isn't made."

"So?" he scoffed.

"So I don't think I have ever been in here when it has been this messy. And I seriously don't ever remember your bed not being made."

"Oh, that. I will make it," he said, but he still made no move to take his eyes off his monitor.

"What are you looking at? Is that a new computer?" Dusty asked curiously.

"Oh, this? It's new to me. I bought it at the pawn shop a few weeks back."

"Welcome to this century! What did you do with the Commodore 64?"

"It was a 128, and I got rid of that long ago," Justin said with contempt.

"What did you do with that old clunker?"

"I had to throw it away; the pawn shop wouldn't take it for trade."

"You can sell those old things to collectors on Amazon or eBay."

"Do what?"

"Never mind," she said as she rolled her eyes and laughed. "Here." She handed him a beer.

"Oh, thank you," he said as he grabbed the bottle and popped the top.

"What kind is that?"

"A laptop."

"No, dumbass, what brand."

"Oh, it's a Dell."

"It's nice."

"Thank you. Did you say hi to Momma?" Justin asked as he sipped on his beer.

"She isn't here."

"What? Oh, right, she is down at the church, getting things ready for tomorrow. I didn't even hear her leave."

"What's tomorrow?"

"Um, church. People still go to church on Sunday—or did your big city life get rid of that habit?"

"I haven't been in a while," Dusty replied, feeling embarrassed.

"Neither have I," Justin said with remorse.

Dusty sat stunned. For as long as she could remember, the Walker family—especially Justin—had always been sitting in the third pew on the right, every Sunday, no matter what the weather.

"You haven't?" she asked incredulously.

"Not since Joleen left."

Dusty glared at him.

"I mean since *she* left," he corrected himself.

"Why?"

"Me 'n' Jesus have been in a bit of a disagreement."

"Well, I hope you find you way back," Dusty said encouragingly.

He went back to looking at his computer.

"What are you hunting for?" Dusty asked, peering over his shoulder.

"Interesting word choice."

"How so?"

"Looking for a new rifle. I want to go elk hunting this year, and I don't think the old thirty-thirty is going to do the trick. I had no idea you could buy all of this stuff on the internet."

"Oh, it's 'internet' now?"

"Apparently you sound like a moron when you say 'interweb,'" Justin said sarcastically. She laughed and took a long pull on her beer.

"You know," she said as she wiped her mouth, "you can find a girlfriend on the internet as well."

"You mean like buying one of those Russian wives for sale?"

"No, you dork, there are dating sites you can go on and find girls around here that are single and just waiting for a handsome cowboy to ask them out."

"Really?"

"You have never heard of internet dating?"

"I have; I just thought it meant something else," Justin said as he shrugged.

"What else could it possibly mean?"

"I don't know, like you meet someone on the internet and then date them that way."

"That's exactly what it means."

"No, that's not for me, I want someone I can go out on real dates with."

"You do go out on real dates. Wait, you want to go out on a date with someone now?"

"Yeah, I thought about what you said, and I guess a year is long enough to wait to get back out there and try again."

"What about Suzie?" asked Dusty quickly.

"I went in to ask her out and, well, we got talking. She thought you and I were dating."

"That's hilarious. I mean, I love you, but no."

"That's what I told her."

"Then what did she say?"

"She said she was going out on a date with some guy she met on a fishing site on the internet."

"Fishing site?"

"Yeah, I couldn't remember what she was said it was, so I looked up fishing sites, and a bunch of sites came up."

"And you found it?"

"No. Actually there was a fishing store that I started looking at, and then I remembered I wanted a bigger rifle and went to this site, and here we are. I still haven't found any chat areas on either of these sites. Do some of them not have chat areas on them?" Justin asked, trying his best not to sound like a moron again.

"Wait, did she say she found a date on a fishing site, or did she say on Hooked on Dating?"

"Yeah, that sounds right—Hooked on Dating."

Dusty set her bottle down and started rubbing her temples. "Dude, you have to get out more. Hooked on Dating is a dating site, not a fishing site."

"Well that's a new one on me," Justin replied, realizing he had failed at his quest not to sound so foolish.

"Ugh. It's named because of that saying, 'There are lots of fish in the sea.' You know, like when you go through a divorce or breakup, some moron always says, 'Don't worry; there are lots of fish in the sea.' This site is along that theme so you can go out and hook ya one, or something like that."

"Oh. So it's not for people who like to fish? 'Cause I like to fish."

Dusty let out a long, agonized breath.

"Okay, cowboy, I am going to break it down for you. It is a dating site. Like lots of dating sites, you can put on it that one of your hobbies is fishing. Some girls will do the same."

"Works for me," he replied, trying to wrap his mind around this new foreign world.

"You cannot be this technologically challenged, can you?" Dusty asked in a more serious tone.

"Not really challenged. Maybe a little behind the times is all," he replied, matching her tone.

"How so?" she urged him.

"I used to have a social media site or two, and once Momma found out how to use spreadsheets, she would email them to Dad and me to keep track of everything on the ranch. There is a spreadsheet for everything now."

"So you do know how to navigate the internet?"

"A little."

"What about social media?"

"That I could do without. Jo, I mean my ex, was always on those different sites. It was always weird to me how involved she could get in those things."

"You didn't?" asked Dusty.

"I would follow a few things, but it seemed like a waste of time."

"They can take up a lot of time," Dusty agreed.

"I think I finally decided to get off when I saw her get in arguments with people she never met."

"People do like to argue on social media."

"The dumb thing is that someone would argue with her over politics, religion, or even the best way to make a salad dressing," Justin said, sounding exasperated.

Dusty giggled. "Everyone is an expert online, and people hold nothing back to try to get you to believe what they believe."

"Well, that was it for me. I didn't need that kind of extra drama in my life. She still did it, but I wasn't interested in someone telling me how to run my ranch, plow my fields, or even feed my horses. It just became too frustrating. Once I was off, it seemed like my blood pressure went back down and I had a lot more time for other things. I wish I knew more, and I do realize that there are a good things about the internet, but it didn't seem worth it."

"There are a lot of good things about the internet." Dusty confirmed.

"I am sure there are, but it's like a fire."

"How so?"

"It can heat your house or burn it down—depends on how you use it."

Dusty smiled at the saying; her dad used to tell her that about money.

"I guess I am not smart enough about how to control it and opted to play it safe and stay away from it," Justin added.

"What about now?"

"Now I guess I need to learn how to control it and use it for good."

"That's a good plan. I will help you avoid the pitfalls."

"I would appreciate that," Justin said as he saw his friend smile again.

Dusty reached out her hand for him to help her up from the bed. He reached out and grabbed it, but instead of pulling her up, she planted her feet on the floor and thrust her body back, twisted, and threw Justin on the bed. She then got up and went and sat in the chair and started punching keys.

"Okay, here is the site; we have to make you a profile," Dusty said as she took up station in the comfy office chair.

"Okay, my name is Justin Walker and I live at—"

"Just shut up and let me do this."

He shrugged. Dusty kept talking as she was setting up his profile.

"You know, just because Suzie found a date on this site doesn't mean she is going to marry the guy. He could turn out to be a sleazeball or just want to get laid, or he could even ghost her."

"Ghost her?" Justin asked, now not fearing sounding like a moron.

"It means he doesn't show up or return her texts or phone calls. It's like he became a ghost and disappeared."

"Do guys do that?"

"Oh yeah, all the time. Girls too. So be prepared."

"So there might be a girl that doesn't show up or return my calls?"

"And texts. You are going to be dating women who are avid texters, so you need to get good at that."

"Jeez, what ever happened to phone calls?"

"Texting is better; you can continue your life without having to stop it while carrying on a conversation."

"I see. Okay, will you help me?" Justin pleaded.

"I am helping you. See, your profile is all set up; we just need some pictures."

"No, I mean help me learn how to text."

"Jesus, dude. How the hell have you been making it all these years?"

"Never really needed to text. Me and, um, her … we were always together, or she called me if she wanted to talk. Then we moved in together, and there was no more need for phone calls."

"What are you doing with your house?" Dusty asked, changing the subject.

"Why? You already have yours; why do you need another one?"

"I guess what I am really asking is, Why did you move back in with your mother?"

"I didn't like being in my house alone. Too many memories. I sold it. In fact, your dad helped me with everything. He made it seem like it was no big deal and sure enough had it sold pretty quickly."

"Girls don't really want a guy that lives with their mother," Dusty remarked.

"They don't?"

"No, we prefer a man that lives with his wife, apparently."

Justin laughed at that. Dusty had told him about a couple of different guys she had dated that were married that had promised her they were going to be divorcing their wives soon. As it ended up, they were just trying to get into her pants, and once they had done that, they made the excuse that they were getting back together with their wives.

That was a dumb move on their part, as Dusty was as ferocious as she was beautiful. She told him that she had and made sure the wives in question were informed of their men's infidelity. He figured that they were now really getting divorced or would be living in the doghouse for a long time.

"How did you know how to get a hold of the wives?" Justin asked.

"I won't let a man see my lady parts until I take a photo of their driver's license."

"Why would they agree to that?"

"Because they really wanted to see me naked."

"Smart move," he conceded.

"Besides, in the big city, there are a lot of creeps, and some guys are just awful. I knew that if I ever got raped, kidnapped, or killed, my dad could access my cloud—that's the term for a place that stores your pictures online. He would be able see the last picture I took and find the slimeball."

"You let your dad see your pictures?"

"Yes, that's why I don't take nudes and send them to guys. I won't make that mistake again."

"You send naked pictures to guys?"

"I did. Not anymore. Lots of girls do that."

"Really? Why?" Justin asked incredulously.

"'Cause some guys want to see the boobies before they get to play with them."

"This is going to be a nightmare." Justin said with a groan.

"Oh, honey, you have no idea what you are getting yourself into, but don't worry; I will be your wingman."

"My wingman?"

"Usually a wingman is a dude that helps another dude get laid. Like, he is a reference for the girls, to let them know it is okay for her to go out with him. His role is also to give advice, to help dissuade the guy if he is too drunk or horny, or both, and to see if a chick is not right for him. It's kind of like in the air force—the pilot that has your back."

"Like in the movies?"

"I guess you could say that, but it happens in real life all the time."

"Who helps him?" Justin asked, confused.

"Not the point. Stay focused here, cowboy."

"All right."

"Put on some nice clothes. Never mind, I will pick out a few outfits, and we will go out and take pictures."

"For what?"

"For your profile. We need pictures, and they cannot look like you took them all today," Dusty informed him.

"But we are taking them all today."

"Stay focused, cowboy. Listen to your wingman; I will help you with this."

"Got it."

Twenty minutes later, Justin was driving his truck with Dusty sitting shotgun on their way to the lake. During the fifteen-minute trek, Dusty tried to explain why they were doing this and how pictures of him doing things he liked were appealing to women.

"Couldn't we do this at one of the ponds at the ranch?" Justin asked.

"We could but getting people or boats in the background will help you establish that you actually go out for fun," Dusty fired back.

They took a lot of pictures of him standing next to his truck, fishing, standing on a hill, and even up a tree. It took a minute for Dusty to convince him that they weren't really here to fish and had to drag him back to the truck to change for his next session.

When they got back to the ranch, Dusty made him saddle up his horse and took some shots of him sitting astride his old girl.

"These are great!" she said as she sat once more at his desk, sending the pictures into the dating site.

She punched in some more information that she had left blank on his profile and changed a few things, giggling as she did so.

"What?"

"This is fun! I have never gotten to do someone else's profile," she happily remarked.

"Did you mention I like fishing?"

"Yes, I did."

"What else?"

"Come here and read it for yourself, but don't change anything."

"Why?"

"Because you aren't good at this, and this is a good profile," Dusty said, standing her ground. "Girls will like it and respond to you."

"They won't respond if I do it myself?"

She shook her head. "Too many guys are constantly bombarding us girls, and we usually get the same shirtless dudes bragging on all the stuff we couldn't care less about. This one is wholesome and, well, a little exciting."

His eyes widened as he read, occasionally shaking his head. He did laugh a few times, and when he was finished, he just looked at her.

"What a load of crap."

"Believe me; that is what girls like to read."

"I just don't know."

"Tell me what part isn't true about you."

He shrugged. "I guess it's all true, just not how I would put it."

"Exactly," she replied, and she hit the send button.

Chapter

Four

Two days later, Justin walked into Dusty's new house carrying a large moving box. "Where do you want this one?" he asked her.

Dusty was in the kitchen, unpacking and placing silverware into an organizer that was seated in a newly lined drawer. She didn't even look up.

"What does it say on the box?" she asked pointedly.

"Kitchen," he responded after glancing at the top of the well-taped box.

"Well then, Mr. Einstein, where do you think it should go?"

"The kitchen?"

"Yes! This really shouldn't be that hard."

"I have helped lots of people move, but they usually only want the basics in the designated room and the rest somewhere they can unpack it later," he retorted as he looked around her new digs.

The house was an old farmhouse built back in the thirties that had been updated over the years, but most recently many modern touches had been added by the flippers to try to bring modern and rustic together under one roof. They had started in the kitchen, bringing in all new modern appliances. They had removed all the carpeting that had been added to the old wood floors sometime in the sixties and brought them back to life. The kitchen had all new tile that matched the updated countertops.

The house was triangular from top to bottom. The house had a storm cellar / utility room in an unfinished basement that could be accessed only from the inside by a stairway just outside the kitchen door that led outside to a partially covered deck.

The main floor consisted of a living room in the front and kitchen in the back. To the immediate left was a small hallway that led to a bathroom, laundry room, and small spare bedroom that was going to serve Dusty as her office and library. Next to the hallway was a stairway leading up to the second floor, where there was a massive master bedroom, a slightly smaller bedroom, and a bathroom dividing the two.

"I don't have that much stuff, and the boxes can go into the room they are labeled for."

Justin put the box in the kitchen and then surveyed the rows of boxes stacked on the table, the island, and all over her counters. He then took inventory of the living room, seeing the line of boxes on one side of the stairs leading to the upstairs bedrooms. He took off his hat and scratched his head.

"You have a lot of damn stuff," he remarked.

"Not for this house. I was living in a one-bedroom apartment when I was in Coeur d' Alene. This is a three-bedroom with a full basement. This kitchen is almost as big as the apartment I was staying in."

"Still a lot of stuff for one chick."

"I am just getting started. I have so many ideas for furnishing this place," she said with a smile.

"Speaking of which, how are you going to pay for all of this?"

"I am sure I will find something. There are always people hiring someone like me."

"Like you?"

"Yeah, you know, smart, hardworking, daughter of the bank owner," she joked.

"You just up and left and came out here with no plan, no job, and no idea what you are going to do?"

"You are starting to sound like my dad."

"He is a brilliant man," Justin said, beaming.

She took the box she'd just emptied, broke it down, and then grabbed another one.

"Honestly, my life was a train wreck in the city. I had been through a few really bad relationships, mostly with cheaters or just scumbags that wouldn't leave me alone. The job I was working at was okay, but it seemed like I wasn't going to move up anytime soon since the owner's family was always coming to work, and heaven forbid they start at the bottom and work their way up. The last raise I got was a joke, and I felt underappreciated, and the job was starting to become so mundane I could do it in my sleep. I just didn't feel challenged. The last time I came home, I really had a hard time going back. So when the lease was expiring on my apartment, I called Daddy to ask his advice."

Justin nodded in acknowledgment. "He didn't give you any, did he?"

"You know how he is; he just asks a lot of questions to get me to figure out what I want."

"And you figured you would come back?"

"Daddy said there are always people asking him if he knows anyone that could help out running their ranches or needing someone to fill in during the busy seasons."

"That is only seasonal work, though."

"Justin, there are also a lot of old people around here that are retiring or need to retire."

He laughed. "Truer words have never been spoken."

"I will find something."

"What if you don't?"

"How's the dating site going?" she asked, changing the subject.

"I don't know," he replied slowly, not really wanting to change the subject.

"No one is responding?" she asked as she moved to a new box with her pots and pans in it and started putting them in their places.

"I don't know," he said again.

She stopped working and looked at him.

"You haven't checked the site?"

"Nope. You said they had to approve the pictures first."

"Have you at least looked on the girls there?" she asked with exasperation in her voice.

"Nope. I don't know how."

"Oh my God, dude."

"What?"

"How much do we have left to unload?" she asked, looking at the ever-growing stack of boxes and furniture.

"There are a few lamps and two more boxes."

"Grab those and then go home and shower. I will be over in a bit, and we will go on and see what is happening on your profile," she said enthusiastically.

"Deal." He started walking out but stopped and turned around. He pulled out a phone from his back pocket and held it up. "I got a new smartphone like you told me to."

"Great," she replied as she ducked back down behind the island. He could hear her as she kept rearranging the pans until she was satisfied.

Ten minutes later, he had everything cleaned out of his truck and was folding up the tarp they had used to bring her stuff from storage room to the house. She walked over to him, stood on her tiptoes, and gave him a big hug.

"You are a lifesaver; thank you so much for your help. How can I ever repay you?"

"Being my wingman."

She smiled; he could tell she loved that title.

"What kind of phone did you get?" she asked curiously.

"Notebook."

"That's not a phone; that's a tablet."

"No, it's a phone. See?"

He pulled it out and handed it to her. She looked at it carefully.

"This is an Android Note. An old one. But it will work."

"Yeah, they wanted like a thousand dollars or something ridiculous for the newer ones."

"You can just have them add it to your phone bill and pay for it over time."

"This one was only two hundred dollars. Still pricy, but the lady said it would do what I wanted it to do."

"What's your passcode? Never mind, you haven't entered one yet."

"Passcode? What do I need that for? I am the only one that is going to be using it."

"What if someone steals it? Never mind; I will show you how to enter one. What is a four-digit code you won't forget?" He gave her the year his mom was born, and she entered it. "You can also use your eyes to unlock it." She held up her hand as she realized her mistake. "The code will work fine. Now nobody can access your phone but you. Now go home; I am going to grab something to eat, freshen up, and then head over there." She headed back to the refrigerator.

"Momma is making pot roast tonight."

"Oh, I will definitely wait for that." Dusty said as she did an about-face and headed up the stairs.

Chapter

Five

Two hours later in the Walkers' kitchen, Justin and Dusty had just finished up doing the dishes and then headed up to his room. Dusty showed him how to download the dating site's app to his phone, after explaining what an app was and that he could call it an application if he wanted to, though it wasn't necessary and doing so would once again cause him to sound like a moron.

They logged into his app, and she showed him how to navigate the site. They entered his credit card number so he could take full advantage of everything the site had to offer. She went to his desk and booted up the site there. She explained that it would be easier for her to teach him on the larger platform rather than them fighting over space trying to view it on the smaller screen.

"Okay, you ready for this?" she asked him as she poised her finger over the mouse.

"Sure," he said as he opened up his fishing chair next to her.

She clicked on the icon that brought him to the screen where he could start viewing the ladies on the site.

"Whoa, Dusty!" he exclaimed.

The image was of none other than her sitting in a raft in a very revealing bikini. She blushed a bit and clicked on the green check mark.

"What just happened?"

"I just told the site you might be interested."

"I am a little interested in seeing that picture again," he joked.

This time Dusty turned beet red and slugged him.

"Focus, dude."

They spent the next hour clicking red Xs and green check marks. They sent messages to each girl they put a check mark by. The last girl they viewed was Suzie Ferguson, or "Never Leave Me Blue," as her profile name read.

"What kind of name is that?" Justin asked.

They had already been through the discussion about how many girls used aliases so creepers could not find them on social media or use other devious ways to figure out who they were.

"Remember when everyone called her Suzie Q in high school?"

"Yup."

"Well, that's a line in the song. She is hinting toward her name. If a guy guesses it, she will know they are paying attention."

"I guess that is better than 'Summer Princess' or 'Aeries Goddess' or 'Must Love Dogs.'"

"You know of that movie?" Dusty asked, astonished.

"Yeah, Mom made me watch it after dad died. I really didn't pay attention because Mom cried through the whole movie."

"That's so sad."

"I know."

"Yes or no?" Dusty asked, trying to return their focus.

"About Never Leave Me Blue? Can we put her on hold for now?"

"What is you deal with her, dude?"

"What do you mean?"

"I mean she has been very flirty with you, and you are avoiding her like the plague."

Justin got up and went and sat on his bed. There was a growing silence in the room, but Dusty didn't want to speak and give him the opportunity to veer off subject. Joleen had left him about fifteen months previously. Their divorce had been finalized almost six months after that, so he had been single for almost nine painstaking months. Before Joleen, Justin had doggedly pursued Suzie Green for over two years. She had allowed him to "date" her in the ways dating went in the 1800s. They spent a lot of time together, but she never kissed him, and only occasionally hugged him; there was no other physical contact that usually goes with dating—no holding hands, no kissing, and definitely no sex.

"Dusty," Justin began slowly. "I tried for two years to get that girl to go out with me."

"You guys went out a lot," Dusty retorted.

"Well yes, but we weren't dating. She would always remind me that we were just friends."

"I see your point, but that was a long time ago; now she is giving all the signs that she wants to be more than friends."

"I don't see it that way. She was always giving off signs that I totally interpreted as her wanting to be more than friends. Every time I brought it up, she would gently remind me that we were just friends. Honestly, I am not up for rejection right now, especially from her."

Dusty shrugged and exited out of the site.

"Why don't you just go ask her out? See what happens."

"'Cause I like her."

"That's exactly the reason you *should* go ask her out," she said.

"I don't think I am ready, and like I said, I don't want to be rejected again by her."

"What the hell does that mean? They say women are complicated, but you sir are a train wreck."

"I mean I don't think I am ready to date someone like Suzie."

"Ohhhh, I get it; you want to sow some wild oats, eh?"

"No, no it's not like that," Justin replied, trying to figure out exactly what he wanted.

"Well, what is it like?" she asked impatiently.

"I think I need rehearsal or a warm-up date first—something that will get me back into the dating world. If I get rejected after that, I don't think it will hurt as much."

She nodded in understanding. "I see your point," she said slowly. "Okay, let's set up some dates that you can, for lack of a better term, throw away."

"Okay, but I don't want to hurt anyone."

"What about getting laid?"

"Wait, what?"

"You know—sex."

"I know what getting laid means; I have done it once or twice before."

"Jeez, only once or twice in fifteen years—no wonder she left," Dusty joked.

Justin saw the horror in her expression as she realized her mistake and started to apologize, but he grinned and returned the joke with his own.

"It was more than that; I'm just not that good in the sack."

"I really didn't mean—" she started, but he waved her off.

"I am doing much better, thanks to you. Do all wingmen snuggle with their projects? Because if that's the case, that is probably a job I'm not interested in," Justin continued.

She giggled a bit.

"What the hell is that noise?" Justin asked on noticing a beeping sound that had been happening every few minutes.

"Justin Davis Walker! What have I told you about cursing in my house?" Doreen exclaimed as she came into his room with milk and cookies for the pair.

"Sorry, Momma."

"Doreen, you brought us cookies, yes please!" Dusty interjected, trying to deflect the scolding.

"With a mouth like that, I should have brough a bar of soap," Doreen scolded.

"Sorry, Momma." Justin said again.

"I didn't curse; I should get all of the cookies," Dusty pleaded.

"Don't think you are so sly, young lady. More than once have I heard filth pour out of that mouth of yours," Doreen said, turning her attention to Dusty and then back to plate of cookies.

"I am sorry, Doreen." Dusty pleaded again, watching the steam coming off the freshly baked cookies.

"Yes, well, when you are in my house, you will mind your p's and q's." She eyed them both in mock anger. "Both of you."

"Yes ma'am," they both replied in unison.

Doreen placed the cookies on the dresser next to Justin's upside-down hat and then smiled sweetly at them and closed the door as she left.

"There it is again. Shut off your phone, Dusty; it's annoying," Justin said, reaching for cookies and one of the glasses of milk.

She pulled her phone out to check it and saw she had many alerts. There were a few texts from her dad and some friends, and some emails, and her own Hooked on Dating app informed her that she had twenty-four messages she needed to address. The symbol at the top of the phone caught her eye.

"Dumbass, that's not my phone; it's yours." She covered her mouth and listened for Doreen. Not taking any chances, she snatched a handful of cookies and shoved the first one into her mouth.

"What?" Justin asked after he had downed a cookie himself.

"See, mine is on silent," she said through chews.

Justin handed her one of the glasses of milk, and she took a drink quickly. There was another beep, and she eyed the culprit sitting next to the keyboard and grabbed it up, entered the passcode, and showed him all the activity on his own dating app.

"Twelve notices. Good job for a rookie," she said as she booted up his computer so they wouldn't both be trying to strain to see what was on the small screen.

"What does that mean?" Justin asked, looking over her shoulder at the monitor.

"It means someone either liked you, messaged you, or matched with you."

"Okay, slow down, city girl; explain it so I get what you are saying."

When the site came up, she went through the status bar and showed him what each alert meant, who had sent it, and the next steps he should take.

"Uh-uh. No way, she is a scammer for sure," Dusty said as she pointed to the picture of the cute girl on the monitor.

"How can you tell? She sure is pretty," Justin remarked.

"Yeah, scammers don't use ugly girl pictures."

"I still don't see how you can tell she is a scammer. I mean, she is from Kalispell; that's not that far, really."

"Believe me; she is a scammer. Just read her profile."

She pulled up the place to text on her profile and entered, "Hey beautiful."

"If she responds to that, she is definitely a scammer."

"Girls don't like being called beautiful?"

"Of course we do, but all guys say that or something dumb like that."

Justin felt confused but continued to read her profile as Dusty pointed out some of the key words or phrases to watch for that people from other countries used because they were not familiar with American slang.

"Am fine, how are you doing today handsome?" came the reply from Desert Star.

"See, not a scammer; she replied," Justin said as he pointed to the text.

"Oh, no, no, no. *Definitely* a scammer."

"Why, because she called me handsome?"

"No, because she said, 'am fine.' Two immediate wrong things pop out. Watch this."

Dusty scrolled through the list of women that popped up, reading their profiles carefully, looking for the telltale signs of a scammer.

"Here!" she exclaimed as she typed in the same message to Forever Love.

"I am not following," Justin said, watching for the reply.

The computer chimed, and a message came up from Forever Love. Dusty read it out loud in her best Asian accent.

"Am fine. Am looking for someone to be my ultimate soulmate, who will be faithful and kind and will be a good, responsible husband and father to our children. What are you looking for?"

"Jeez, she is pushing the accelerator pretty hard, isn't she?"

"She is a scammer as well," Dusty informed him.

"I still don't see how you can tell they are scammers."

"Look at the first line. What true red-blooded American woman says, 'am fine'? Not one. We always say, 'I am fine' or 'I am great.' We Americans are in love with using the word 'I.' Secondly, we didn't even ask how them how they were doing; we only said hello. Who responds to 'hello' with 'am fine'? Even if it was 'I am fine,' you still didn't ask, but they don't know American protocol, so they always seem to say something along those lines. That is important to watch for."

Justin looked hard at the profile for Forever Love. "Any other signs?'

"Sure. It's sometimes hard to tell by looking at the profile pictures. Some will even steal pictures of other women on social media and even steal their whole profiles, including their names. The better the scammer, the more realistic the dating profile will appear. They will research an area they claim to be from and add a local restaurant as their favorite place to eat."

"I see," Justin replied, nodding slowly. "But what makes them scammers?"

"Eventually they will tell you some sad story like a family member died or is in the hospital or injured and if they could only come up with a few hundred dollars, they could take care of them."

"Oh, so they try to get money from me with a bleeding-heart story."

"Exactly, although sometimes they say they only need like fifty dollars to replace their phone that they just broke or to add minutes so they can talk to you longer, or really ambitious ones say that if you buy them a plane ticket, bus ticket, or gas, they will come right out to visit you. No woman says that to some guy she doesn't know. Its unsafe and, quite frankly, dangerous if someone is really thinking about doing that."

"But they aren't, right?"

"If they do, they are stupid, but no, they aren't going to come out and visit you for sex all night." She said the part in her Asian accent again.

"How do you know all this?" Justin asked curiously.

"Different guys I have dated have told me stories, and I have had my share of scammers trying to get me to help them out of a jam."

"Gotcha," he replied, feeling apprehensive about this new world.

"So we will delete these and report them as fake users."

"We can do that?"

"I think so, I know on some dating sites you can. I never have; I just swipe left and am done with them."

An alert popped up, and then they both heard the Walkers' home phone ring. They looked back at the screen and noticed that someone had liked Justin.

"Well, click on it," Justin said impatiently.

"Hold on, cowboy; I am still trying to find where to report them." Dusty said, navigating the site.

"Don't worry about that; just swipe left. How do you do that, anyway?"

"You can't on the computer, only your phone. On the computer, you just click on the red *X*."

"Well, do it, I wanna see who likes me."

"Justin, there is a phone call for you! I think it is Suzie Ferguson." They heard Doreen call up the stairs.

Justin and Dusty both looked at each other, and then a slow, devilish grin spread across Dusty's face.

"Your lover girl calls," Dusty said with an impish grin.

"Shut it!" he retorted as he got up to go downstairs and talk on the archaic rotary phone that was still mounted to the wall in the kitchen. Dusty was laughing and whistling after him.

When she heard his footsteps hit the creaky bottom step, she turned back to the monitor and grabbed the mouse.

"Okay, let's see the next victim on our list."

Her finger froze as the image of Cowgirl 86 popped up on her screen. It was Joleen.

"That bitch!" she muttered under her breath. "Yeah, she's out finding herself. Finding herself a new man—that's what she's doing. The fucking bitch."

Dusty wasn't sure where Doreen was in the house, but she was pretty confident she was eavesdropping on Justin's conversation and not trying to catch her cursing. She hovered her cursor over the red *X* button and then decided to wait for Justin to return before she decided his fate on whom he should like or message. She shook her head and returned the cursor over the red *X* and pressed the button.

Another face popped up, but now she didn't see it; she was still feeling angry and hurt. *I can look at who liked him*, she thought, and she clicked on that screen.

She read the name "Honky Tonk Girl" and saw the image of a girl they had gone to school with in middle and junior high school till her family moved to Great Falls.

"Damn, Sarah Beth, you aged well," she said as she looked jealously at the picture.

Chapter

Six

Justin grabbed the phone receiver that Doreen had left on the counter.

"Hello?" he said in his friendliest voice.

"Hi, Justin. It's Suzie Fer … I mean Green. I guess it's going to take me awhile to go back to my maiden name. How are you this afternoon?"

"I am good, Suzie. You?"

"Well, I am okay, but I have a problem I was hoping you could help me with."

"Sure, what is it?"

"Well, it's actually two things."

"Okay."

"First, and most important, I think my tire is getting low on my car, and I was wondering if you could fix it?"

"Sure, I can come take it off and take it down to Donny's and have them fix it."

"Oh, that would be wonderful," she replied gleefully.

"What's the second?"

"Well, um, my bathtub. It's not draining very fast. I poured some of that stuff in it, and it's not helping—not really."

"Okay, I will come right over."

"Oh, thank you so much. I really appreciate it."

"Anytime," he replied as he went to hang up, but he heard her continue.

"Um, Justin."

"Yeah?"

"I um … well, I uh … I don't really have any way to pay you this week for helping me out."

"No problem, it's on the house."

"Oh, thank you, I was afraid to ask because of that," she replied, sounding relieved.

"Nonsense, my momma would beat me if I took any money from you," Justin assured her jokingly.

Justin heard Doreen giggle from her hiding place around the corner.

"Suzie, I have to go. Apparently this conversation is being monitored. See you in a few."

"Okay and thank you again."

Justin hung up the phone and almost ran into Dusty bringing in the tray of cookie crumbs and empty glasses.

"Want to go for a ride?" he asked her as she maneuvered around him to the kitchen sink.

"Sure, let me just clean up here," she replied, turning toward the sink and reaching for a dishcloth.

"Nonsense," interjected Doreen, who also came into the small kitchen. "You two run along; I will finish up."

"But—" Dusty started to insist.

Doreen waved them away with her hand.

"Momma, you gonna be okay?" Justin asked, sounding concerned.

"Of course."

He kissed his mom on the cheek and headed up to his room to grab his hat.

"Brandy," Doreen said.

Dusty froze. Doreen never called her by her real name unless she was scolding her.

"Justin has really been in a mess the last few months. He helped me a lot when I lost Benson. He was always there until I was able to function again."

Dusty looked at Doreen in aguish but let her finish.

"I have been at a loss. Nothing I have done seemed to pull him out of this funk. I just wanted to say I am so glad you are here for him."

"Of course" was all Dusty could get out.

"Brandy, he is really hurting. When I told him you were coming, it seemed to draw him out a bit, and I finally saw him brighten up."

"Friends will do that."

"Do what?" asked Justin as he reappeared.

"Kick your butt if you don't get a move on," Doreen said cheerfully.

Justin turned and headed for the door with Dusty following close behind. When she reached the door, she looked back. Justin saw them both nod to each other. He shook his head, figuring they were scheming something, but thought better and kept his mouth shut.

Chapter

Seven

Justin pulled his truck out of the driveway and headed for Suzie's house. Dusty was doing something on her phone while he sat in silence thinking about the girl who had crushed his dreams and heart those many years ago.

The ride took less than ten minutes, and when he started to slow the big truck down, Dusty looked up. The big white Chevy 4×4 pulled into Suzie's driveway.

"Oh God, no!" Dusty exclaimed.

"What?" asked Justin.

The door opened, and Suzie stepped out onto her porch.

"No, no, no, no!" Dusty exclaimed.

"What?" Justin asked again, growing impatient.

"I don't need to be here. Not here, not now!" she exclaimed.

"Suzie needs our help; she has a flat tire and a clogged drain."

"Dude, look how she is dressed."

They both peered out at Suzie, who was busy fumbling with her shirt.

"She looks fine."

"No, dummy. Look: she is buttoning up her shirt."

"Well, we did get here pretty fast; maybe she didn't have time to get dressed."

"She was already dressed when she made the phone call. She didn't expect me, so she was showing off her cleavage for you."

Justin looked at Dusty and then looked back at Suzie, who had finished with the two buttons she had unfastened and then had to refasten. She then leaned nonchalantly against a post on her deck and started waving. She wore a smile, but Justin noticed her face showed frustration and dismay.

"I can walk back to my car; it's only a couple of miles, and lord knows I could use the exercise. Then you will get to see *more* of her," she said with a sly smile.

"No, it's okay. Please stay," Justin pleaded.

They exited the truck and went to greet Suzie.

"I will have the usual," Dusty said jokingly.

"Coming right up!" Suzie joked back. "Hi, Justin," she said as she turned her attention to him.

"Hi, Suzie," he replied, already looking at the tire.

"I am so glad you came by; I was concerned about that tire."

"It looks like only a nail. We might not even have to take it off. I will grab my kit and fix it up in no time," he assured her.

Five minutes later, he had used water pump pliers to extract the nail and quickly plugged it with his kit. He then took a compressed air can out of the back of his truck, added the appropriate amount of air to the tire, and then listened closely for a leak.

"Okay, that should do it. How about that drain?" he asked as he approached the women.

He paused a long second, looking at them both, and could feel the tension in the air.

Suzie shook her head. "I am so sorry; can we make it for another time? The girls just called me and are having a problem with one of the machines at my shop, and I need to run into town really quick to see if I can get it going."

"You are still open?" Dusty asked curiously.

"We started selling lunch, and one of the customers convinced me to buy a pizza oven since the Pizza Shack closed down. So now we do sort of a dinner as well, although we still close at six. I am also getting ready to put in a grill and friers so we can make burgers, fries, and hot sandwiches."

"Wow, that would be awesome!" Dusty said excitedly.

"But your shop is so small," Justin added.

"The thrift store next to us is moving to their new building they just built, so the space has come available, and I bought it."

"Oh wow, that will give you plenty of room," Dusty said approvingly.

"Yes, but it has left me strapped for cash. Between hiring new employees, buying new tables and chairs, and everything else that will go into the new place, I am just broke right now."

"Well, let me know what I can do help," Justin said, and Dusty nodded in agreement.

"Actually," she said a little hesitantly, "I am in a bit of a bind."

"Sure, anything," Justin said, eager to help.

"Um, it would be from you, Dusty," Suzie said as she turned her gaze to her.

Dusty and Justin both looked a bit shocked.

"Dusty," Suzie continued, "your dad told me that you haven't found a job yet, and if you say no, I am okay with that."

"Well, I do need a job. What is it?"

"My great-grandmother in Pennsylvania is entering her end-of-life phase, and she doesn't want to die in a nursing home. She requested that I come take care of her in her own home until she passes. Since I am, or was, a CNA, she worked it all out with the insurance so I will still get paid. Unfortunately she did this without telling me and before I bought the coffee shop, and I am kind of in a bind. I trust my employees, but not indefinitely while I am not around to monitor them on a day-to-day basis."

"So you want me to look in on them?" Dusty queried.

"No, I want you to run it. I want to hire you as my general manager while I am gone."

Justin saw Dusty's face and knew she was just as shocked as he was. Dusty was a brilliant choice for this job. She was dedicated, hardworking, and always had a positive attitude. Her experience as an administrator was going to help her tremendously, but her experience at working at the Pizza Shack for four years in high school was the icing on the cake. He knew this was definitely the opportunity she needed for a challenge and to keep her from falling back into some mundane job. He also knew she would be appreciated and valued, which was exactly what she was looking for.

"And when you come back?" Dusty asked.

"You are free to go, or you can stay. I will need a manager anyways—when we get fully operational, that is."

"I think that sounds like a great idea. I would love to work there, as long as I can have free coffee."

They all laughed, and then Dusty said, "You must have been pretty close to your great-grandma for her to trust you with this."

"We were," Suzie replied. "She would always talk about me coming out east to take care of her, but I never really thought I would. She also felt it was good for me to get away from Russel for a while."

"Oh, you mean that lying, cheating bastard you were married to?" Dusty asked, seething.

"Yep, that's the one," Suzie confirmed.

"See, she is not afraid to call her ex what he really is," Dusty said, looking Justin's way.

"We can follow you into town so you can start showing Dusty the ropes. I mean, I can't think of any better way to start her training than fixing something your employees are unable to fix," Justin added, changing the subject.

"Great idea," Suzie said as she put her hand on Justin's forearm.

Chapter

Eight

Two days later, Justin opened his eyes and stared at the ceiling in his dark room. The phone next to his head was ringing, and he leaned over and grabbed it and then hit the green phone that was lighting up on his screen.

"Hello?" Justin said sleepily.

"You ready?" Suzie's voice asked Justin in his ear.

"I am; I will be over there in a bit."

"Okay, I will see you soon." Justin said as he half wished he hadn't agreed to take her to the airport all the way over in Spokane, Washington.

Justin looked at the clock on his phone. It was 4:18 in the morning. He shook his head and got up quickly and dressed. He wasn't tired; he always used to wake up at four so he could drive over to this ranch. He would start his day by feeding the horses and milking the cows; then he would start on his long list of chores that kept his family's ranch in business.

When his dad died, not much changed except that he was doing the work of two instead of one. They had hired some help but always had to lay them off in the wintertime. There were no more afternoon jaunts down to the fishing hole that his dad had encouraged him to take to get some rest before the evening chores kicked in. He laughed; Dad did not really have to encourage him much to go fishing.

Now getting up before eight was a struggle. He felt depressed, and since it was late in the year, he didn't really have much of a purpose around the ranch with most of the animals having been sold and the fields being dormant for the winter.

Damn this feeling, damn this whole situation, and damn her! he thought as he grabbed his hat and headed to the living room.

He stopped to grab his boots, and he looked up to see his mom standing there with two sacks and a case of bottled water.

"I made you two lunches," Doreen said.

"Momma, you are up and dressed already?"

She nodded as she handed him his lunch and water after he put his boots on. He

34

grabbed them, kissed her on the cheek, and walked out the door, putting his hat on as soon as his heels touched the porch.

"Be careful," Doreen called after him.

"I will be back tomorrow. I told Dusty to swing by here and check on you."

"I can take care of myself," Doreen retorted.

"I asked for Dusty's sake; she will worry about you if she doesn't."

"Okay, for Dusty's sake," Doreen replied, relenting.

Justin grinned and pulled open the creaky door on his truck. He hopped in, put the key in the ignition, and turned it over. He panicked for just a second, as the old truck didn't want to start after a couple of turns, but the third time was the charm. He stuck his head out the window and hollered to his mother, whose face showed much concern.

"Just the cold, Momma. I will put in the oil heater when I get back, so it doesn't happen again," he assured her.

"Justin, be careful. There is a winter warning all the way from here to Spokane," she hollered back as the truck slowly eased up the dirt driveway toward the road.

Justin immediately wished he had waited for the truck to warm up, but he was too impatient and thrifty to let time or fuel waste while they could do that during the ride. This was a trait he had inherited from his father.

When he pulled the truck onto the asphalt, he tapped the brakes and turned the tires while driving slowly to check how much traction he had on the icy road.

"No need for four-wheel drive, at least not yet" he said out loud to himself.

Suzie was waiting just inside the door with a suitcase, a laptop bag, and her purse. When the truck rolled to a stop, she quickly ran out and threw her items in the back door while Justin helped her. He then opened the passenger door, and she paused a beat and put her gloved hand on his arm.

"You know, the entire time Russel and I were married, he never once opened a door for me," she said in dismay.

Justin stood there a little dumbfounded and remembered all of the times growing up his dad had kicked him in the rear for jumping into the back of the truck before he opened the door for his mom.

Suzie squeezed a bit and used the passenger's handle mounted to the door frame to boost herself into the cab.

Justin wasted no time hoofing it around to the driver's side and swung the door open.

"I think I forgot to lock the door," Suzie exclaimed as she looked at the front of her house.

Justin ran back and swung open the screen door and pushed on the handle while his momentum carried him into the locked door. His hat flipped off, and he lost his footing on the icy porch; but in a wild display of athleticism and semi coordination, he was able to catch himself and the hat, although not gracefully.

When he recomposed himself, he rushed back to the truck and jumped in. Suzie was laughing so hard she couldn't catch her breath.

Justin put the stick shift into reverse and maneuvered the truck into a K turn then headed toward the road.

"Not a word to Dusty," he told Suzie.

She muttered something between breaths, but it didn't sound too reassuring to Justin that his dance wasn't going to make the front page of the local paper.

Suzie finally composed herself and said genuinely, "Thank you for checking for me."

"Your door's locked," he said with a grin, and the laughter from the passenger side of the truck started again and filled the whole cab.

Chapter

Nine

The first leg to the airport was slow and tedious as the snowplows were not running in full force yet and after a few hours of driving brought the daylight and the on ramp to interstate ninety.

"Before we get on, can we stop so I can freshen up?" Suzie asked Justin.

"Freshen up? You look great."

She blushed a bit and then blurted out, "I have to pee."

"Oh," he said, a bit embarrassed as he swung the old Chevy into the truck stop.

They drove to Spokane International Airport with little trouble. The transportation departments of Montana, Idaho, and Washington did their jobs to perfection, keeping the roads in top shape and ice free. The Chevy's all-weather tires never lost their footing but whined the entire time.

Justin and Suzie passed the time with idle chitchat and, to Justin's chagrin, listening to music from Suzie's phone that she plugged into his radio. He realized that although some songs hit harder than others, he was not feeling the same hurting in his heart—and, more importantly, in his eyes—when they came on. Suzie was different from most of the small-town girls he was raised with; she mixed in some big-hair bands, eighties and nineties, and her favorite, the entire *Top Gun* soundtrack. Justin found himself subconsciously tapping his foot to many of her selections.

"So you can play all those songs through your phone?" he asked her in wonderment.

"Yes, and you can Bluetooth it to your car, although I don't think your truck has Bluetooth capabilities."

"That's why you plugged that cord from your phone to my radio?"

"Yes, this is called an aux cord." She saw the confusion in his face and laughed.

"Why do they call it an ox cord?" he asked curiously.

"Not ox, aux. Short for auxiliary cord."

"Oh. Can I get one of those applications on my phone?"

"Sure." She giggled. "There are lots of music apps that you can get for your phone to play on your truck or on your computer or home radio. I have mine set up at the shop to play for the customers during the day, and when we shut down at night, we blast the music we like while we are cleaning up and closing down."

"I see. I will have to get me one of those apps."

Justin parked his truck and walked Suzie into the airport, where he went with her to the line for the check-in counter.

"You don't have to stay; I got this," she said, but Justin saw her facial expression saying otherwise. Besides, he was hoping to catch up with his friend from high school. Despite his failed efforts to romance her, he had enjoyed her friendship and spending time with her back then.

"I have never seen how this works; I am kind of curious in case I ever need to fly," he said as he rejected her offer to leave.

"Okay, but once I go through security, you will have to stay behind; then you can leave."

"Deal."

Suzie did all the things one does when one flies, explaining each step to Justin.

She approached the kiosk and got her ticket, and then they stood in line, waiting to check her baggage. Once that was done, Suzie checked her phone for the time.

"I still have about an hour before I need to be at the gate," she informed him. "The way the line is moving, and considering the small crowd, that should give us about forty-five minutes."

"Works for me. What are you thinking?"

"Well," she said thoughtfully, "You can walk me to security, or we can grab a coffee and talk for a while."

"Dealer's choice," he responded, wanting to talk to her but still a little hesitant. Dusty's words were swirling through his head about him being in and, most importantly, her wanting him to see her naked. He blushed at the thought.

"What?" she asked seeing him shift uncomfortably.

"Actually, a drink would be nice."

She beamed. "I am glad you think so; we can catch up without distractions."

Over the next forty-five minutes, they caught each other up on the past few years since their junior year. Suzie and her family had moved away from Hackamore when her parents had both taken jobs at a feed mill in central Montana that was run by an aging distant relative that needed help running the business. Suzie had started dating Russel, the son of the local district attorney, and they marred right after graduation and then moved to Seattle, Washington, where they had stayed for the last seven years until she found out about his infidelity with his secretary.

"You know, I would have never found about her if he hadn't gone to the Virgin Islands," Suzie lamented, staring into her to go coffee cup.

"He took her there?"

"No, his company was doing a team-building retreat there."

"Oh, and she went with him?"

"No, she wasn't high up enough in the company. The way I found out is our cell phone company did not have service there, and the idiot didn't realize that it was costing us about two dollars a minute in roaming fees when he made phone calls."

"Two dollars a minute?" Justin said with a low whistle.

"Yes. When I got our phone bill, it was outrageous. I wasn't worried, because his company reimburses us for him using his personal cell instead of the company having to buy and pay for company phones. Anyway, I wanted to see why it was so high, and I found a number I did not recognize. It was hurtful because right before he would dial that number, he would dial mine and talk to me for like ten minutes. He was always checking in on me and joking about not having any Sanchos over and how tired he was, how much he loved me, and how he would be home before I knew it. Then the bastard would hang up and dial the mystery number."

"What did you do then?"

"When I got the bill, I saw the number, so I called it. His secretary answered it. I was crushed."

"I'll bet."

"So I confronted him about it, and the asshole didn't even deny it. He tried to blame me for all my shortcomings and tried to blame the whole thing on me."

"What a jerk," Justin said angrily.

"Yeah. So I left that night and came back to Hackamore with my grandma and grandpa. I filed for divorce the next day, and six months later it was finalized. That was almost two years ago."

"I am sorry to hear that."

"It's okay. What about you? What really happened with Joleen?"

Justin shrugged and his heart paused when he heard her name.

"She just left," he told her matter-of-factly.

"Did she give a reason?"

Justin's insides started to ache again, but this time anger was added to the mix. He had loved that woman and everything about her and the life they had together. No, it had not been perfect, and there were things they'd had to work through, but they always did. He had felt cheated for being left alone and cheated for not been given a reason why.

"Only that she had to go find herself," Justin informed her slowly.

"Oh."

"Yeah, I know. Dusty explained what she meant by that."

"You were married for how long?"

"We started dating right before I graduated. I met her at a rodeo in Cody, Wyoming, my senior year. They have a big one there every year. It is weird because we always lived so close together but never met. After she graduated high school, we moved in together, much to my momma's objections, but we then married two years later. We stayed married for fifteen years; then she just up and left."

"That's awful. Do you have any kids?"

"No, she wanted to wait, so we waited and never did. How about you? Any kids?"

"No, same story. I did get pregnant once but lost the baby after two months."

"That sucks," Justin said softly.

"It did. That's why I planted the tree in my new front yard … in honor of the baby."

Justin nodded his head. He did not know much about the tradition, but more than once he had been recruited to help plant a tree for someone in the community that had lost a child that way.

"How did you know what Dusty's usual drink was? I mean, she has been living in Idaho for the last seven years; how could you possibly know what she liked to drink?" Justin asked, changing the subject.

"She comes into town during holidays and on her vacation. When I started working at the shop, she would come in all the time while she was here and order the same thing. When I see certain customers that order the same thing drive up, I start making their drinks right away. I learned early on that this really helps on the tips."

"I see."

"So what's next for you?" Suzie asked.

"Well, I sold the house, I couldn't bear to live there anymore. I moved all of my stuff out and left a message on her voice mail to come get her stuff."

"Did she?"

"She never answered, but when I went back with Mr. Mann to get it ready to sell, someone had cleared out most of the rest of the stuff. We hired the auction company to clear out and sell the remainder of the things, and we then hired another company to get it ready to sell."

"Were you able to sell it?"

"Yes, the housing market is a lot better now than when I bought it, plus a new strip mall was built a mile down the road, so the value increased quite a bit. I made out surprisingly good. I got back my down payment and a lot extra."

"What are you going to do now?"

"I am going to stay with Momma for a while. She insisted that she could not make it without me, but that is a lie; that woman has never asked for help in her life. I think she only said that so she could keep an eye on me."

"You have a great mom."

"I sure do. Dusty said that women don't like to date a man that lives with his mother."

"No, we only like the ones that live with their wives."

Justin laughed out loud. "That's exactly what she said."

"So are you two dating?" Suzie asked.

"No, like I told you the other day, we are just friends. I am not her type apparently."

"Do you want to date her?"

"I don't think so. I mean, I have known her forever, and she is a bit too wild for me. We are great friends. I was told that is the foundation for a great marriage, but I don't know."

"You should approach her and ask her what she thinks about it."

"What is it about you two?" Justin asked with a smirk.

"What do you mean?"

Justin turned his head and looked sheepishly away. He then cleared his throat and looked Suzie right in her big, beautiful green eyes.

"Both of you are trying to set me up with each other," he finally blurted out.

"What?"

"Well, Dusty said I should ask you out."

"Oh? You didn't want to?"

"No. I mean yes, I did, but now."

"Because I am leaving?"

"Yeah."

Suzie looked a little disappointed.

"I am coming back; I don't know when. We can still talk."

"I would like that."

"Me too. I will tell you what, you go out and date while I am gone. If you meet someone, then good for you."

Justin was taken aback by this statement. He could not get his mind wrapped around why so many people were worried about him being single. Since Joleen had left him, he had been busy selling his house and working the ranch. Now that winter was upon them, the ranch required only a little of his time each day, and he was completely done with the house, he was getting a little bored not having things to do during the day. He had been out hunting a few times, but his heart really was not in it, and the cold was definitely letting him know he was getting older. Then he looked back at Suzie. She was watching him carefully as he mulled through his thoughts.

"If I don't?"

"Then when I get back, we can see what that brings. Look, we haven't hung out in such a long time, and I remember how you always wanted to date me in high school, but more than that, I remember how much fun we always had just hanging out."

"Those were some good times. Why wouldn't you date me?"

Now it was her turn to grow quiet and mull through her thoughts. Justin watched her as she navigated her thoughts back to high school and looked for an answer she could not find. She finally looked at him and said, "I really don't know."

"Oh?"

"I mean now, looking back on what I said …" She paused for a second as it looked as if she were searching for the words to appear out of the air.

Justin interrupted. "Seems like a lot of things we did back then don't make sense now, doesn't it?"

She shook her head slowly. There was an announcement over the terminal's intercom system announcing the time and some safety rules. They both perked up when Suzie realized that she had only half an hour to get to her terminal.

"Oh my gosh, I need to go!" she exclaimed as she got up.

Justin jumped up as well, and before he could react, Suzie gave him a big hug and then pulled him toward her, and she planted a short kiss on his lips.

"To remember me by," she said as she turned and ran toward the security line.

Justin stood there a little dumbfounded but savoring the afterglow of feel of her lips against his.

Chapter

Ten

Justin left the airport and spent the night in one of the many motels offered along I-90 as he headed back to Hackamore. The weather had relented, so he drove the maximum amount the law would allow, plus a little more. Justin returned home to find Doreen sitting patiently on the couch.

"Hi, Momma," he said as he started to sit down and take off his boots.

"I want to get out of the house for a spell," she informed him.

"Um, okay," he said, sliding his boot back on.

"Dusty told me she is now running the coffee shop in town."

"Yes ma'am, she is."

"I think it would be a good idea to see how Dusty is doing with her new job," Doreen said as she walked past Justin and out the door.

Justin shook his head but followed her without a word.

When they reached the coffee shop, Justin settled his mom into a booth and then went to the counter to talk to Dusty.

"So," Dusty started with an impish grin. "How was your adventure to Washington?"

"It was good," Justin replied with a wide smile.

"Don't you lie to me; I could see that grin for a country mile."

"Nothing happened, Dusty." Justin said, realizing he wasn't very good at lying.

Nothing had really happened. He looked back at the kiss scene in his mind and realized that if anyone had been watching Suzie kiss him, they would not have had viewed it as anything out of the ordinary. It seemed to him that nowadays people were getting all sorts of physical with each other and pushing many boundaries that the generations before would have saved only for their mates.

To Justin, the kiss was spectacular. It seemed to him he had been waiting all his life to kiss that woman, and when he had the chance, he missed it, because by the time he knew what was happening, it was over. He had thought about grabbing her, spinning her around and kissing her like she needed to be kissed, but he was no Rhett Butler, and he wasn't sure whether the kiss they had shared was a friendship kiss or something more. He was still wary of Suzie; after all, he had poured his whole heart and soul to her only for her to place him in the friend zone. He wasn't angry about that—at least not anymore, but he was going to be very cautious with her, because he wasn't interested in getting let down again.

"Something happened," Dusty prodded.

"Just a kiss."

"You kissed her? Good for you."

"No, she kissed me."

"Oh, did you kiss her back?"

"Didn't have a chance; it was a short kiss."

"Uh huh," said Dusty.

Justin noticed she almost looked hurt. "What is wrong with you?"

"What?" asked Dusty, watching a couple leave the coffee shop.

"You aren't going to be satisfied till I get laid, are you?"

She shrugged and laughed. Then she summoned one of the waitresses to go bust the table that had just been deserted.

"I just want to see you happy," she told him, turning her attention back to him.

"Did you know she wanted to set me up with you?" Justin said as he leaned in conspiratorially.

"Ah ha. That was a test. What did you say?"

"Isn't it little weird that both of you want me to date the other?" Justin asked, grabbing his hat with one hand and scratching his head with the other.

"No, not really. I am doing it because I care about you; she is doing it to see where you are. Both of us are doing it because women think no one should be single and we all are part-time matchmakers."

"Now that is weird."

"So what did you tell her?" Dusty asked while wiping down a spot on the counter.

"How about you get my cocoa and my mom's coffee so I can go spend time with her."

"Ugh. All right, Mr. Romeo, here you go," Dusty said, taking the drinks that had been brought up by the barista.

"Thank you, ma'am." He tipped his hat and then grabbed the drinks and went over to his mom, who had been watching the interaction with great intent.

"Don't be so nosy, Momma," Justin scolded.

"I did nothing of the sort," she rebutted.

"Uh huh," Justin replied, sounding not so convinced.

"Is Dusty coming over tonight?" she asked after sipping her coffee.

"I think so. It might be late since she has to help close down the shop."

"Why didn't you tell me you were going to start dating again?" Doreen asked, looking hurt.

"How did you know about that?"

"A mother knows everything."

"Bullshit."

That was the only curse word that was acceptable in the Walkers' house—mainly because they dealt with it and played the game, and it was the only word powerful enough to use in situations like this. Besides, Doreen could never get Benson to not say it, so she finally relented and decided to focus on winning the other important battles a wife and mother has to fight.

"We had a long chat when she came over yesterday to check on me."

Uh oh, Justin thought. *Maybe I should have let her rattle on about her eavesdropping innocence.* "I dunno, I am just seeing what is out there, not really interested in getting in something right now, just looking," he finally told his mother.

"Suzie Ferguson is out there."

Justin smiled unconsciously and realized Doreen noticed right away and smiled a smug smile back.

"Well, um, she goes by Green now. Besides, she is heading back east till her great-grandmother passes," Justin informed her.

"She won't live forever," Doreen commented offhandedly.

"Momma!" Justin exclaimed.

"Well, she won't, and then Suzie will be back," Doreen offered before taking another sip of her coffee.

"That could be years," Justin said, looking out the window.

"Okay, then wait; you are young, and she is a good woman."

"Momma, seriously."

"Just saying."

"What seems to be all the commotion over here?" Dusty asked as she brought some sandwiches over and laid one each in front of them.

"We are talking about Justin's love life," Doreen said with a smile.

"What love life?" Dusty asked, fully engaged.

"There is no love life," he replied tersely with a mouth full of sandwich.

"Justin, manners," Doreen scolded him.

"Sorry, Momma," he apologized after chasing his sandwich with his drink.

"What time will you be over, Dusty?" Doreen asked, turning her attention away from her son.

"Not too late. We close at six, and it doesn't really take that long to close down since we try to keep cleaning during the day."

"I cannot wait to see what you all are going to do to this place." Doreen commented, looking around the shop. It wasn't anything fancy, and it had been forever since it had been updated. The original design was a small restaurant, but when the Pizza Shack was in business, it couldn't compete. The previous owner decided to focus on coffee, and it made a name for itself in the small town. It didn't have a drive-through window like most coffee shops in bigger cities did, but it still drew enough business to prosper. Many of the older folks in town would stop by and spend a few hours chatting with their friends during the mornings. The shop faced the north, where Main Street ran east and west. The main entrance was on the west side, near the northwest corner. When you pushed your way through the glass door, your options were to go straight ahead to the dining area or make an immediate right to get to two very small restrooms. As you entered the dining area, you were met by the beginning of a bar that ran over halfway down the dining area. At the very beginning was a register and order / pickup area. After you ordered, you could choose between one of four booths along the front, pressed up against the bay windows, or you could choose from six small round tables: one up against the western wall with two chairs, three that were spread across the middle of the dining room floor, and two tucked away in the back past the end of the bar. The bar was impressive; it was an old fifties-style counter that had been loaded up with different coffee machines and the equipment normally used to mix specialty coffees. The bar stools had been taken out to make room for the extra tables, and they were no use anyway because of all the equipment on the bar.

"Yeah, what are you going to do to this place, Dusty?" Justin asked her as he finished up his sandwich.

"It's a surprise," she told them giddily.

"No, really. What do you have planned?" Justin insisted.

"Suzie made me promise not to tell anyone until she was ready."

"Even me?" asked Justin, feigning sadness.

"Especially you," Dusty shot back with a smile.

"Maybe she will tell us when we bribe her with food," Justin told his mom.

"You never know; I guess you will have to try when I get off."

"Okay, we will see you then; I will bake a cake," Doreen said sweetly as she arose to leave.

"You are bound and determined to make me fat," Dusty joked.

"Well, you could use a little meat on those bones. Men like some meat with their meal."

"Doreen!" Dusty laughed, and then she went back to her station behind the counter.

"Leave her a big tip, son."

"Yes, Momma."

Chapter

Eleven

After dinner and some failed interrogation tactics at the Walker kitchen, Dusty and Justin made their way up to his room to find him a date.

"Okay, a few rules," Dusty said as she sat in Justin's fishing chair, perched on his office chair in front of the computer. She hated this chair, especially using it in his room. Fishing chairs are notorious for being awkward to get in and out of, and they always seem to poke people in their backs and arms. This one also stunk.

"Rules?"

"Yes, I am making them; you have to follow them."

"Why?"

"For your own protection. Besides, I am the wingman here, and I am helping you."

"All right."

"First, no scammers; don't even waste your time on them."

"Okay."

"Second, try to get your matches to meet sooner than later."

"Why is that?" Justin asked curiously.

"Because some girls are just a waste of time. They want to think, evaluate, talk. It means they are wishy-washy or are married or are talking to too many guys and can't decide. Usually, though, they just want the attention because they have low self-esteem and having conversations with a bunch of different dudes is their way to cope. You don't want those either."

"Really?"

"I'm not saying they are bad; some are just careful, but if you have chatted with them for more than two weeks, they are not ever going to meet you or make up their mind to meet you."

"I see."

"Number four."

"What was number three?"

"Okay, number three. Don't come off as a Chad."

48

"Who is Chad?"

"A Chad has several meanings in the dating world. First, a Chad is a guy who only wants sex and will say anything to get it. This Chad is generally good looking and really doesn't have to say much to get women in bed."

"So, a user?"

"Exactly. Another Chad is pretty much a moron. He is full of himself and thinks he is God's gift to women. He doesn't know how to talk to women, especially when he wants them to go out with him. He makes stupid jokes and says stupid things, usually derogatory toward others—especially women. He thinks his macho attitude turns women on or is what they want to hear, but it's the exact opposite. Some women have been in abusive relationships, and they seem to flock to this kind of moron."

"I've seen quite a few of them in bars."

"Yeah, me too. The third Chad is really someone that is clueless. He might even be a good guy with a good heart, but he still doesn't know how to make that connection that will get him digits."

"Digits?"

"Phone numbers. You really need to get out more," Dusty said with a mock sigh.

"No one has said 'digits' since the nineties, Dusty," Doreen said as she brought in a platter holding two plates, each with a slice of cake, two glasses filled with milk, and some napkins.

"How would you know, Momma?" Justin asked, staring at the cake.

"Cosmopolitan," Doreen replied nonchalantly.

Justin remembered seeing the magazine on the nightstand next to his mom's bed, along with the fat Sharpie she used to "edit" pictures and articles that were not to her taste.

"Doreen, you read *Cosmo*?" Dusty asked, sounding shocked.

"Well, the parts I find appropriate," she said indignantly. "It has gotten a little too risqué over the years for my taste, but they still produce a lot of good articles in there, so I just read what I like and don't read what I don't like. I also like the quizzes; those are so much fun to take." She placed the platter down on Justin's bed and went back downstairs.

"Your mom!" Dusty exclaimed.

"Yes, I know," Justin replied, reaching for one of the plates of cake.

"She is full of surprises."

"Don't I know it."

"Anyway, back to business. There are other kinds of Chads, but those three are the most common I run into."

"How many more kinds are there?"

"Tons, but your goal is not to be like any of them."

"Any more rules?"

"Probably, but I can't think of any right now. I will let you know as we move forward."

"I was thinking," Justin started slowly.

"Okay …" Dusty said cautiously.

"It's about her."

"No," Dusty answered quickly but calmly.

"You haven't even heard."

"No."

"But I …"

"What part of 'no' don't you understand?" Dusty asked, frustration in her voice.

"You don't even know what I am going to say."

"It's a bad idea."

"But."

"Look, whatever it is, forget it," she said, debating whether or not to tell him about her profile on the dating site. That would mean breaking his heart all over again. More importantly, he might not let her help him anymore.

"I need closure."

This caught Dusty off guard. She saw him tensing up and knew he was frustrated and getting irritated. This was not a trait she often saw in the laid-back cowboy.

"Okay, what is it?" Dusty asked, resigned to help her friend move forward.

"Rules," Justin said, mimicking her.

"Rules?"

"Yes, number one—you cannot say anything until I am finished."

"Okay, this might be difficult for me to follow."

"Two, you cannot object to it, no matter how foolish you think it is."

"That's not fair," Dusty objected.

"These are my rules. I make them; you follow them."

"Ugh," she replied, hating him using her own words against her.

"Lastly, I am going to do it whether you like it or not."

"Damn it!" she said. She then covered her mouth, listening for the hall monitor.

"Promise me, Dusty."

"Promise you what? You already made up your mind."

"I just want to run this by you. I have put a lot of thought into this, and I am hoping for your blessing."

"Ugh, okay, okay."

"Promise me."

"I promise," Dusty replied, finally giving in to the idea she knew she wasn't going to like.

"Did you know you can send flowers over the internet."

"Oh, no, no, no, no."

"That sounds an awfully a lot like an objection. Remember your promise."

"Damn it." Dusty was careful to whisper it this time.

"I already did it anyway."

"You didn't. You sent your ex-wife flowers?"

"Yep, they arrived last week."

"Was this before you signed up for the dating site?"

"They arrived the day before we signed up."

"What did you send her?"

"Her favorite. Tulips."

"Ugh. Did she reply to you?"

"Nope. She doesn't have my new cell phone number, but I guess she could have called here, but Momma hasn't said that she did call."

"Okay," Dusty said, feeling a little more encouraged.

"You can also send a message with the flowers," Justin continued.

"Oh, no. What did you say?"

"I am still here waiting to see what happens when you find yourself, no matter what that brings."

Dusty started to tear up.

"What?" Justin asked as he handed her a napkin from the tray.

She shook her head and started crying.

"Jeez, Dusty, what did I say?"

"You still love her."

"I think I will always have some love for her; she was such a big part of my life for a very long time. Why does that make you cry?"

Dusty thought back to her own love life over the years. She had dated quite a few guys but only slightly loved a couple of them. There had been many that told her they loved her, only for her to realize that their kind of love lasted only until another love came into their lives. Her dating life was a train wreck at best. It was always exhilarating when the relationship began, but in this culture of online dating, friends with benefits, and sex-driven motives, the options for finding someone that she truly loved and who loved her back were few and far between. She sighed and wished someone would truly love her for her, not because of her looks or her body or even because her father was wealthy. She wanted someone to love her for her.

"Because I have been looking for that someone my entire life that would love me the way you love her. I have always hoped that whomever I ended up with would cherish me for me—not for my face or my body, but for me. A kind of guy that would risk everything, including humiliation and rejection, to chase me down. If I ever had a guy that would put his whole heart on the line for me …" She started to cry again. Justin leaned over and held her as best he could until her crying turned into sobbing. She tried to blow her nose in the degrading napkin and ended up with snot all over her fingers.

He smirked but killed the laugh before it got to his mouth and handed her the entire stack of napkins.

"Thank you," she said, and she blew her nose hard into the stack and then started laughing.

"You okay?" Justin asked with concern.

She nodded and threw the used napkins in the trash.

"Thank you for that."

"For making you cry?"

"I guess I needed to get that out. Are you okay?" Dusty asked, composing herself.

"Yeah, of course."

"What if she doesn't ever reply?" Dusty asked, looking at him intently through bloodshot eyes.

"I don't expect her to."

"Then why did you do it?"

She watched Justin closely as she saw him mull over his words.

He began slowly. "Because I needed closure," he finally said. "Besides, sometimes you have to risk it all; you have to do something spectacular and put your heart on the chopping block. If it gets smashed, then I win. I win because I tried. I care about her, so I had to try. I was not going to let defeat, defeat me. I would never bow down to letting her go away without letting her know she was loved, and I will make sure she never forgets me. Every new man her life now has a huge hurdle to overcome. I didn't set the standard; I am the standard."

Dusty started bawling again. When she finished, she used the rest of the napkins to freshen herself up.

"Holy shit, dude. Where did that come from?" she asked when she finally composed herself.

"I just thought of it, really."

"I am so proud of you. That was pretty deep."

"Thank you. You okay?"

"Yes, now what?" Dusty asked, looking over his shoulder at the monitor that had just gone black.

"Now we find me a girly friend," Justin replied with an impish grin.

"You know I hate it when you say it like that," Dusty replied with a scrunched-up face.

"Then why do you think I say it like that?"

She punched him in the shoulder and giggled.

"I am so glad we are friends," she said with a deep breath, washing her body with relief.

"Me too, sometimes," Justin said with a smile.

Another punch and he pulled up the dating site.

Twelve

Justin spun around in his office chair to face his computer and then moved his mouse to wake up the screen.

"Whoa!" Justin exclaimed after he navigated to the "likes you" area on the dating site.

"I know." Dusty replied.

"Sandra."

"Sandra?" Dusty said as she leaned forward to see who liked Justin. "No, dummy, that's Sarah Beth."

"Oh, right," he said, looking at their old high school mate.

"She is beautiful," Justin said, admiring her photo. "And she likes me."

"That doesn't mean you are going to see her naked."

"It could."

"Are you doing this to get laid or to find a relationship? I mean, either is fine, but you cannot go into this trying to achieve both."

"At this point?"

"Look, if you just want to get you some booty, there is another site for that."

"This internet is great!" Justin said sarcastically.

"Shut up! Seriously, if you want to wait for Suzie, then just get off and we can go grab a beer at the bar."

"If I wanted to just get laid, I would go there."

"So what are you looking for then? I mean, I am being serious. Do you want to wait for Suzie?"

"Yes and no. I want to practice dating before she gets back. I mean, there is no guarantee we will get together when she gets back, however long that will take. I really liked her in high school, but she would never really date me, even though we did everything a normal dating couple would do."

"There is no such thing as a good or bad date," Dusty said, trying to refocus their conversation.

"Really?"

"No, it's the experience and the getting to know the opposite sex. Take your time and date around. If you find someone you like, then you might want to pursue her instead of waiting for Suzie."

"That sounds fair. What kinds of things do I need to learn?"

"Who knows. You seem like you can handle yourself okay around women, but you have been out of the dating game for a long time. You need to learn how it works now. Like, some dudes I went on dates with were perfect gentlemen. They did everything right, and we really had a good time, but it ended up being a bad date to me."

"How is that a bad date?" Justin asked, sounding a little concerned.

"When the date ended, then they suggested we go get a motel room, or make out in the back of their car, or they just came right out and asked where we should go to screw."

"Wow, I can see how that could made it a bad date."

"Yes. Sometimes when they didn't ask for sex, it made it a bad date."

"Wait, so it's a bad date if they ask for sex and it's a bad date if they don't ask for sex?"

"You wouldn't understand," she said a little defensively.

"You're right, I don't understand."

"Women send off signals. Sometimes we just want a date, other times we want to be thrown over our date's shoulders like a Viking warrior would do and then ravaged."

Justin blinked, trying to wrap his mind around what came out of his sweet, innocent childhood friend's mouth. Obviously, he knew she wasn't a prude, and growing up she would debrief him on her exploits with some of the various boys and men who swung through town or the ones they went to school with. Once it was even a teacher. He shook the thought off and refocused.

"So how would a guy know the difference?" he asked slowly.

"The signals."

"Oh, gotcha. Um, what signals?"

"Sometimes she will laugh at your stupid jokes."

"You laugh at my stupid jokes."

"Stay focused, Cowboy. It's different. They will also play with their hair, look seductively at you, try and touch you as much as possible, lean toward you, show you their cleavage, and use the other womanly ways they have in their dating book to attract a man."

"You have a dating book?"

"Figure of speech. There are lots of different ways a girl will tell you she is interested in seeing more of you. If a woman wants to see you again or try to build a relationship with you, she will give you the signs or signals and hope you catch them."

"Jeez, that's a lot to remember."

"You have to remember it's not always about them wanting to have sex with you; it's about them being attracted to you."

"Isn't that the same thing?"

"Oh, no. A woman can be attracted to a man but not want to sleep with him. Yes, I know that if a guy finds a woman attractive, he wants to sleep with her."

"Truer words have never been spoken. How do I know if they are signs or if she is just being nice?"

"Enough with the lessons. I will teach you as we run into real-life experiences. For now let's talk to Sarah Beth."

He rubbed his hands.

"Stop it!" Dusty exclaimed.

"What?"

"You are going to message a woman, not eat a meal, dummy."

"Okay, okay."

He started typing.

"Dear Sarah, it has been a long time. How have you been."

"You are a dumbass." Dusty commented as she watched him type.

"What?"

"Erase that."

"Wha—"

"Erase it now."

"Okay, it's erased. Now what do I put?"

She talked through a few of the lines that had worked on her.

"No, no, and hell no," he replied after he realized that coming up with a pickup line was harder than he thought.

"Well, what did you use on that bit … I mean, on you ex?" Dusty asked, trying not to mutter her name.

"You from around here?" Justin said with a shrug, remembering the first time he got to talk to Joleen. They had both finished their morning events and were sitting next to each other, watching others compete at the rodeo.

"That worked?" Dusty asked, sounding confused.

"Well, obviously."

"Okay, whatever."

He typed in, "Sarah Beth, it's been a day or two," and he hit send.

"She's never going to respond to—" Dusty started.

Bing went the computer.

"Oh, look, she responded," Justin said conceitedly, pointing to the awaiting message.

"Beginner's luck. What did she say?"

He read it out loud.

"Justin, I didn't know if you would remember me from high school."

"Damn, she remembers you. Don't be all Chad-like in your response," Dusty said encouragingly.

"You just sit there, little lady, and let me handle this."

She rolled her eyes and got up and kissed him on the cheek.

"I am going home—long day tomorrow. It looks like my work here is done."

"Thank you, Dusty."

Justin continued just after midnight, messaging with Sarah. He also viewed other profiles when there were breaks in the conversation. With some, he just pressed the like button; others he messaged.

He discovered that Dusty was right. Sarah was a fluke, probably because they knew each other. He wasn't getting any responses from other women; it was late, and they all probably didn't sit by their phones, waiting on some dude to contact them. He thought about calling Dusty, but then he remembered she was probably sleeping.

He remembered Dusty had mentioned icebreakers, or messages that might get a woman to respond, so he decided to look them up on the internet. He wasn't impressed; nor did he feel comfortable with many of the suggested lines, but he found a few that weren't perverted or inappropriate and messaged them to a few women. Still nothing. It was now nearing one, and he figured that many women were probably sleeping. He decided he would check for any results when he woke up later.

Dusty had told him that women constantly get bombarded when they get on these sites, and he needed to find a way to separate himself from the pack.

"Your pretty face will only get you so far on any dating site; you'll have to figure out some way to catch their attention," she had told him with a teasing smile.

Thirteen

The next morning, Justin's boots clicked loudly on the floor as he walked into the coffee shop. He approached April, the waitress, who was running the counter.

April was fifteen years old and full of life and awkwardness. Her five-foot-ten-inch frame put her taller than most of the boys in her class, but she seemed to carry it with all the grace her growing body would allow. Her blonde hair was tied in a ponytail complete with a blue bow to match her big blue eyes, which were now staring up at the cowboy she had known since she could remember. They never ran in the same circles, but they did go to the same church, and Justin had been a volunteer counselor at the church camp she had attended over the years. They weren't friends but were familiar with each other enough to be friendly whenever they were around each other.

"Hi Justin," she said with a smile.

"Hi April, is Dusty around?"

"You don't want to talk to me?" she asked as she did her best seductive lean against the counter.

"Okay, about what?"

"I heard you are dating again."

"Trying to."

"You know, there is someone right here that wouldn't mind being asked out."

"Dusty and I are just friends."

"I am not talking about her," she said while she faked pouting.

Justin looked around the shop at the few customers.

"Who?"

"April, go clean something," Dusty said as she came around the corner, scolding her employee.

"Yes ma'am."

When she had gone to the back, Dusty burst out laughing.

"What?"

"Maybe I was wrong."

"About what."

"Your pretty face might be all you need."

"You forgot about my outstanding physique," he said as he did his best Schwarzenegger pose.

Dusty took a long gaze at his six-foot-two-inch frame. She had to admit the years of working on the ranch and preparing for the rodeo had done him better than most guys that had hit on her in the gym. The Stetson and Wranglers didn't hurt either. He was always the topic of discussion among her staff when he left.

"You are all right," she lied, feeling a bit too flustered for her own comfort. "How did it go with Sarah?"

"We have a date this weekend."

"Really? Good for you. Where are you going to take her?"

"She mentioned a family-owned restaurant near where she lives. We are going to meet there on Saturday after she gets off work."

"Any others?"

"No. Not really. Nobody is responding to me."

"Really? Nobody?"

"Well, a few um, well, women I am not interested in."

"Why?"

"Well, um, I am just not interested." Justin looked uncomfortable.

"Because they are fat or ugly or both?" Dusty pried.

"I am just not attracted to them."

"Good answer, Mr. Politian. Look, it's okay not to go out with someone if you don't find them attractive."

"It isn't?"

"Yes, you are going to have to look at that mug the rest of your life, so make it one that you are attracted to."

"Gotcha."

She handed him a sandwich and a bottled water.

"I didn't order this."

"Do you want it or not?"

"I want it."

"On the house."

"Wrong," he replied quickly as he laid a twenty on the counter and walked out.

Chapter

Fourteen

S unday morning, Justin had finished his early morning chores and breakfast and made his way up to his room, where his mom had mentioned she wanted him to look over "the state of the ranch," as she put it. He flipped on his computer and found the email. He dived into an updated spreadsheet his mom had emailed him. He was pouring over the ranch's expenses and looking at what Doreen had figured for the upcoming year. There was a column for repairs on the equipment they were going to have to pay. Justin had already been working on repairs. Justin was impressed at how accurately his mom had been on some of the repairs.

"Hello," came the familiar voice outside his door.

"Come on in, Dusty," Justin called out to his friend in the hallway.

"So how was the date with Sarah Beth?"

He grimaced.

She walked into the room and saw him rubbing his temples and let out a loud sigh. "Welcome to the wonderful world of online dating," she laughed as she saw the results of a bad date. "That bad, huh?"

"Well," he started; then he stopped.

"Look, we have been friends all of our lives, and I am helping you here, so you need to be honest."

"Oh, my goodness, she has changed. I mean, I didn't really know her that well in school. But damn, it was awful. No, she was awful. Did you know she has three kids?"

"Yup."

"How did you know? And why didn't you tell me?"

"I stalked her on social media. If I had told you everything about her, you wouldn't have asked the right questions."

"Stalked her?"

"On social media. That's different than stalking her in real life. Besides, people post everything on there, so I found out about her kids, that she likes doing crafts, and that she went to Hawaii a few years ago."

"Jeez."

"What happened?"

"We met at a diner; she was pretty normal up to that point."

"Normal?"

"Yeah, we just talked a bit until we ordered, and then she just started talking and wouldn't stop."

"What did she talk about?"

"Like, everything: her kids, her divorce, her life. Like, *everything*."

"That's not bad. Do kids bother you?"

"Well, no, but I was surprised she told me about them; isn't that dangerous to be talking about to a stranger?"

"Under normal circumstances, but she knows you."

"Oh."

"Anything else?"

"She did the hair thing."

"Oh, so she was into you."

"Yes, yes she was."

"Did you get to see her naked?"

"She invited me back to her place; she said the kids were at their grandmother's."

"Did you see her naked?" Dusty asked again.

"She wanted us to go there to have a nightcap."

"That's a code word for sex," Dusty informed him.

"Yeah, I got that."

"Did you see her naked?"

"What is with you and sex?"

"One of us needs to be getting some. I certainly am not. Besides, I want to live vicariously through your sex life."

"No, I did not go and have a nightcap with her."

"Dude! You were so in, why not?"

"I didn't want to lead her on."

"Dude, she wanted to bang you. Probably with no strings attached."

"I just don't want that kind of relationship."

"Who said anything about a relationship? She needed some dick."

"Dusty!"

"Look, its fine you didn't sleep with her. I was just saying."

"Okay, but I just wasn't feeling it."

They worked on his profile a bit more and then went through the different likes and messages; then Dusty told him she needed to get going and left.

He worked a few more hours on the site and then got tired and shut the computer down.

He texted Dusty: "I have a couple of more dates lined up, and I am now chatting with a couple of women."

Fifteen

The next evening, Justin arrived at the restaurant a little bit early and sat on one of the benches just outside the door. The building had been home to Pizza Hut before they moved to a better location. It still had the same frame, but the new owners painted the red roof green and had painted or changed other aspects to try to separate themselves from the former owners. This place served comfort food, and the smells coming from inside were reminding Justin he should have eaten the other half of the sandwich his mother had made for him while he was changing out the starter on their tractor.

"Justin!" said a rather plump blonde walking across the parking lot.

"Megan?" Justin asked, a little surprised.

"It's so good to meet you! You look exactly like your pictures."

Justin wished he could say the same, but this woman before him was not exactly represented in her profile. She was much heavier, and her face was somehow different in real life from the pictures she had posted online.

"Nice to meet you," Justin said slowly.

"I was afraid I was going to get catfished again," she told him as they were led to their table in the small diner.

"Yeah, me too," Justin replied, scratching his head.

They sat down, ordered their drinks, and started perusing the menu. Justin barely saw any of the words, as he was still trying to wrap his mind around what catfishing had to do with dating and, more importantly, to figure out what it was so he wouldn't do it. He sure hoped it didn't mean "look like a catfish," because he surely wasn't interested in being thought of like that.

He resisted the urge to text Dusty; he was sure she would know, but she warned him never to look at his phone while on a date. That was the number-one rule in first dates.

"Isn't it awful?" Megan asked as she peeked over the top of the menu.

"What is? The food?"

"No, people who catfish."

He wanted to say he liked catfishing and eating catfish, but he was sure he would somehow sound like a moron, so kept that thought to himself.

"It's a shame" was the only appropriate answer he could find.

"I can't believe people would do that to another person."

"People are jerks sometimes."

"You get it," she said as she smiled seductively, grabbed a lock of her dirty blonde hair from around her ear with a finger, and ran it down to her chest, where she held it for a minute.

"Yes, yes I do," Justin lied nervously.

"What will we be having tonight?" the waitress asked as she realized Justin was struggling a bit.

"Burger and fries," he answered quickly.

"I will have the chicken alfredo and a salad," Megan replied.

"Great, anything else?" she asked as she looked at Justin.

He returned her gaze like a deer caught in the headlights. Justin was definitely wanting an out and was trying to plead with the waitress using his eyes, but then he realized she could offer no assistance that wouldn't cause a scene.

"I am good," he finally lied.

"Me too," Megan added.

"Okay, I will go put these in right now." She left quickly to place their order.

"What do you do for a living?" Megan asked as she went back to fiddling with her hair.

"I work my family's ranch. You?"

"Mail carrier. That must be hard work. Do you have to work sunup to sundown?"

"In the summer, much longer than that. Right now the fields are bedded for the winter; we only have a few animals to tend to."

"Oh, so what do you do all day long?"

"Plenty. There are still fences to mend, barns to fix and clean equipment that needs to be maintained, and errands to run—and to get everything ready for spring."

"Sounds exciting."

"Not really, but it keeps me busy. Delivering the mail sounds fun; everyone is excited to see the mail carrier," Justin said, as he struggled to keep the conversation going.

"Eh, sometimes. I mean, we do bring bills. No one wants those."

Justin felt a tap on his shoulder and looked up.

"Sir, I think there is a phone call for you."

"What? Who?"

The waitress shrugged. "I don't know, she just described a tall cowboy. As you can see, you are the only one in here that matches that description."

Justin looked around and confirmed he was the only one there to match that description. The waitress stepped away and waited for him over by the wall next to the rear of the restaurant.

"Excuse me, I know I am not supposed to do this, but I need to see if everything is okay," he told Megan as he pulled out his phone and called his mother.

"Hello, Momma, are you okay?" he asked when she picked up the phone.

He clicked off when he confirmed she was okay. He immediately dialed Dusty.

"You okay?"

"Your date over already?" Dusty asked curiously.

"No, are you okay?"

"Why are you calling me while on your date?"

"Because."

"No, hang up and do your date."

"Are you okay, though?"

"Yes," she reaffirmed, and she hung up on him.

Justin looked a little confused but raised his hand as if he were back in school. The waitress came back to their table.

"Sorry, ma'am, they must be looking for someone else; all my women friends are …" He paused and thought about Suzie.

"Are what?" the waitress snapped.

"They are all right; must be looking for someone else," he continued as he realized there was no way she would have known he would have been there tonight, and she would have called is cell.

The waitress let out a deep sigh and turned to go check on other guests as she shook her head.

Justin shrugged and turned back to his date.

"I guess because I wear a Stetson, I am labeled."

Megan was beaming and really going at her hair.

They talked a lot during dinner and even had dessert. When they had finished, Justin walked her back to her car and opened the door. She threw open her hands in the universal sign for giving her a hug, so he moved forward, but she grabbed him quickly and planted a kiss on his lips. He stepped back in surprise.

"There is more where that came from," she said seductively. "A lot more."

"I, um, well," Justin stammered.

"Why don't you come back to my place; we can Netflix and chill."

Justin figured this statement as an invitation to get laid if he wanted to. He didn't want to. It wasn't that Megan was unattractive, maybe a little heavy, but it was the things she said in the conversation that made him think twice. She was more of a homebody, while he loved the outdoors. She liked to travel, whereas he felt more comfortable staying in Montana. He also felt deceived by her pictures and her appearance. He didn't like to be lied to, and her alteration of her photos made him wonder what else she was hiding.

"I, um, I am too tired to watch a movie, sorry," he said, and he quickly walked back to his truck, fired it up, and tore out of that parking lot as if the devil himself were after him.

Chapter

Sixteen

Justin drove over to Dusty's house the next evening. She invited him in, gave him a beer, and then led him outside.

"Oh, hell no!" Dusty exclaimed as Justin told her about the kiss.

They were sitting in the sun porch at Dusty's house, watching the sun set. He hadn't been able to talk to her because he had been busy all day spending time with his mother and running errands. First, they'd had a big breakfast, and then they'd gone off to church. They went over to an elderly couple's house to deliver them some food and supplies. Mom fed him a late lunch and then had him take her to town so she could get their own supplies. When he had finally finished, he rushed over to Dusty's. She had been pestering him all day with texts about his date, which he kept ignoring. Having a conversation via text wasn't his thing anyway; he preferred to talk face-to-face with her.

"Yup."

"Just like that? She just up and kissed you?"

"Yup."

"Did you want her to?"

"No, she wasn't attractive, like in her pictures."

Dusty glared at him.

"You said I had to be attracted to her. I wasn't."

"But you went out with her anyway?"

"No. Well yes, but her pictures were way prettier than her in real life."

"Filters!" Dusty exclaimed as she got it.

"Filters?" Justin asked, seemingly confused.

"Yeah, there are apps for your phone that can make you look different; you still look the same, but better."

Justin thought about it for a minute.

"That must have been it, because she did not look in real life like she did in her pictures."

"Did she have one with kitty cat ears and nose?"

"What?" Justin asked in astonishment.

"There are filters that add that to you picture," Dusty informed him.

"Oh, no. Wait, she had one of a dog. I thought she had some kind of mask on."

They sat there sipping their beers, slowly rocking, and watching the sun slip behind the mountains.

"What the hell is catfishing?" Justin asked suddenly. "I mean, I am not a moron, but she kept talking about how she had been catfished."

"Oh, dear, what did you say?"

"I just lied and said it was a terrible thing to do."

Dusty explained the dating version of catfishing.

Justin listened as she explained that some people make fake profiles for themselves using pictures and even personalities to try to lure others into liking them. Their hope is that someone will fall for them and, when they finally meet, not worry about their real appearance.

"So *I* was catfished?"

"Kinda. I mean, not really. The pictures were of her, only altered. Usually when someone catfishes you they use pictures of someone entirely different. Any other surprises on this very entertaining date?"

"It wasn't entertaining."

"Oh, it is to me," Dusty joked.

"Whatever. That was about it." He thought about the date and then commented, "That whole date was a damn circus."

"Oh, so something else did happen. What did she do?"

"It wasn't her; it was the waitress."

"The waitress?"

"Yeah, after we ordered, she said some girl had called and described her to me as sounding like she needed help."

"Is that why you called me?"

"Yes, you and Momma. But both of you were fine, so I told her she must have been looking for someone else."

"Oh my God, you really are a moron."

"You mean someone was really in trouble? Who? You and Momma were the only ones that knew I was going there."

"No, you dumbass, she saw you were struggling, so she tried to give you an out. Did you even follow her to the phone?" Dusty asked.

"No."

"Why not?"

"Because I didn't want to talk to some stranger that needed her cowboy."

"There was no girl."

"Yes there was she said so," Justin insisted.

Dusty took a few deep breaths.

"The waitress was trying to help you," she said calmly.

"What?"

"Where do most people go for first dates?"

He looked at her blankly.

"To restaurants or bars. They see that kind of thing all the time. They know when someone is not having a good time and use excuses like that to help get them out."

"How did she know I didn't want to be there? I didn't tell her anything."

"Because you don't hide your emotions well."

"Okay, so how would that have gotten me out of the date?"

"She probably would have told you to go back to the table and apologize, saying that your sister—"

"I don't have a sister."

"You don't have a friend in trouble, either."

"Oh, right."

"Anyway, she probably would have said your sister, your momma, your aunt, or some female friend blew a tire or fell off her porch or some other emergency and you had to leave immediately."

"That works?"

"All the time."

"Oh. Okay, next time, I will be ready for that."

"Did you at least have a good conversation with her?" Dusty asked.

"It was okay. She is kind of boring, and I don't think we would get along."

"Oh, how so?"

"Her favorite thing to do is binge-watch TV shows."

"Yeah, that wouldn't work," Dusty agreed.

"Do you know she even invited me back to watch Netflix and chill?"

Dusty laughed.

"That's another sex reference, isn't it?" Justin asked, scratching his head.

"Yup."

"Jeez, there are a lot of them."

"Damn, boy. You get offered more sex than a prostitute."

"Well, I do have a pretty face."

"I never should have told you that," Dusty said as she grimaced.

Chapter

Seventeen

Justin had just left Dusty's and made his way quietly to his room. He figured his mom was in bed but probably not sleeping, and he didn't want to disturb her. He looked at his phone and the three numbers he had saved in his phone list: Dusty, home, and Suzie.

His heart leapt when he saw the last name and remembered the kiss at the airport. He had spent a lot of time with her in high school, trying to win her heart to no avail. She had not been in his life that much recently, but the time he had spent around her had stirred some old emotions. He compared the girl she was to the woman she is now. She was older now, but still beautiful. He smiled to himself as he remembered watching her walk away at the airport in her suit pants, and how he stole a glance at her butt, which hadn't changed at all.

The pain of losing her still lingered in his heart from all those years ago, and the thought of losing her again was something he had been debating in his head and heart since he learned she was available.

He checked his phone again. She had told him to call her whenever he wanted when she gave him the number. He took a slow, deep breath, pressed her name, and then hit the call button.

"Um, hi Suzie," Justin stammered into the phone.

"Justin, it's so good to hear your voice," she replied sleepily.

"Are you in bed?"

"Yes," she said, trying unsuccessfully to stifle a yawn.

"It's only ten p.m."

"Justin, it's after midnight here."

"Oh, I am sorry; I guess I didn't realize," he said as that familiar moronic feeling came back to haunt him.

"No, it's okay. Hold on for a minute."

He waited patiently as he listened to dead air for a minute.

"You still there?" she asked, a little more chipper.

"Look, I am sorry; we can talk tomorrow, or the day after," Justin offered.

"No, it's okay. I am awake now."

Justin grabbed a notebook and a pen from his desk and started writing.

"What are you doing?" Suzie asked.

"I am writing down that we have a two-hour difference."

"Aw, that's sweet."

"I don't want to wake you again."

"You know, Russel never cared about things like that. He would call me at all hours."

"Oh."

"Many times he was too cheap to take a cab or an Uber after hitting the bars and would make me get out of bed and come pick him up. Then he would try to get some when we got home."

"Oh."

"I am so sorry; I shouldn't talk about him," Suzie said quickly.

"No, it's okay. I sometimes want to talk about Joleen."

"So why don't you?"

"I can't really tell things to Momma about her."

"What about Dusty?"

"She doesn't want to hear anything about her."

"Have you tried a therapist?"

"No."

"Why? Too macho?"

"No."

"Then why?"

"Joleen was seeing one. I have been thinking he might be the reason she left me."

"You think they were having an affair?"

"I doubt it," Justin said with a laugh.

"Why? Things like that do happen," Suzie insisted.

"She wasn't, um, his type."

"She was too young? He was married?"

"He was gay."

Justin heard Suzie unsuccessfully stifle her laughter.

"Sorry," she apologized.

"It's okay. I thought it was a little weird she wanted to go in the first place, but she said she wanted to deal with a few things that only a therapist could help her with."

"That seems normal. Did she tell you why she wanted to go?"

"No, she never did. I didn't really ask, because I felt if she wanted me to know, she would tell me. I guess deep down I was afraid it was something I had done."

"Usually if a woman wanted to fix a relationship, she would want to go to a couple's therapist and bring you with her."

"I guess I hadn't really thought of that. You think it was something else?" Justin asked, feeling encouraged.

"I don't know. It could be because of a million different reasons."

There was a brief pause while Justin processed this new information.

"Why do you think it was because of him?" Suzie finally asked.

"Well, she had stopped seeing him for a while, and then one day he contacted her and told her he would give her a free session to do a final follow-up."

"That seems normal. What happened at the final follow-up?"

"I don't know, exactly. When she came home, she had somehow changed."

"Changed?"

"I dunno, she was acting weird."

"How so?"

"I can't really describe it, but it was just different."

"Then what?" Suzie asked, encouraging him.

"Then a day later, she was gone."

"She just left?"

"Yeah, I was at work. When I got home, she had packed a lot of her stuff and left me a note on the kitchen table."

"What did the note say? If you don't mind me asking."

"It said she had to go find herself."

"That's it?"

Justin teared up and then cleared his throat and continued. "Not to try and find her or contact her."

"That's awful! Are you okay?"

Justin thought about it. That memory had haunted him since the day he read it, and he hadn't told anyone about it. Letting it out to Suzie made him feel better. It still hurt, but now that it was out, he felt as though a fog had been lifted off his chest.

"I am. I do feel better, Suzie. Thank you."

"Anytime, stud. Well, I am exhausted and have a busy day tomorrow."

"Okay, good-bye Suzie."

"No, wait."

"What?"

"Can you call me on Wednesday night?" Suzie asked.

"Sure, what time?"

"Eight o'clock my time, if that's doable."

Justin wrote this down.

"Okay, six o'clock my time on Wednesday."

"Good night, cowboy."

"Good night, Suzie."

Chapter

Eighteen

Justin walked into the coffee shop and looked around. Dusty and her staff were definitely getting ready for the expansion while trying to keep the current business running. His boots echoed on the hardwood floor as he walked up to the counter.

"Hi," he said, trying to read the name tag on the girl standing behind the counter. Her name tag rested on her enormous breasts, and he strained to read the faded writing on it. She waited patiently with a smile as he finally gave up. When their eyes met, he realized he had been staring at her chest for way too long.

"You must be Justin," she said a little flirtatiously.

"Uh, I ... yes ma'am," he replied as he tried to recover from his embarrassment.

"I am Lori, nice to finally meet you."

"Uh, oh. Hi, Lori. Same here," Justin stammered, trying to regain his composure.

Lori had moved to Hackamore a few years back, and Justin had only seen her from the grocery store where she used to work before she recently found employment at the coffee shop. She was barely over five feet tall and had short auburn hair and brown eyes. She wasn't thin, but not fat either, and she carried herself with confidence. Her bubbly personality and friendly smile had made her a good choice for waiting at the expanding coffee shop.

"I'll bet," April, another waitress, said as she walked up and stood next to Lori.

"Girls!" came a voice from behind them.

"Ugh, I know, I know," snapped April as she grabbed a rag and went to go wipe down the tables. "Bye, Justin, nice seeing you again."

"You too, April."

"How can I help you, Justin?" Lori asked him.

"You can help him by buttoning those top two buttons on your shirt and putting this on your name tag," Dusty said as she handed her a label sticker with her name on it.

Dusty sent Lori to grab a broom and join April in cleaning the dining room.

"April Thompson is sure growing up fast," Justin remarked.

"Too fast if you ask me," Dusty replied.

"You really need to hire some dudes to work in here," Justin told Dusty.

"I have; they are mainly cooks. No dudes are applying for front of house."

"Well, at least they are friendly. They need to be friendly to make better tips."

"Only to you, eye candy," she said with a smirk.

"Is that what I am to you?"

"No, to them. To me you are still the same old dumbass."

"Glad to hear it."

"So what's up?"

"Momma wants one of those sandwiches you made her the other day. Oh, and the largest cup of coffee that you make."

"Venti."

"Yes, one large venti."

Dusty laughed.

"No, silly. 'Venti' means 'large.'"

"Why don't they just call it large?"

"Because some famous coffee chain decided it would be called venti, and all of us small-town coffee shops have followed their lead."

"Okay, whatever."

"What sandwich did I make her the other day?" asked Dusty.

"It had some meat in it, and she dipped into some brown soup."

Dusty rolled her eyes.

"What?"

"It's called au jus."

"Oh right. Okay, one au jus sandwich and a venti coffee to go, please."

"Anything for you?"

"Naw, I have a date later."

"Ooooh, with who?"

Before he could speak, she raised a finger and ran to the back to get the cook working on his order. When she came back, she gave a stern look at the two Nosy Nancys that had crept closer to eavesdrop on their conversation. They started to turn, and then Dusty spoke to them.

"Would you two like to join in on this conversation?" Dusty asked the pair.

They looked at each other and then back at Dusty with wide eyes.

"Um, Dusty," Justin asked, sounding confused.

"Shush," she told Justin. She then turned to address her waitstaff. "Well, would you?"

They both nodded eagerly, and she waved them over. They stood to Justin's left, and Dusty folded her hands, rested her elbows on the counter, and put her chin on the perch.

"So who is it?"

"Well, it's um … well." He paused and looked at the two new participants. Justin wasn't shy, but having the pair eavesdrop definitely took him out of his comfort zone. He studied the pair and then looked back at Dusty.

"Well?" asked Dusty.

The other two joined in.

"Well?"

Justin was definitely feeling uncomfortable. He wasn't much for group discussions unless it was to a herd of cattle he was trying to calm during a lightning storm, or horses when he was training them. He had spent many years trying to get a horse to take a saddle and then a rider. He had been bucked off more times than he cared to remember. This was certainly different; horses and cows weren't so judgy. Justin took a deep breath and plowed on.

"All I know is that her name is Pinwheel 79 and she lives in Evergreen."

"Is she pretty?" April blurted out.

"Yeah, is she pretty?" Dusty chimed in.

"Well, not as pretty as you three," Justin said as smoothly as he could muster.

April blushed when he looked at her, Lori smiled brightly and started fiddling with her hair, and Dusty remained solid on her perch.

"Of course she isn't," Dusty replied coolly with a smile. "Tell us about her."

"Well, she is a blonde, about five feet ten inches tall." He scratched his head. "She moved up here from New Mexico a few years back. She is divorced with a five-year-old boy. I think she said she does something with transportation in the government."

"What's her real name?" April asked.

"Don't know; she said it had something to do with her name."

"Kids are trouble," April offered.

"Pinwheel 79 … Does that mean she is forty-one years old?" asked Lori.

"Yes, at least that is what her profile said."

"Oh, we want to see," Dusty interjected.

"Yes!" The other two said in unison, quickly and enthusiastically.

"Here ya go," said Ralph the cook as he placed a bag containing Justin's order on the counter.

Justin quickly grabbed the bag and the coffee that Dusty had set on the counter earlier. He pulled a twenty from his chest pocket and threw it at Dusty and made a quick exit.

The girls laughed as he quickly departed.

"Good luck with Miss Cougar!" April hollered after him.

"What?" asked Ralph.

Chapter

Nineteen

That evening Justin stood in front of his closet door, which also doubled as a full-length mirror. He was putting the final touches on his outfit and made sure everything looked just right on him.

There was a tap on the door, and then he heard Dusty.

"Hello?"

"Come on in, Dusty."

"Whoa, you look good! What's the occasion?" Dusty asked as he was putting on some cologne. She sat down in his office chair. "I thought you said your date with Miss Pinwheel was this afternoon."

"It was."

"A second date already? You are moving quick with this one."

"No, this is a different one."

"What?"

Justin shrugged as he wiped the excess cologne on Dusty's face.

"Jerk. Now I'm going to smell like a dude."

"About time," Justin joked.

"You are getting awfully cocky since you are going out with all these women."

"It has been good for my morale."

"I can tell. Did you ever find out what Pinwheel's name was?"

"Yeah, Wendy."

"How the hell does she get that out of pinwheel?"

"I guess they used to call them wind wheels, and her name is Wendy."

"That's a stretch."

"She's a thinker."

"You like her, don't you?"

"I did enjoy my date with her," Justin replied with a smile.

"So why are going on another one with a different woman?"

"Working on my Chad degree."

"Where the heck did you get that from?" Dusty asked.

Justin heard footsteps creeping down the hall.

"She and I had a great conversation and a great meal, and everything went pretty good."

"You like her. I can tell."

"I told you, I really enjoyed our date."

"Maybe you should stick with older women," Dusty remarked.

"Maybe."

"Who is the lucky girl tonight?"

"Melissa."

"She sounds sexy."

"So does her voice."

"Is she older than us?"

"Two years older. Another cougar, as April likes to call them."

"What about Wendy?"

"She left her husband."

"Oh," Dusty said. "That doesn't mean she will leave you."

"Yeah, but I really don't want to take that chance. Once is enough for me."

"Maybe he did something wrong—hit her or mentally abused her, or something else."

He shook his head.

"She told you that?"

"She told me he did nothing wrong—that she just fell out of love with him, but he would not leave, so she did."

"That doesn't mean—"

"That means I don't want to hope she doesn't do it again and then does," he said firmly.

"Okay, okay. I get it, you want to play it safe."

"I just don't ever want to hurt like that again."

"Didn't you say you have to put your heart on the chopping block?"

"Yep, but not for her."

"Wait, you said you don't want to hurt like that again."

"Yeah, so?"

"Does that mean you don't hurt anymore?"

Justin froze. He tried to remember the last time he really hurt. It had been a while; there was still some sadness, but it felt more like numbness than pain.

"I guess I still ache a bit, but yeah, I guess the pain is going away."

"Good for you!" she said as she got up and hugged him. "Good luck tonight."

"Thank you."

"Go get 'em cowboy," she told him, and she headed home.

"You look so handsome," his mother commented as she fussed with his collar. "Just like your daddy."

"Thank you, Momma."

"He would be so proud of you," she commented as she straightened is shirt and smoothed out some wrinkled areas.

"I know he would."

Doreen stepped back, looking puzzled. "Aren't you going to fuss at me for messing with your clothes?"

"Never again, Momma. I remember you always saying that Daddy didn't mind it when you did that."

A tear slipped from Doreen's eye.

"Go have a good time, son. Be careful out there."

"I will, I promise."

He kissed his mom on the cheek, grabbed his hat, and made his way down the stairs.

Chapter

Twenty

Wednesday night at exactly eight o'clock Eastern Time, Justin lay back on his bed and pressed the third number saved into his phone.

"Hello, Suzie. How's your great grandma doing?" Justin asked Suzie when she answered the phone.

"Hey, cowboy. She is fine, fighting the good fight."

"Is she in pain?"

"A little; her body is old, and she has arthritis. It is hard for her to get around, but she is doing it."

"Good for her."

"Yeah, I am not sure exactly why she wants me here."

"What do you mean?"

"I mean ever since I got here, she has cooked for me, gone shopping with me … she even made my bed the other day."

"You don't make your bed?"

"I do now," Suzie said with a laugh.

"Well, good for her," he replied, chuckling.

"Yes, but I am feeling kind of useless."

"Don't be, she needed a friend—someone to talk to and to make her feel useful again."

"I didn't really think of it like that."

"Sometimes being a blessing to someone is allowing them to be a blessing to you."

"Wow! That is really insightful," Suzie said admiringly.

"Yeah, my momma is full of good insights. I am starting to realize that all those years she was drumming those sayings into me, she was really teaching me some good lessons."

"Your mom really is a good woman."

"That she is, even though she is awfully nosy," he said a little louder to the shadow he could see under the crack of his door.

"Stop it! It only means she cares about you."

"I know. I like to give her a hard time. I don't have any secrets from her."

"It is good to have someone you can talk to and be completely honest with."

"I am three times as lucky then."

"Oh?"

"Momma, Dusty, and you."

There was a long pause on the phone.

"So are you still on that dating site?" she asked abruptly.

"Yep."

"How's that going?"

"Honestly?"

"No, Justin, I want you to lie to me," she said with a giggle.

"Well then, amazing," he shot back sarcastically.

"That bad, huh?"

"I never knew women could be so, um, different."

"Well, of course we are different."

"No, I mean, like, single women."

"Oh, how so?"

"I am digging a hole here, aren't I?" Justin asked sarcastically.

"Depends on what comes out of your mouth next," Suzie retorted.

"I mean, these girls are crazy. They say crazy things, they make crazy choices, they do crazy things. A lot of them just want to have sex. Others, I think, are just trying to get attention from guys."

"Why do you think they are single?"

"Well, I guess for maybe the same reason you and Dusty are."

"Why is Dusty single? She is so beautiful."

"She is a bit crazy too."

Suzie laughed at that comment. "Great, that's the woman I left in charge of my business."

"Oh, you have nothing to worry about. She is solid there."

"So what makes her crazy then?"

"She has bad taste in men."

"It seems we all do."

"Joleen didn't."

"Ah, point taken."

"I was just kidding. But Dusty really seems to attract the wrong kind of men."

"No, Dusty attracts all kinds of men; she just picks the wrong ones."

Justin thought about that for a minute. He could remember growing up how she would always go after guys that were totally wrong for her.

The gym teacher was probably her worse choice. She had just turned seventeen, and he had come to the school as an assistant football coach right out of college. They had hit it off pretty quickly. He couldn't really blame her; the guy was full of charisma and had taken on the job of gym teacher when the current gym teacher had to take time off to care for his wife who was battling cancer. She had been working out in the weight room with some of the guys, and the teacher had been there to make sure there was no roughhousing and to make sure no one tried to break any records without doing it safely. They had stayed late working on her glutes, and one thing led to another. Of course it was illegal, and Justin felt it was immoral, but he kept his mouth shut, and when the teacher got a job at a big college, he left her without saying good-bye.

That result seemed to be the mantra of her life; the guys would get what they wanted from her and then leave her crushed.

He looked over to his bed. There were many nights she had come over to cry herself to sleep while spilling out her most recent tragedy. That is why he always had kept tissue in his room.

When he had gotten married, there were many times he had been sitting at his kitchen table with Joleen and her on the speakerphone as she poured out her tears trying to figure out what was wrong with men, her, and the dating world in general.

"That is a true statement, more accurate that you know," Justin said pointedly.

"I know, I went through the same thing." Suzie said with a sigh.

"But you were married."

"No, I mean before that."

"In school?"

"Yes. Well, in college, you always made me feel good about myself. Then I met Russel. He wasn't always the most proactive in our relationship, but there was something about him that always made me feel good about myself. That is until about a year after we were married; then he changed, or I did."

"What about now? What about the guys on the site?"

"Well, I learned. When you get hurt like that, you start getting pickier, or less involved."

"Less involved?"

"I have a hard time trusting now. I mean, Russel never led me to believe that he was a liar or a cheater. Honestly, I can see why he wanted to have sex with his secretary, but never in a million years could I ever believe that he would have cheated on me."

"I can understand that. With Joleen, I never saw any signs that she was unhappy or wanted to leave me. I still struggle with that a little bit."

"Therapy helps."

Justin cringed at that suggestion. "Do you think Joleen told the therapist about us?"

"Probably. He might have even tried to talk her out of it, given her some things to work on to help her stay."

"I never thought of that."

"What did you think?"

"I thought he might have wanted to keep her as a client so he gave her advice that would make her keep seeing him."

"There are bad therapists, but I doubt he told her to leave."

"You think so?" Justin asked, starting to alter his opinion about the therapist.

"I don't know. I don't know what he was like or what they discussed. I do know keeping her in a troubled relationship would guarantee more sessions than telling her to make a clean break," Suzie postulated.

Justin mulled this new information over in his mind.

"Justin, you still there?" Suzie asked after the long silence.

"Yeah, just thinking. It takes me longer than the average human."

"Shut up; you are smart."

"Well, thank you."

"Hey, don't worry about it; only worry about the things you can control, and try not to make the same mistakes you did before."

"Now you are sounding like my momma."

"I will take that compliment."

They sat there in awkward silence for a moment.

"How did Dusty get her nickname?" Suzie suddenly asked.

Justin laughed. "It started when she was about three. She would walk around after messing around outside, slapping her hands together and saying, 'I am dusty, I am dusty.' She would pat down her shirt and pants and watch the dust fly off and say, 'Yep, I am dusty.'"

"That's funny."

"Pretty soon everyone started calling her Dusty."

"She is a good a friend, isn't she?"

"The best."

"So why aren't you dating her?'

"I told you before, we are just friends."

"Is that all?"

"She always tells me I am not her type."

"Do you want to date her?"

There was another long silence.

"Justin?"

"I don't know. I mean, there were times in high school that we slept together."

"You had sex with her?"

"No, I said we slept together."

"Isn't that sex?"

"No, I mean she would come over after some dude broke her heart or she was too drunk to go home and face her dad, so she would climb into bed with me." He quickly added, "With her clothes on."

"And you never fooled around with her?"

"No, never."

"Why?"

"I am not her type," Justin reiterated. This was only a half-truth. The real reason was that Justin believed that if had ever slept with Dusty, then his chances with Suzie would have gone from slim to none. He had never wanted to take that chance no matter how much the temptation had been.

"That doesn't mean you can't have sex with her."

"It just never seemed the right time, especially when she was heartbroken or drunk."

"So you wanted to?"

"I am a dude, when a hot chick climbs into bed with you, of course, that thought crosses your mind," Justin reminded her.

"So you do want to have sex with her."

"What is it with you two?"

"What?"

"Both of you want me to have sex with the other one. She has been trying to get me to ask you out since she came back into town."

"Why didn't you?"

"It's complicated."

"No, it's really not. Is it because I am divorced?"

"No, not at all."

"Then why?"

"You are so far away."

"I wasn't you had your chance before I even knew I was going to be out here."

"It's, um … Well, it's, umm … Like I said, it's complicated."

"Ugh. Okay, Mr. Complicated. So how is your dating life going? You never told me."

Justin spent the next half hour sharing his limited experiences in his bid to try to find someone he could date. He lamented on the different social blunders and hoops he had to jump through to try to even get a girl to chat with him, the few that had actually gone out with him, and the fiascos he realized he had worked so hard to get himself into once they were out on dates. He told her how he had been kind of catfished, that on one date he really was catfished, and that at other times the girl never showed up.

He did spend a lot of time covering his date with Wendy.

"You like her, don't you?"

"I did."

"Just because she left one dude doesn't mean she is going to leave you."

"I'm not willing to take that chance. Besides, you were the one that said once you have been hurt like that, it makes it much more difficult to trust someone else that exhibits those same qualities."

"Yeah, I guess I did," she replied.

"I think it is especially hard in both of our cases."

"Why is that?"

"Because we didn't think they would do that to us."

"We never think the one we choose and that chose us is going to betray our hearts." Suzie sounded defeated.

"I am learning that there are signs to watch for. Neither Joleen nor Russel displayed any of those signs, so it hit us twice as hard," Justin reminded her.

"I see your point. I know I am overly cautious now when I go out with someone."

"But you don't know what signs to look for, because there were none last go-around."

"That is true," Suzie agreed.

"I am in the same boat. I have no clue what I am looking for, nor signs that I should be watching out for."

"What are you looking for, then?"

"Big boobs," he replied jokingly.

"I guess that would be a good start. At least you could get some fun out of them."

"Really don't know what I am looking for, I guess I will know when I find it."

"So what are you going to do till then?"

"I guess keep going out until I find the one," Justin replied, and then wished her good night and hung up.

Chapter

Twenty-One

The next morning, Dusty woke up early and headed to work. She wanted to start cleaning out the new space Suzie had purchased for the restaurant. She was feeling excited about having purpose in her life. She giggled to herself as she looked at the clock on the dash: 5:18 a.m. She would still be sleeping for at least another hour and a half, dreading the alarm clock that would wake her up way too early. She also thought about how many times she could hit the snooze button and what she would have to sacrifice in getting ready so she wouldn't be late to work. Sometimes she would give up showering, sometimes her morning workout, and in very rare instances she would miss her makeup routine, putting on only the bare minimum.

She pulled up in front of the coffee shop and looked at the space next door. It looked a little creepy with nothing inside and only the streetlight shining in a small pool of light through the big bay windows. Dusty grabbed her phone and sent Justin a text to meet her later at her place so they could discuss his game plan and the phone call he'd had with Suzie last night.

After one last deep breath, she shut down her car, ran up to the shop and unlocked it, and stepped inside. The warmth hit her and gave her energy to start her tasks.

All day she kept looking at the clock, wondering when Justin would be able to come over. Her staff was now trained enough to continue business without her, except the occasional question that could be answered with a phone call. Dusty had made Lori the shift supervisor, and she seemed to be competent enough.

Dusty felt a buzz in her back pocket around 3:00 p.m. She read Justin's text that informed her he had finished his work for the day and was going to shower and then head over to her place.

"Finally!" she said out loud to herself.

"Finally what?" Lori asked.

"Finally, time for me to go home. You got it from here?"

"Sure do, boss lady."

Dusty grabbed her coat and headed to her place. She had just unlocked the door to her house when she heard Justin's truck pull into her drive.

He came in and sat down on the couch.

"How did your chat with Suzie go?" Dusty asked Justin as she handed him a beer and sat in her chair.

"It was good, I guess."

"You guess?"

"I think I really like her, but I don't know when or if she will be back," Justin said with a sigh.

"So?"

"So I am not sure what I should do."

"You said you wanted to practice date till she gets back. Do that; it will be okay."

"Won't she get jealous or be mad?"

"She won't get mad, and you want her a little jealous."

"I do? Why?"

"Because women want what they can't have."

"That doesn't make sense."

"Neither do women; just do it," Dusty said jokingly.

"What if I find someone I really like?"

"Then good for you and sucks for her."

"There is another problem."

"Oh?" Dusty replied as she sat up quickly.

"I am, um … well, I, uh …"

"Spit it out, cowboy," she said impatiently.

"Dusty, I haven't had sex in over a year now."

"Want to go do it now?"

"Wha- what?" Justin stuttered.

"Sure, let's go do it. I haven't gotten laid longer than that."

She could see that he was clearly uncomfortable with that suggestion, but he didn't seem dismissive of the offer either.

"I uh, well, I don't know," Justin replied his cheeks turning red.

"Easy, big boy, I was just joking." When the words left her lips, Dusty was not sure whether she was joking or not. They had come close a couple of times, but that was usually when she had been hammered or trying to rebound, and Justin would not have any of that.

She always told him he was not her type, which she believed back then, but now things were different. She was different, and he was different as well.

He was good-looking and definitely well built—more so than many of the guys she had let see her naked. Justin had depth, though, and he was her best friend, and she knew she probably could do it without changing her feelings for him or ruining the relationship on her end. It was him she was worried about. The most important question would be their friendship and how it would change. Justin wasn't like most guys, and this would definitely change him and his views toward the relationship.

"Dusty, it's not that I don't think you are attractive or—"

"I know, I know, I feel the same. I love you too much to lose our friendship. Besides, once you have me, every other girl will seem bland," Dusty said, trying to ease the situation.

"Oh, really?" he asked sarcastically.

"Yeah, I am pretty good in the ol' sack," she bragged.

"Even if I threw you over my shoulder and took you to your room and ravished you?"

Her breath caught as that thought crossed her mind.

"Do you even know how to ravish?" she said quickly, recovering from the thought she was trying to desperately push out of her mind.

"Well, I, um, guess I could start with the shirt rip."

"What the hell is a shirt rip? That's probably a bad idea since no woman wants her shirt ripped."

"No, no. I mean grab the front of the shirt and rip it open where all the buttons come flying off."

Dusty's face flushed.

"What?"

"I would like that. No one has ever done that to me. In fact, they always bitch about how it is taking too long to unbutton all of them. Where did you learn how to do that?"

"Joleen saw it in a movie or something. She said she wanted to try it, so we did. After a while, she got tired of sewing buttons back on, so we bought her some shirts with snaps. She would always wear one of them when she wanted to have sex."

"I think it would take me a while before I got tired of sewing buttons."

"There is something about the sound of them popping off and then hitting the floor, the bed, the dresser."

"I bet," Dusty said as it was her turn to feel flushed.

"The snaps were cool too, but it doesn't replace the sounds of the buttons."

"You should do that."

"Do what?"

"Go find a girl and just bang one out."

"Bang one out?"

"Yeah, just screw her brains out; get rid of all that built-up tension. It will do you good."

"Okay, but who?"

"What about Wendy?"

"Wendy? Oh, I, um … what's that word?"

"What word?"

"When you don't call or text them back."

"Ghosted."

"Oh, right. I ghosted her."

"So? Tell her you got busy and you want to see her again. If she invites you back for a nightcap, or Netflix and chill or whatever, take her up on it and screw her."

"What if she doesn't want to go on another date? I did ghost her, after all."

"She will. And if she doesn't, then find someone else."

"What if she doesn't ask for a nightcap?"

"Then ask her to come home with you. Be a man; take control of the situation."

"What about Momma?"

"Bring her here," Dusty said, waving her arm around, indicating her house.

"What about you?" Justin asked, warming up to the idea.

"I want to listen," she said with an impish grin. "Remember: I want to live vicariously."

"I couldn't. There is no way I could with you listening."

"All right, have it your way. I can go stay at Daddy's. Just text me before you come, and I will be gone. You have the key, so just make your way here."

"Your room looks like a girl's room."

"Use the spare; I will fix it up a bit so it will look like you are staying here. I can't promise I can make it stink like your room. Maybe I can go get some cow shit and put it under the bed to add your special smell."

"You are having too much fun with this."

"It is kind of exciting."

"Okay," he said slowly.

"Don't think about it; just go out and do it. Do *her*."

"What if—"

"What if nothing. You are thinking again—something that is not your strongest suit."

"Shut up."

She laughed and took a swig. He let out a little chuckle and followed suit.

"She basically let a guy screw her and then left him; you will be just returning the favor, and you will be releasing a bunch of pent-up energy. It will be good for you."

"Suzie?"

"Who cares? You aren't with her. She might be banging someone in New York."

"Pennsylvania."

"Whatever."

"I am going to get a second opinion."

"Suit yourself," Dusty said as she took their empty bottles to the kitchen.

Twenty-Two

Justin left Dusty's house and headed home. His mind was a blur. He reached his place much sooner than he wanted to. He wanted to call Suzie and discuss what Dusty had told him, but he could not help but think that that was some wrong on so many levels.

When he got to his room, he decided to take a chance and do it anyway.

He pushed the button to call her.

"Hello, Suzie."

"Justin, what a surprise. I was not expecting you to call till this weekend. Is everything okay?"

"I know, I apologize. I am in sort of a dilemma and wanted some advice."

"What about Dusty? Can she help? Oh my goodness, is it about Dusty? Are you going to ask her out?"

"Slow down, lady! No, nothing like that. She did offer to have sex with me last night."

"She didn't! I can't believe it!"

"She did. She just blurted it out that we both needed it."

"You didn't do it, did you?"

"No. Of course not."

"Is that your dilemma?"

"No, but that's kind of part of the problem."

"So you wanted to?"

"No, well maybe. I mean, I do like her, but this not about that."

"Well now I am curious," Suzie noted.

"It's a bit embarrassing, and kind of complicated."

"Relationships usually are. Go on."

"Well, she told me I needed to have sex to blow off some steam."

"I can see that."

"You can?"

"Sure, everyone needs some wild rough and tumble every now and then. Just because we are single doesn't mean we are now monks or nuns."

"You included? You said 'we.'"

"Of course, why do you think I was coming on so strong?"

Justin swallowed hard.

"So you just wanted to have sex with me?"

"Yes. Hallelujah! The cowboy finally gets it," she mocked.

"I am being serious."

"Me too."

"Is that all you wanted from me?"

"No, but that part would be so much fun. Besides, I have needs too."

"I see."

"Does that help your dilemma?"

"Actually, it makes it worse."

"Okay, let's back up and start from the beginning."

"Dusty and I were talking last night, and she said I should take one of these dates up on their offer to have a nightcap or Netflix and chill, or whatever the code word for sex is these days."

"Okay."

"She said it would be good for me to go out and just use one of these women for sex—Wendy in particular."

"Do you like her?"

"I do, but she left her husband. I really don't want to get roped up in that again."

"So just sex and then ghost her?"

"Pretty much."

"You don't want to do that?"

Justin thought hard about what he was going to say. He remembered his big speech to Dusty about risking it all. Right now he was feeling he should just lay it all on the line and then handle whatever came next.

"Justin?" Suzie asked into the silence.

"Suzie, I like you. The only reason I did not ask you out is because I am a bad dater. I went through something that completely caught me off guard, and I do not know what I did wrong. I would hate to make the same mistakes, or even all new ones, and you wouldn't want to be with me."

Suzie was quiet on the other end. Justin figured she was processing, so he let her have a moment.

"So what you are saying is that you want to practice date and have sex with other women so you can get it right for me?"

"When you put it that way it sounds really bad, but I guess that is what I am trying to say."

"I don't know if I should be flattered or offended," she shot back.

"I am sorry."

"Stop it. I was joking, of course. I am flattered. Justin, we aren't dating. We are friends at best right now. What you do right now is up to you. No, I don't think I would like to hear about you having sex with other women, but it is up to you."

"When you put it like that, it scares me."

"Why?"

"Because it means that you are saying one thing but are probably meaning another."

"You are probably right," Suzie agreed.

"Then why not be honest with me?"

"I cannot tell you what to do or not to do or who to do or not to do. This is all kind of weird."

"But you don't want me to go out with anyone and wait for you?"

"No, Justin, I don't know how long I will be here. I don't want you sitting around pining away for me. Really, I am good; I just don't want to hear about all your sexual conquests."

"Agreed."

"I have to admit, I have been a little jealous of the other women that get to go out with you, but I don't want you to be miserable either."

"I am not miserable."

"Yes you are."

"What do you mean?"

"You are struggling so hard to do the right thing for others, you are forgetting about yourself and to have some fun," Suzie pointed out.

"Okay."

"Don't okay me. Go out, date, have fun. Practice up so you can sweep me off my feet."

"And you are okay with that?"

"Justin, I want you to be happy. You cannot be happy worrying about me or about what you should or should not do. Go have fun."

Justin sat back on his bed, not knowing how to handle this. His relationship with Suzie in high school had always been one of openness and communication. They had always talked about everything, even covering sex, relationships, politics, homework, and their hopes and dreams.

He felt comfortable with this conversation and seeking her advice just as he had back in high school. However, this conversation was a little different, and the subject had higher stakes than those of pointers for a chemistry exam or which color fingernail polish went with which outfit.

The sound of silence was growing in his ears as he drifted back from 1998 and all those feelings he had experienced back then, including when she had left him without ever even kissing him.

"You think that will work?" he asked.

"When Russel first left me, I was devastated. You are lucky to have Dusty; I really had no one to turn to. All of Russel and my old friends didn't want to take sides, so they shunned both of us. Everyone I knew, except family, treated me like a contagious plague."

"Dusty has been a blessing."

"She is pretty awesome."

"You are pretty awesome as well," Justin said, trying to grasp the situation.

"Thank you, but I didn't feel that way when I was going through the divorce."

"No?"

"No. In fact, I wasn't going to tell you this, but since we are being honest, I slept with quite a few guys during that time and shortly after."

"You did?"

"Yes. I am not proud of that, but I needed reassurance that I was still pretty and sexy."

"How could you think that?"

"How are you feeling about yourself?" she asked him abruptly.

"I see your point. Did it help?"

"Yes, some. I regretted some of them."

"Only some?"

"Some were smoking hot, and others made me feel so sexy. Not just because of the way they looked, but because of the words they said and the way they treated me; they helped rebuild my ego."

"I see."

"So go rebuild your ego; it will be fun."

"Okay."

"And Justin."

"Yeah?"

"If I had been in your position, I would have screwed Dusty."

Chapter

Twenty-Three

The old coffee shop was starting to change. Suzie had wanted to keep the coffee shop as close to the same as it had always been for the sake of the old-timers who always seemed to vehemently fight anything new or different. They were an important part of the business, as they would meet in groups in the morning to discuss how to save the world and what was wrong with all the politicians. They would purchase pastries and some hot brew and then take station with their friends and begin their committee meetings.

Sales to the younger crowd were becoming a larger part of her income, but they usually grabbed a premium drink and then rushed off to wherever they were needed. Their interest wasn't in the décor or the nostalgia, but only in how well the wi-fi was working. Still Suzie wanted to add some upgrades besides what was behind the bar.

Suzie budgeted some of her loan to go into the coffee shop itself to try to please all ages and was having some luck in achieving her goal. She didn't want to go all progressive and lose her regulars but wanted to get the younger crowd to stay. A staying customer is a paying customer she had once heard.

Justin walked into the coffee shop and stopped short halfway in as he saw Dusty bent over a table, trying her best to clean with one hand and rearrange the condiments with another. Her dirty blonde hair was highlighted by the morning sun, which was peeking through the big bay windows. Her body was silhouetted through her clothes, and he took a long swallow.

"Quite the view, huh?" asked April as she hip-bumped him and then reached up and placed her elbow on his shoulder.

"Huh?" asked a bewildered Justin, trying to regain his composure.

"Uh huh. The pretty ones always get those kinds of looks."

"What?"

"I wish someone would look at me like that."

"April, you are very pretty," Justin reassured her.

"I know, but Dusty is smoking hot. I want to be smoking hot."

"Give it a couple of years," he said with a grin and a wink.

"What are you two conspiring about?" Dusty asked as she approached the duo.

"We were just admiring the view," April said slyly.

Dusty turned around and looked at the sun creeping over the mountains.

"I have always loved the mountains in the morning," she commented, watching the snow-capped peaks reflect the sun.

April and Justin looked at each other and smiled.

"It is breathtaking," Justin commented.

"So beautiful," April added.

April took her elbow back and gently pressed it into Justin's side. Then she smiled at him and left him to gaze at the scenery in front of him.

"How was your talk with Suzie?" Dusty finally asked, turning to face him.

"Who said I talked to her?" he rebuffed.

"Dummy, we talk almost every morning, usually about business, but this morning we were discussing—"

Justin quickly interrupted. "Gossiping, more like."

His face flushed as he remembered Suzie's final words.

"It was good," he said when he composed himself.

"What? There must have been something she left out. You don't blush easily."

"Nothing. I mean, we talked about just normal things."

"Bullshit, Justin, you are turning red. What did you talk about?"

"She agrees with you," he said, trying to find his words.

"About?"

"Releasing tension."

"I knew I liked her. Are you convinced now?"

"I don't know, maybe a little more convinced, anyways."

"Good. Go call Wendy and set something up for tonight."

"I have a date tonight."

"Oh really? With whom and where?"

"Whom?" Justin asked.

"Its proper English, caveman. Get with the program."

"Okay, college girl."

"So, with whom?" Dusty asked again emphasizing the *m* in "whom."

"Her name is Evelyn, and it's at that restaurant where they have video games and a place for kids to play," he said slowly.

"What kind of date is that? Is she fourteen?"

"No, It's her kid's birthday." Justin said slowly, feeling embarrassed.

"She wants you to meet her kid on the first date?"

"I guess she is busy, and this was the only chance we had to meet."

"And you agreed?"

"Yes."

"Well, that's weird."

"There is something else."

"Oh dear, what else is wrong with her."

"Well, um … Well, she is sort of … well … young looking."

"How young? She can't be fourteen, so what is she, like, twenty?"

"I mean like eighteen, or maybe younger."

"You are not going out with a minor! Does her profile say how old she is?"

"Thirty-nine."

"But you don't think she is?"

"She did one of those fancy pictures—you know, where the girl gets all dolled up and wears kind of sexy clothes."

"Oh, a glamor shot. Yeah, those are fun."

He looked at her in surprise.

"You have done those?"

"Of course, a few times. I really like doing them; it makes me feel good about myself."

"Why haven't I seen those?"

"Because they can be revealing. There are a few where you can see my lady parts."

Justin swallowed hard. Dusty laughed and led him over to a table where they sat down.

"So, tell me about Miss Glamor Shots."

"They didn't show her lady parts in the picture she had on her profile," Justin assured her.

"The site won't allow nudity on those profiles. Even with subjective ones they sometimes will deny the picture."

"Oh."

"She might have used a filter; they can take years off," Dusty suggested.

"So I have noticed."

"You aren't buying it?"

"I don't know what I know any more about the women on these sites."

"What do you mean?"

The door opened and an elderly couple came in and shed their coats and hung them up on a tree next to the door.

"Don't go anywhere. Also, remember that thought; I want to get back to it."

"Okay."

"Cocoa?" asked April as she brought the mug over to Justin.

"Thank you," he replied, and he took a sip.

"You should really ask her out," April encouraged.

"We are friends."

"Friends don't look at other friends the way you look at her."

"Really?"

"No, and don't think I haven't caught her looking at you the same way."

"Really?"

"Yes, there definitely seems to be a spark there."

"We are just friends," Justin said pointedly.

"Ugh, have it your way!" April exclaimed. She then turned and went to tend the new customers.

"Okay, where were we?" Dusty asked as she sat back at the booth with Justin.

"The dating site. It really is confusing. Every woman on there says she wants a guy that doesn't lie or cheat and is good with kids, responsible, single—the list goes on and on."

"That's what we want."

"Then why don't they pick that exact guy?"

"What do you mean?"

"I was talking to a girl a couple of weeks ago; she told me that she found her dream guy."

"Okay."

"Then she messaged me last night saying Mr. Perfect already cheated on her."

"Oh, I see. Then what?"

"She wanted to go out on a date with me."

"Was that Evelyn?"

"No, some other girl."

"Do you have a date with her?"

"Hell no. I am not plan B. If she didn't want me first, then she shouldn't have me second."

"I really don't know how to react to that."

"Why are you taking her side?" Justin asked, sounding confused.

"I am not really taking her side. I just know what she was thinking."

"What was that?" asked Justin, now getting frustrated.

"That she was hoping this guy was like that. She made her choice, and it was wrong. I mean, the guy didn't come out and say he was a cheater. He probably told her all the things she wanted to hear."

"But he still cheated."

"Remember the Chads?" Dusty reminded him.

"Yep."

"He was a Chad. He just wanted to get into her pants and then move on to the next one. He will be calling her in a week or two, saying he was sorry and didn't know what came over him. Then his story will be that she is the one for him. He will apologize and say he wants to try again."

"She will believe him?"

"Maybe, maybe not. Either way, he is going to try."

"What if she says yes?"

"He will romance her till he gets back in her pants, and then he'll go after another girl."

"What an ass," Justin remarked, shaking his head.

"Welcome to online dating and endless possibilities."

"I don't know how anyone finds a real relationship doing this."

"It works sometimes. But there are lots of Chads and Karens on these sites."

"Karens?"

"Female versions of Chads."

"Oh, okay."

"There are those people on these sites that just want to screw around, others that want to rebuild their confidence, and yes, even some that actually want a real relationship," Dusty informed him.

"So how do you know? It's not like they are very truthful on there."

"You are."

"Kinda. You embellished a bit for me."

"Eh, it's all true."

"How do you know then?"

"Time. That is usually the big revealer of who a person really is."

"Sounds like good advice."

"Just take your time if you find someone you really want to get to know, but if you want to screw her, then do it."

"Okay."

"Don't fall in love too soon either—not at least until you know that you know."

"Agreed."

"And most importantly, listen to your friends."

"I am trying," Justin said with a shrug.

"You should have taken your friend Suzie's advice."

"About dating and releasing tension?" Justin asked.

"No."

"What advice then?"

"You should have screwed me when you had the chance," Dusty said pointedly.

The sound of the server's tray hitting the floor was deafening in the small café. April stood there looking at them both, obviously shocked at what she had heard.

"I am so sorry," April told the elderly couple.

Justin watched as the old lady smiled, patted April on the arm, and then said something softly. April nodded, grabbed the tray, and headed off to the kitchen.

"So you know about that?" Justin asked Dusty nervously.

"Suzie tells me a lot, like you do."

"You talk to her?"

"I sorta have to; she's my boss."

"Oh, right."

"Yes, we are becoming quite the friends," Dusty said with an evil grin.

"I think I am in trouble," Justin replied worriedly.

"Yes, you are," Dusty said with a smile. She then got up. "Well, back to work. Good luck, cowboy."

Justin slipped a blushing April a twenty and a wink as he headed out the door to get ready for his date.

Chapter

Twenty-Four

Justin paused just outside the restaurant he was going to meet his date, Evelyn. He listened to the muffled sounds from inside. There was music and kids screaming and laughing. The smell of pizza and fried foods filled his nose and reminded him he was starting to feel hungry, and he hadn't had pizza in quite a while. He shrugged his shoulders and walked into the busy restaurant at exactly fifteen minutes before noon. He had never been in a place like this, so he took a minute to get the lay of the land and watch the chaos of children running around yelling and whooping, dressed up characters and staff busily attending to their guests' needs, and tired, disheveled-looking parents trying to desperately to keep their kids under control.

He soon spotted the girl called Evelyn and made a beeline to her. When he reached her, he realized there was something definitely wrong. No matter how good filters were, no matter the amount of makeup used, real life always revealed the truth behind the shroud. Real life was telling Justin that this was a girl, not a woman—not even a young woman, but still a girl. The awkward way she stood, the innocence in her eyes, and the clothes she wore spoke of a teenager, not a fortysomething divorcée. Justin started to get a terrible gnawing in his stomach and turned to leave.

"Hello, Justin," came a voice from his left.

He turned to see a much older and more well-worn version of the teenager in front of him. The teenager had noticed him approaching her and was now staring up at him in wonder and a little bit of fear.

"Um, hello," he said, a bit unsure of this new stranger. She looked more like a fortysomething divorcée.

"I am Evelyn," said the new stranger. "And this is my daughter, Rebecca."

"Oh" was the only thing he could muster. Evelyn was dressed in jeans and a rock band T-shirt. Her graying blonde hair was tied back into a ponytail. Her makeup was heavy, and time was starting to show on her face, he noticed she had the starts of crow's feet forming at the corners of her eyes. She had a big smile under bright red lipstick. She was not unattractive, but not what he was expecting.

"I am so glad you could make it to my son's birthday party," Evelyn said as she gave him a quick hug.

"I am a little confused here," Justin said as he looked at Rebecca and then back at Evelyn.

"Yes, I understand that. I use Rebecca's picture because if I don't, no guy wants to have a date with me," Evelyn said quickly.

"I see," he said, still trying to process what just happened. *Catfished? Bait and switch?* No, this was definitely one of those catfish scenarios Dusty had warned him about.

She wasn't unattractive—not what he was expecting, but not the beauty queen he was led to believe he was having a date with. He had two choices here: one, to turn and leave, or two, to throw himself into this nightmare. Justin didn't have time to decide, as Evelyn made the choice for him. She grabbed him by the elbow and led him over to a table that was occupied by four boys eagerly awaiting her return.

"Did you get us some tokens?" asked a younger boy with a birthday boy hat on his head.

"I told you we will get them when we order our pizza," Evelyn said sharply.

The boy seemed a little discouraged and looked around for a waitress so they could place their order and, more importantly, get his tokens quickly.

Justin studied the group, who were now all seated at the table, as he sat down and was introduced to them. The boys were not all the same age, and Justin thought it was a bit odd that he would invite only children that were not his same age to his birthday party. Then he got it; they all looked a bit alike. These were not friends, but siblings.

The waitress came over and asked to take their order.

"We have great specials that include pizza, drinks, and tokens," she said with a smile.

"We want the one with a medium cheese pizza and twenty tokens," Evelyn said nervously.

Justin did the math quick; no way was one medium pizza and four tokens each ever going to satisfy this rowdy bunch.

"Drinks aren't included in that special," the waitress said with a frown. Justin saw this and suspected the waitress was starting to realize her tip wasn't going to be spectacular if she was even going to get one at all.

"No, that won't do," Justin interrupted as he saw the downcast faces also doing the math.

"Well, what would you like to order instead?" the waitress asked him with hopeful eyes.

"What are your specials?" he asked.

She went through the different packages with the different combinations of food, drinks, and token packages. He ordered one that came with two large pizzas, breadsticks, drinks, lots of tokens, and even a small birthday cake for the birthday boy.

"I can't afford that," Evelyn said.

"I've got it, no worries," Justin replied.

"You don't have to do that," Evelyn pleaded.

"It's okay; I've got this," Justin reassured her.

The faces at the table went from downcast to all smiles.

"Okay, but there is no way I can pay you back," Evelyn said as she leaned over to where only Justin could hear.

"Nonsense, it is my pleasure," he whispered back.

With that, the waitress scurried off to place their order. She rushed back with the tokens and handed them to Justin, who divvied them up to the boys. They all thanked him enthusiastically as they hurriedly grabbed their treasure and excused themselves from the table and headed to the game room.

Justin took the last pile and slid them over to Rebecca. She shook her head vigorously.

"She is a bit shy," her mother commented as she rubbed Rebecca's forearm.

"Too shy to play the games?" he asked Rebecca.

She shrugged, staring at the pile of coins in front of her. One of the younger boys came back and grabbed Justin's hand.

"Please come help me, I want to get lots of tickets, and I am not very good at this game."

Justin looked at the boy and then to Evelyn, who nodded her head with a smile. She was twirling her hair with her finger, smiling, and giving him very seductive looks with her eyes and body.

Justin spent the next hour and a half playing games and eating pizza, and when the birthday cake was delivered, he watched the boy blow out the candles and open his gifts. He told them he had to go and got up and left. As he was leaving, he stopped to tip the waitress forty dollars.

When he reached the door, Evelyn was waiting for him.

"Want to come back to my house? We can continue the celebration there; I have to drop the kids off at their dad's house first so there won't be any distractions," she said with a wink.

"I am sorry, but no."

"No? Didn't you have fun?"

"Yes, actually I did."

"Don't you think I am pretty?"

"I think you are attractive."

"So why don't you want to come home with me?"

"I am not that kind of guy."

"If you were, would you?"

"No."

"Why not? What is wrong with me?"

"You lied to me, Evelyn. You lured me here with a picture of your daughter. You are pretty and you need to use your own picture. I cannot be with someone that starts a relationship with a lie. I am sorry, but being truthful in a relationship is paramount to me."

"Okay, I am sorry," Evelyn said, deflated.

He tipped his hat to the waitress, who had taken up station nearby. She smiled and waved to him. With that, he turned and walked out the door and headed to his truck. Justin fired up the motor and sat there for a minute thinking on what had just happened over the last couple of hours. He was conflicted between his reasons he had given Evelyn and something that had been gnawing at the edge of his brain for the last couple of weeks. Was he making excuses not to get back into a relationship, or was he really being picky? Was he being *too* picky? Evelyn wasn't a bad catch; her self-esteem was a little low, but other than that she seemed solid as a woman.

He shook his head, put his truck in drive, and pulled onto the highway, headed back to Hackamore.

Twenty-Five

Justin pulled into Dusty's driveway and let himself in and threw himself on her couch. Dusty was in the kitchen, finishing up doing her dishes. She grabbed two beers out of the fridge, handed him one, and then settled herself on the chair opposite him.

Justin didn't wait for her to ask; he jumped right into his play date.

"She did not!" Dusty exclaimed as he finished up.

"Every word is true."

"I don't doubt you are telling the truth; that is just unbelievable. I can't say I haven't heard of being catfished before, but using your kid is gross."

Justin took a sip of his beer and wiped the spittle off his lips. He then glanced at Dusty with a smirk.

"What?" she asked.

"I think I just made my first booty call ever."

"You did not. With Evelyn?"

"No, someone else, but I did."

"With Wendy?" asked Dusty after a short pause.

"Yup."

"What did she say?"

"Well, I didn't exactly tell her it was a booty call; I just told her I wanted to see her again."

"I am sure she is suspicious; I mean, guys don't write a woman off and then call them back later just wanting to go out on a date. I am sure she is thinking you want sex."

"I thought of that, but I made the call anyways."

"And she said yes?"

"Yes, she seemed pretty excited to hear from me."

"Where are you going to meet her?" Dusty asked.

"That same place I was at today."

"Where you met the liar, liar pants on fire?"

"The same."

"Why there? Did you tell her to bring her kid?"

"No, no kids, and because it was fun. I never knew places like that existed. I mean, I did; I just never had been to one. I thought it was a great place for a date."

"Does she know about that place?"

"Yeah. She was a bit hesitant at first, but I convinced her it would be fun."

"I think I would be a little hesitant as well."

"What? Why? There are games and food and a cute waitress," Justin said in defense of himself.

Dusty thought about it for a while.

"Maybe that is a good idea; no one has ever taken me to a place like that before."

"It really was a lot of fun. I really enjoyed hanging out with the small people."

Dusty laughed. "You thinking you want kids now?"

"I kind of always have. Joleen wanted us to take care of a few things first; I guess we never got there."

"What about being a stepdad? That is something you will have to consider now that you are older and a lot of the women you are going out with have kids."

"I will cross that bridge when I come to it."

He stood up, kissed Dusty on the forehead, and headed to his truck.

"Good luck, cowboy!" she hollered after him. "Let me know ahead of time if I need to leave."

Twenty-Six

Justin pulled back into the parking lot of the restaurant he had left a few hours previously. He saw Wendy sitting in her car, and he parked next to her. She jumped out when she saw him. They gave each other a quick hug and headed toward the entrance. Justin took a quick look around to make sure Evelyn and her brood were no longer there. They weren't. The same waitress that had taken care of him earlier greeted Justin and Wendy at the door and then brought them to their seats. She eyed Justin suspiciously as she took their order.

"Well, this is a first," Wendy said with a smile.

"What's that?" Justin asked.

"Never have I ever been brought to a place like this for a date."

"Do you want to go somewhere else?"

"Oh, no. I think this will be fun."

"Me too."

"I need to go freshen up; I will be right back." She got up and headed to the restroom amid a sea of children.

"Weren't you here earlier?" the waitress asked as she placed his drink on the table and dropped a huge cup full of tokens next to his drink.

"I was, and I would appreciate you not mentioning it to my date."

"What's up with that?" the waitress asked with her hands on her hips.

Justin couldn't wrap his mind around why all these teenaged girls were so interested in his dating life, especially since they were no way connected to it.

"I don't think I have time to explain it before Wendy gets back."

Justin and the waitress looked over toward the restroom and saw Wendy waiting patiently in line to get into the ladies' room and chatting it up with a young girl who seemed to be pelting her with questions.

"Our girl's restroom only has two stalls; she will be there for a long minute; you have time," she reassured him.

Justin quickly explained the fiasco he had been roped into earlier and the conversation he'd had at the door with Evelyn; he hoped this would help the waitress understand this situation and that she wouldn't make a scene or ruin it for him.

"You set up two dates on the same day at the same place? Ballsy," the waitress said when he had finished.

"This date was more an impromptu decision."

"So if one girl doesn't put out, you just go get another one?"

"No, it's not like that. I went out with this one once before," Justin said defensively.

Justin started to understand how those people on TV that were getting questioned by a Senate committee felt. He turned to see that Wendy was next in line and staring hard at him and the waitress.

"Don't you have other tables to wait?" Justin asked the waitress with a smile.

"No, I am almost off, and the other crew is already here. We are good," she said with a rebellious smile. Justin had seen that smile before in both April and Dusty and knew he wasn't going to get rid of this kid unless he satisfied her curiosity.

"Okay, yes, it is a booty call, I guess. Last time we went on a date, she invited me back to her place, but I refused," Justin said pointedly.

"What is wrong with her that you don't want to date her? I mean, she is awfully pretty."

"I am a bit skittish about dating her."

"I see. Well you should at least tell her this is a booty call or that's what you want so you don't waste the whole night trying to make it happen."

"What do you mean?"

"Just tell her. It's either yes or no, and then you can relax and have fun either way."

"That is pretty astute for someone your age."

"Both of my parents are bartenders or were. My mom still is my dad owns a flower shop now, so they both have great stories I get to listen in on."

"You aren't trying to steal my date, are you?" Wendy asked as she sat back down in her seat.

"No ma'am, I was just curious why two adults with no children were meeting here."

"It's okay, um …"—Justin looked at her name tag—"Sam. I am going to tell her the story."

"What story?" asked Wendy curiously.

"Tell her everything?" Sam asked pointedly.

"Yes, everything. Your advice included," Justin reassured her.

"Okay, I will make sure you are well taken care of. Have a great night, you two," she said as she flitted off.

"What story?" asked Wendy, a little bit more cautiously.

Justin told her about the day's events from start to finish.

"That's terrible."

"It wasn't so bad; I got to meet Sam."

"So I am your plan B?" Wendy asked slowly.

"No, it's not like that."

"What is it like?"

Justin had a hard time finding the words. After an awkward silence, Wendy asked, "What advice did she give you?"

"Um, well, that's what I was trying to tell you."

"Okay."

"Look, you are spectacular," Justin said quickly before he lost his nerve.

"Well, thank you; you are pretty all right yourself," she replied as her cheeks reddened.

"The fact that you left your husband for no reason really bothers me," Justin continued.

"I can see that."

"I don't see us having a relationship, but I do like our conversations and being with you."

"Did you ask me out so I would invite you back to my house so you could get you some?"

"Well, I, um …"

"Not happening."

"Okay, I understand," said Justin, a little deflated.

"No, that's not it; my mom is babysitting my son at my house. She warned me not to bring any damn man back with me."

Justin's eyes widened.

"So," she continued, "we will have to go back to your place."

The pizza was set on their table by the new waitress, Tonya.

"Anything else I can do for y'all?" she asked in a slight southern accent.

"We are great," Wendy enthusiastically replied.

"Let me know if you need anything," she said, and she left them alone.

"You really okay with this?" Justin asked Wendy when Tonya had left.

"Of course. The pizza looks better than I thought it would."

"No, I mean about the sex."

"I am a little disappointed that we can't make a go of the relationship, but yeah, I do want you. I have never been with a real cowboy before."

They ate and played the games, and Justin even won her a small teddy bear with all the tickets they had acquired. As the night went on, the sexual tension built between them. They decided to play a two-player game that had them shooting aliens with small futuristic rifles. When Justin realized he was losing the battle, he grabbed Wendy, who was still concentrating on not losing her last player, turned her to him, and kissed her hard on the lips. She, in turn, embraced him and kissed him hard back.

"Ewww" came from a bevy of youngsters standing nearby.

They smiled and went on to some competitive Skee-Ball. There was much hip bumping as their bodies anticipated the hip bumping they would be doing later with no audience and no clothing.

"Get out now" was the message Justin texted to Dusty when they were on their way to her house.

"Okay, okay, Jeez, Mr. Horny Pants" came the immediate reply, but Justin paid no attention to it as he made the speed limit and just a bit extra on the painfully long drive to her house.

They burst through the door, both eagerly kissing and exploring each other's bodies with their hands. Wendy went to start unbuttoning her shirt, but Justin stopped her. The expression on her face was one of confusion and dismay until Justin gripped it and ripped it. The sound of buttons hitting the various furniture around the living room was exhilarating to both of them. She smiled widely, and Justin could see the lust in her eyes.

He threw her over his shoulder and carried her up the stairs to the room Dusty had prepared for them. True to form, she had done a bang-up job of imitating his own room, including a picture of his mom, which he quickly put face down on the dresser.

They quickly undressed each other and spent the next few hours frolicking around the bedroom, exploring various positions and techniques. Near 1:00 a.m., both exhausted and satisfied, they fell asleep spooning.

Chapter

Twenty-Seven

Justin opened his eyes and realized immediately he was not in his room. He blinked twice and started to take in where he was and why he was there. The night's events flooded back into his mind as he realized he wasn't alone in the bed. He rolled over to see a smiling Wendy watching him.

"Good morning, sleepyhead," Justin said with a grin as Wendy rolled over and opened her eyes.

"Good morning yourself, cowboy."

"You were quite the cowgirl yourself last night."

She blushed and looked around the room. "Whose room is this?"

"What do you mean?"

"Come on, it looks like this is someone's spare room. I mean, you don't even have clothes in your closet."

"You checked?"

"Not on purpose. I had to use the restroom last night and must have gotten disoriented; after all, I was carried in here upside down."

"I remember."

"So I opened the closet door and there was an empty closet."

"Oh."

Justin told her about Dusty and how she offered her place for activities that would not meet his momma's approval. He had a hard time focusing as she was lying on her side, propped up on her elbow. The sheet was at her midriff, and her entire top was exposed to him.

"It's okay, you can look—and feel if you have the urge to."

Justin quickly complied, and they started kissing as they slowly moved their bodies into position for another round.

"Wait," Wendy said quickly as she looked to the open door.

"What?"

"Where is Dusty now?"

"Visiting family."

"When will she be back?"

"I am sure she won't come back until she sees your car gone, or at least until I give her the okay."

"She sounds like a great friend."

"She was the one that suggested I take you up on your offer."

"Well, I am so glad she did."

They continued to relieve their pent-up frustrations till the afternoon, stopping only for bathroom and snack breaks. Dusty had left sandwiches and lots of Gatorade in the fridge so they could fuel their vigorous calorie-burning adventure.

"Whenever you want to do this again, feel free to call me," Wendy said after she kissed him lightly on the lips and stumbled out of the house to her car.

Chapter

Twenty-Eight

The doorbell clanged as Justin walked into the coffee shop. The entire staff stopped what they were doing and looked at him. He felt a bit self-conscious as they stared at him.

"You feel better, cowboy?" Dusty said as she rounded the corner, pulling some loose hairs off her face and putting them behind her ear.

"You dirty dog, you did it, didn't you?" April said a little too loudly with an impish grin.

"Jeez," he said as he did an about-face and headed back to the door, but Lori beat him to it and stood guard.

"Going somewhere so soon?" she said with a smirk.

"I would like to leave, Lori," he said, not feeling the words.

"I bet you would, but we have some catching up to do."

"We all want to know what happened," Dusty chided.

April chimed in. "Besides, if you won't tell us, Dusty will."

"We would rather hear it from the horse's mouth," Lori added, standing firm.

Justin shrugged and went over to a four-top table, which was quickly filled by the three conspirators.

"Not much to tell. We met and then went back to Dusty's."

They all turned to look at Dusty in astonishment.

"You were there?" asked April incredulously.

"No, I just let him use a room. I was at my dad's all night. Thanks, blabbermouth," she replied, wishing Justin had left that part out.

April went to say something, but Dusty cut her off.

"No, April, that is definitely a no for you—and forever, so don't even ask."

"When did she leave?" April asked, returning to the conversation at hand.

"About an hour ago."

"Holy shit!" Lori exclaimed. "You must have really given it to her."

"I had a lot of pent-up energy to get rid of. By the way, thanks for the sandwiches and Gatorade, Dusty."

"You gave him fuel for his debauchery?" April asked Dusty.

"Now you are sounding like my momma," Justin scolded her.

"Maybe this was a bad idea." Dusty said, a bit flabbergasted.

"What idea?" Justin asked her.

"I told the girls what was going on, and I didn't want to have to explain it and answer all their questions. So I stupidly agreed they could sit in on our conversation so they could grill you instead of me."

"As I said, not much to tell."

"Not true!" April said pleadingly. "Please, you don't have to go into complete detail—just, like, what happened. How did you get her to come back to your—I mean Dusty's—place?"

He told them about the waitress and her advice. Then he thought better of it and started from when he had gone to meet Evelyn. Then he explained the feeling of defeat, followed by Dusty's advice, and then on to the waitress and, finally, his proposal to Wendy. They listened intently, taking in all of his words and processing them as quickly as he led up to the drive back to Dusty's.

"Then what happened?" asked April, hungry for more.

"Then we had sex."

"No, no, no—*details*." This came from Lori, who was more reserved than the present crowd, so it caught everyone a bit off guard as they all looked at her, surprised.

"What?" she asked defensively. "I want to know a little more."

They all turned back to Justin, encouraging him with their eyes and body language, fully agreeing with Lori.

"Well, we um … Well, I uh …" Justin started fumbling over his words, now growing embarrassed.

"Did you do the button thing?" Dusty interjected, trying to help him along.

"Yup, and the Viking warrior thing as well," he said with a grin.

"What the hell is the button thing?" asked Lori.

"And the Viking warrior?" April added.

Dusty smiled, got up, and put her hand on his shoulder. "I need to count the till before shift change; you can handle it from here, cowboy." And with that she went to the register to retrieve the cash.

Justin turned to his eagerly awaiting audience.

He started to explain what Dusty was referring to and then said, "What the hell," shrugging his shoulders.

He went into the steamy details of the previous night's events. He didn't hold anything back and watched their shocked faces as this quiet cowboy unleashed a story some of the smutty magazines would be proud to publish. April's face grew redder and redder, while Lori started fanning herself with one of the menus.

Dusty saw the commotion at the table, gave them a curious glance, and then shook her head and carried the money to the back so she could finish up her accounting.

Chapter

Twenty-Nine

An hour later, Justin followed Dusty back to her house when she had finished at the coffee shop.

"I hate you," Justin said as he sat at his usual place on her couch.

"Why?" she asked knowingly with an innocent smile.

"For roping me into that roundtable discussion."

"Didn't really look like a discussion to me."

"You know what I mean."

"You had them captivated for a while; I don't think April even blinked once the whole time you were talking after I left," Dusty remarked with a laugh.

"Her eyes were as big as wagon wheels," he laughed.

"What were you telling them?"

"What happened."

She pulled two beers out of the fridge and walked over and settled in her chair.

"Everything?" she asked incredulously.

"Everything."

"The sex?"

"Yep."

"April is very impressionable; you might want to try to keep it more PG with her," Dusty said seriously.

"This was your idea, mastermind."

"Yeah, well, I thought you were a little more reserved."

"I am a changed man, Dusty," Justin announced.

"So I can tell."

"April didn't seem as jealous as she usually is."

"I think she is in love with someone else," Dusty remarked.

"Oh, should I be jealous?"

"I think he will take your place in her heart, at least for now."

"Who is it?"

"Charlie Simmons."

"Crap, he is older than I am; what happened between him and Judy?"

"No, dumbass, Charlie Jr."

"Oh, oh right, Little Charlie. He's about her age, right?"

"You know he hates being called that."

"What do people call him now?"

"Just Charlie."

"Got it. How did they get together?"

"Well, they aren't together yet. It seems like they are both trying but are a bit shy to make the first move."

"Shouldn't he make the first move?"

"You know how young guys are; they don't want to be rejected, and they are terrible at reading the signs."

"Old dudes too," Justin acknowledged.

"Yeah, well, she is trying to send off signals, but I think they are confusing him."

"Sounds like a woman."

"Stop it. Anyways, he came into the shop last Saturday to get coffee and snacks for his dad's employees for a safety meeting at their shop. He has been coming in every day after school to buy something from us and to chat with April."

"Sounds like a good start."

"She really wants him to ask her to the dance coming up, but so far he hasn't even indicated he even knows one is happening."

"He knows; he is trying to rope up the courage," Justin said encouragingly.

"April has already been asked by a couple of boys, but she hasn't given them an answer yet."

"Sounds like she has already made up her mind."

"I wish he would hurry up and ask. She is a wreck after he leaves."

"He'll come around. Maybe someone should bump the fence."

"I cannot do that. I am a woman and seriously wouldn't know where to start."

"Bullshit. You got me sorted out; you are a great wingman."

"I only got you hooked up; I feel more like a pimp than a wingman."

"I thought a wingman's job was to get their friend hooked up."

"Point taken. I cannot tell a seventeen-year-old boy that she wants him to ask her out; that would be so awkward for both of us."

"Well, maybe he will come around," Justin said hopefully.

"I hope so."

"Thank you for the beer."

"You are leaving already?"

"Yep."

"Another date?" asked Dusty.

"Of sorts."

"A phone call with Suzie?" Dusty asked.

"Yes," he said with a guilty grin, and then he let himself out.

Thirty

Justin made his way up to his room after he checked on and fed his horses and other barnyard animals that had taken up shelter in the barn from the cold winter night. There wasn't a lot to do when he wasn't having to drive out to each field to give them their dinner. The stairs creaked as he walked slowly up them, debating on what to say to Suzie.

He decided to shower first, and when he had finished, he got into bed and called his friend in Pennsylvania.

"Hello, Suzie. How's your grandma?" Justin asked when his friend answered the phone.

"Did you do it?" she shot back quickly.

"Do what?"

"Sleep with that woman?"

"No 'Hi, how are you?' You just want to start off with that? I thought you didn't want to know one way or the other."

"I am sorry. I heard you were going out with her last night."

"Jeez, word travels fast."

"It's a small town," Suzie stated.

"You are in Pennsylvania," Justin shot back.

"I still talk to my staff."

"Yeah, I know, Dusty."

"April and the cooks, and Lori as well, are coming up with new ideas for things to add to the menu. We are doing those meetings online now, where everyone can join in."

"I heard April has a thing for Charlie Simmons," Justin remarked.

"Old news. What about that woman?" Suzie demanded.

Justin could hear the nervousness in her voice. "Yes I did."

"Well good for you," she said, sounding disheartened.

"You already knew, though, didn't you?"

"Small town. I was hoping it was only rumor and wanted to confirm it with you, though."

"You aren't mad, are you? I mean between you, Dusty, Lori, and April, I felt almost like it was a direct order to sleep with her."

"I know; I am just being stupid."

"You aren't stupid," Justin assured her.

"I told you to do something that I didn't want you to do; that is the epitome of stupidity."

"This is all new to me. I would rather have someone to date and build a relationship with than someone to just try to relieve frustrations with. I am sorry."

"Don't be. Did you have fun?"

"I did clear up a lot of questions that I had."

"Really? Like what?"

"Well, it was definitely a confidence builder, and I still know how to have sex."

"You thought you forgot?"

"It has been a little while."

"Well, I might be in trouble then," she joked.

"Naw, I am sure you will do fine."

"Are you going to see her again?"

"I don't know. I told her I wasn't interested in a relationship with her," Justin said, realizing he wasn't comfortable with this conversation. Years ago this was a normal topic of conversation between him and Suzie, but now it seemed out of place.

"You came right out and told her it was a booty call?"

"Yep."

"And she was okay with that?"

"Obviously. It was a go-for-broke moment, and I took it. I think she was wanting a confidence booster herself. Maybe next time we will conference call you in so I don't have to relive this humiliation over and over again," he joked, still searching for a way to change directions on this slippery slope.

"You are humiliated?"

"I was raised not to share those kinds of details."

"Well, according to April you broke all sorts of boundaries at your little meeting."

"That I did. I am sorry."

"Don't be. She is growing up, and the things on TV and the internet she is exposed to are a lot worse; believe me. I have heard her saying things when I was there that I never would have even thought about saying when I was her age," Suzie said with a softer tone.

"Well, I still don't think I am going to share those kinds of details with them again. It was a one-time deal."

"Justin?" Suzie asked slowly.

"Yes?"

"I met someone."

"In Pennsylvania?"

"Yes. We have gone out twice. He is very nice and asked me out again. I am thinking of maybe dating him."

"Good for you. What's the long game?"

"I haven't thought that far out yet. It is a lot to think about. I met him when he delivered some equipment for my grandma."

"How did that go?"

"Pretty good. We started talking while his employees were setting everything up, and he asked for my phone number. The next day, he asked me out for drinks. The day after, for dinner."

"Good for you. I knew a pretty gal like you wouldn't stay single long," Justin assured her.

"I am a little worried about the third date," Suzie said with some concern in her voice.

"What's wrong with the third date?"

"You really need to get out of Hackamore more often."

"Yeah?"

"The third date is supposed to be the date where you have sex."

"Really? Who made up that rule?" Justin asked.

"Yes, well, that's the social standard anyway."

"Are you?" Justin queried.

"I am nervous about it."

"Do you want to?"

"I do, but I don't either."

"I can definitely understand that" Justin said, remembering his feelings.

"I know you can. That's why I want your advice."

"I cannot tell you what to do or what not to do or who to do." He smirked while throwing her line back at her.

"I know. I guess I really want to know how it is after so long?"

"I guess for me, I just threw myself into it, didn't think about it, and did what comes naturally. We sort of communicated while we were doing it, so that helped."

"Communicated?"

"Yeah, she just told me what she wanted, and I tried to do it to the best of my ability."

"I think that would be embarrassing."

"Nonsense. A man's ultimate goal when having sex is to please his woman," Justin assured her.

"Not all men; maybe some men. Most just want to get you naked, take what they need, and then leave," Suzie said with frustration in her voice.

"I am sorry."

"Not your fault. You are different from those men."

"Maybe this guy is in the minority. Maybe he will want to do what turns you on," Justin assured her again.

"His smile does that. There are other things, but I really like his smile."

"See, he is already trying to please you."

"I haven't told him his smile turns me on. What if he gets weirded out or refuses to do what I ask. What if I tell him what I like or what I want, and he just laughs?"

"You won't know until you try. The only way is to be honest with him. You could talk about it before you end up in the bedroom or figure it out as you go."

"But I don't think I could handle that kind of humiliation."

"What's to be humiliated about?" Justin asked.

"If he says no."

"Why would he say no? Unless it is something really weird or maybe something he hasn't tried, he might not want to do it; but then again, he might refuse now and then later want to do it. If he really refuses to listen to you, then don't sleep with him."

"But what if he leaves me? That would also be humiliating."

"Then he wasn't right for you."

"I guess you are right," Suzie agreed.

"You should talk to him about it. If he is hesitant, then maybe try again when you are both more comfortable with each other. In my experience, talking to a guy about sex will definitely pique his interest. You should just bring it up and see what happens."

"Just like that? I mean, just blurt it out?"

"Worked for me and Wendy. I told her right when we started the date what my expectations were, and I let her decide what direction she wanted to head."

"Just like that? You told her you wanted to screw her but no relationship."

"Yes. It was hard to do, but we talked about it, and then she agreed."

"I am not sure that will work in this situation. We just started dating."

"Well, I am one for one on that advice, but if you don't feel comfortable talking about sex, how are you going to have sex?"

"I guess talking and doing are two different things. I think it is actually easier to have sex than talk about it," Suzie said with a giggle.

"I am still new at this, so I just took the advice and ran with it. It worked out pretty good for me," Justin pointed out.

"Dusty is pretty sharp."

"It wasn't Dusty; it was actually the waitress."

"What waitress?"

Justin took in a deep breath and spent the rest of their call telling Suzie about his entire day. She laughed, and Justin was confident he made her feel better.

"Just like old times," he said softly to himself.

Chapter
Thirty-One

"Well, Suzie is out," Justin told Dusty the next day at the coffee shop.

"Brad?" she asked while she wiped down a table.

Justin grimaced. "Is that his name?"

"Yeah, I am sorry."

"For what? We are only friends; besides, she sounds like she could use a night like I had."

"Suzie does need some romance. She has been grouchy lately; I am sure that will help."

"Are you doing okay?" Justin asked.

"What do you mean?" she asked as she stood up and put her hands on her hips.

"I mean your dating life. We have been concentrating so hard on getting me sorted out I didn't even to think about asking about you."

"I am fine. A bunch of Chads, as usual. I have been so busy here that I really haven't had time to even go out on a date. When I do have free time, I am usually relaxing because I am so tired."

"Is this too much for you?"

"No, I am just used to sitting at a desk all day, working from nine to five thirty and then going home and not worrying about work until the next morning. Here, if I am not opening, I get calls from the morning staff, and when I am not closing, I get about a bazillion calls from Lori on how to close down the place."

"Is she not able to do it?"

"No, actually she is great, but she wants to get it exactly right and worries about every little detail."

"I see. Well, you are a great manager," Justin said encouragingly.

"She is getting it; she only called me twice last time she closed, and last night I worked with her to make sure she saw how I did closing, so she is coming along. We will see tonight how she does."

"That's great. So are you going to start dating again?" Justin asked pointedly.

"I will as soon as I find someone to date."

"Want me to be your wingman?"

"Wouldn't that be fun?" she asked, rolling her eyes.

"What? I would make a great wingman."

"Let's get you sorted out first; then we can work on me."

"Sounds like a plan."

"How is that going?" Dusty asked curiously.

"I have a date tonight."

"Good job! With whom?"

"Her name is Tonya."

"What else?"

"She lives near Kalispell. We are meeting at an Italian restaurant there."

"Is she cute?"

"Yes, very."

"That's my cowboy," Dusty said with a smile and a thumbs-up.

"I am going to go home and spend time with Momma; she is still recovering from me not coming home the other night."

"I am sorry, but I had to tell her where you were when you didn't come home, and you wouldn't answer your phone. Is she doing okay?"

"You know how Momma is with debauchery, like April put it. No, she did not sit well with my soiree."

"I love your mom."

"Yeah, but sometimes I wish she wouldn't be so motherly with me."

"Give up on that, bucko, she will always be that way with you. Besides, you are living at her house, so she has the right to know."

"I know, so I am going to go take my medicine."

"Hold on a minute," Dusty said as she ran off to the kitchen.

"What's this?" Justin asked when she returned.

"Sugar."

"That's two sandwiches," Justin said, looking into the sack Dusty had brought.

"It's the sugar to make the medicine go down."

"What?"

"Okay, it's a peace offering from you to your mom."

"Oh, gotcha, good idea."

"Duh. Now get going and make peace with her; you're probably going to need another one tomorrow."

"I am not sleeping with anyone else until I find the right one."

"Yeah, you can lie to yourself, but don't try that bullshit on me."

"Seriously, I am not."

"Get, cowboy; your momma needs you."

Thirty-Two

Twenty minutes later, Justin pulled his truck into its normal spot in front of the house. He got out and walked into the house and headed to the kitchen, where his mother was sitting at the table, doing a crossword puzzle. He could tell she was mad, as she didn't even acknowledge him as he pulled out the sandwich and au jus in front of her.

"Tell Dusty thank you for me," his mother said, not looking up.

"How do you know it isn't from me; you know, like a peace offering."

"Was it from you?"

"No ma'am, it was Dusty," Justin admitted.

"Have a seat, Justin."

Doreen poured a cup of coffee for herself, grabbed a bottled water out of the fridge, and set it in front of her son.

She spent the next twenty minutes explaining the consequences of having extramarital intercourse. She covered everything from diseases to childbirth. She was also awfully specific on the dangers of husbands, ex-husbands, boyfriends, ex-boyfriends, fathers, uncles, brothers, and cousins that might take offence to him causing their delicate flowers to sin.

Justin offered no argument; he just took it like a man, letting his mother express her feelings and worries to her baby boy. He would apologize every so often and give his mom an honest answer when she asked a question that needed answering.

"I will put off dating for a while," he promised her.

"Nonsense. I want you to find someone; you have been so happy lately, and that does this old heart good to see her boy back on his feet."

"I am confused; I thought you didn't want me to date."

"I don't want you to sleep around, Justin."

"I only did it once, Momma."

"Did you feel proud afterward?"

Hell yeah, he thought. But out loud he lied, "Not really."

"I can see by that stupid grin on your face that you aren't sorry at all," Doreen remarked as she interrupted his thoughts.

"Sorry, Momma."

"Is she the one?"

"No, she left her husband, and I don't want someone like that."

"I can see that."

"No, it was just a boo—" He stopped midsentence and tried to find a softer word to describe the scenario.

"I think the term you are looking for is 'booty call.'" Doreen interjected.

"Momma!"

"I told you, I read *Cosmo*; I am not an idiot. I know what the kids of today are doing."

"I really just needed a confidence boost."

"Well, it looks like it worked. Just promise me she is the only one you will sleep with until you find someone you want to spend the rest of your life with."

"You want me to sin again?" Justin asked, not believing what he was hearing.

"No, but if you have to, just do it with her. You cannot undo what is already done, and I am against it, but I do see that it helped make you happy, and that makes me … well, not happy, but glad that you are not moping around the house anymore."

"But why her?" Justin asked, sounding puzzled.

"Because you don't need to be sinning with every woman you come across. You already visited that well; let her be the one that quenches your thirst. When you find someone that you want to spend the rest of your life with, then you can get that drink from her."

"Is that from the Bible or *Cosmo*?"

"A little of both."

Chapter

Thirty-Three

The Italian restaurant was a national chain that Justin had heard of but never been to. He didn't know whether he liked Italian all that much but was willing to give it a go for his next first date with someone he'd had brief conversations with over the last few days. She finally mentioned that she liked to eat here but never really got the chance, so Justin thought that would be a great way to get to meet this young lady. He was right.

Justin sat on a bench outside the restaurant as he waited for his date to show up. He had went to give his name to the hostess, but she said they weren't busy at the moment, and he didn't need to reserve a seat. It was cold out, but the afternoon sun and some mild weather had encouraged him to take the opportunity to enjoy this change of pace.

His phone buzzed in his shirt pocket. He carefully pulled it out, hoping his date hadn't canceled on him. Nope, it was Dusty, wishing him luck and asking him to text her if the date was a bad one and so she could call him with some fake emergency that he could excuse himself for.

"Justin?" said a voice attached to some very shapely legs moving smoothly toward him. The brim of his hat covered the rest of her. He slowly raised his head as his eyes followed the contour of her body all the way up to her smiling face.

"Um, Tonya?" he asked as he stood up.

"Yes, hello, nice to finally meet you," she said as she stood on her tiptoes to give him a hug. Justin's six-foot-three-inch frame was a huge contrast to Tonya's five-foot-nothing height; even with her heels, the top of her head barely reached his chin.

When she gave him a hug, he noticed a short guy helping a woman out of an old beater truck glaring at him. He thought it weird someone would pay so much attention to him hugging this woman; after all, they were both strangers, and he had a woman with him.

"Is that an ex-boyfriend of yours?" he asked her when she released him from a bit too long of a hug.

She turned around and saw the man trying to help a woman out of the truck. The man continued to glare at Justin.

"No," Tonya said as she slipped her arm through Justin's and quickly led him in through the front door, where the hostess greeted them cheerily.

Not two minutes after they had been seated, the man and woman from the parking lot sat in a booth two down from their own and across the small aisle. The man took up station where he and Justin could see each other; the women had their backs to each other and seemed oblivious to what was going on.

The waitress came and brought them menus, talked about the specials, took their drink orders, and left. Another waitress did the same at the other table. Justin tried to concentrate on his date, but the eyes burning into him made it hard to do so.

Tonya was quite attractive. She was very petite except in her bust, which was a bit too much on display in her red spaghetti straps, which were doing their best to keep them up and under wraps. It was killing his neck not to drop his gaze below her chin. *I mean, she put them on display; why not enjoy the view?* he thought. She was nine years younger than Justin and had spent the last three weeks of chatting with him through the dating site, then through texts and a couple of phone calls, before he finally agreed to meet.

"So what made you finally do it?" Tonya asked Justin, bringing his eyes and attention back to her.

"Do what?" he asked as he stared into her deep blue eyes. He noticed she was fiddling with her bleached blonde hair. She was spectacular, really every man's dream date, all dolled up as she was. There had been more than one head that turned as they had walked through the restaurant to their seat. *Maybe that's the mystery dude's problem—he's jealous of me.* He stole a side glance at the man, who was getting fussed at again. His woman seemed more concerned about him paying attention to her than being jealous of his attention toward another woman.

"Meet me. I mean, what was holding you back?"

"I think mainly your age. You are nine years younger than me."

"Age is just a number; it doesn't matter to me. Does it bother you?"

"I don't think the age itself is the issue."

"Then what is?"

"I don't know; I just never dated someone so young before."

"It sounded like you have never dated anyone but your own age before."

"True. I guess I have never really hung around anyone your age. Occasionally we would hire help during the summer to help with the ranch that were around your age, but I never felt like I fit in with those guys."

"Well, girls are much more mature than boys. That is one reason I decided to try to date guys older than me; it seems older guys have their shit together."

The waitress approached and took their order. While Tonya was distracted with placing her order, he stole a glance at the magnificent cleavage on display. He realized his mistake right away. He had been caught—not by Tonya or the waitress, but by Mr. Nosy.

The dude mouthed something to Justin that he didn't understand, but he figured it was some kind of threat. His girlfriend turned around to see who her boyfriend was talking to. Justin tipped his hat, smiled, and winked at her. She smiled back and almost sent the crazy dude through the roof. She then calmly turned back to her date, leaned toward him, and said something to him, to which he reluctantly nodded and relented.

"And for you sir?" The waitress and Tonya were both staring at him expectantly, unaware of the exchange that just had happened.

He placed his order, and soon after, the breadsticks arrived. Their conversation was uninterrupted until their food came, and then Justin felt the eyes again. He noticed that the dude had resumed his staredown; this time he would not heed the advice of his date and really gave Justin the stink eye. Justin was partly to blame; he blatantly pointed his eyes to the cleavage every time Tonya adverted her eyes from his.

Justin hadn't been in many fights, mainly because when he was in one, he usually obliterated his opponents. His dad had been a fairly good boxer in the Marine Corps and had taught Justin from the first time he had been bullied back in the third grade how to hold his own. After his divorce, he used the punching bag that still hung in one of the barns on the property to release his anger.

This dude was definitely fueling his anger, and finally he decided to do something about it.

"Excuse me, Tonya, I need to use the restroom," he said as he got up and headed toward the sign that hung above the hall leading to the facilities, and right past that all-too-familiar table two booths down and across the aisle. The man squirmed as he watched Justin approach their table, and he then blew out a sigh of relief as he saw the tall cowboy ignore him and head for the restroom.

A few minutes later, Justin came out of the bathroom and placed his huge hand on the same man that had been glaring at him. The man looked up in horror into Justin's cool, composed eyes.

"We got a problem here?" Justin asked the man.

"Justin, we are only here for Tonya," came the response—not from the man, but from his date.

"You are?" he asked her, a little surprised she knew his name.

"I am Lisa, and this is my husband, Brandon," she answered sweetly, albeit a bit tensely.

"Is there a problem here?" he asked again, turning his attention back to Brandon and squeezing his shoulder a little tighter.

"No problem" was all Brandon could say.

"We are Tonya's chaperones of sorts," Lisa continued. "Tonya is Brandon's sister, and we were concerned about her well-being on a first date. You know, in case you got a bit too grabby."

"I see. So why are you glaring at me?"

"I-I-I just didn't want her to get hurt."

"You want to join us?" The words just popped out of his mouth automatically. He didn't want them there, but years of good manners had taken control, and there it was—an offer he could not rescind. To add insult to injury, he added, "My treat."

That was all Lisa needed to hear. She reached out her hand for Justin to help her out of the booth, and he subconsciously reacted quickly—a result of years of proper etiquette training from his parents. Brandon looked unsure but finally made the move and followed the duo to the booth. Justin gently pushed Tonya over with his hip as Lisa and Brandon took their seats opposite them.

"Tell your waitress to bring your food over here," Justin remarked as he saw the confused waitress staring at an empty booth.

Justin noticed both of them staring at the table, and then it registered: the broken-down truck, the ridiculously small ring on Lisa's hand, and their best clothing all were signs of a couple struggling to make it. Justin knew the feeling and could relate. He felt his frustration subsiding and decided to do the right thing. He had pretty much wiped out all of his debt, the last few years had been very prosperous on the ranch, and since Joleen had come from a pretty wealthy family, she hadn't contacted him about wanting anything from the sale of his house or anything else from the divorce; he now had money in his pocket. He decided he was going to do the right thing.

"I bet you haven't even ordered yet," Justin continued as he waved to his own waitress.

She quickly came over and looked confused at the new additions.

"These are our friends and decided to join us," he told the waitress. "Just take their orders and put them on my bill. I insist."

They ordered and passed the rest of the date with conversation and good food.

Brandon looked glum through the entire affair; he never came around to even smiling. It was a stark contrast to the women, who were thoroughly enjoying themselves and chatting away while they chowed down on their meals. Justin was included in much of their conversations, but Brandon only would grunt or reluctantly give an answer when asked a question; other than that, he didn't contribute to the conversation.

After dinner, they ordered desserts, and the women indulged themselves while complaining how many carbs they were going to have to burn the next day to make up for this.

"Well, we should be hitting the road," Brandon finally said as he got up and stuck out his hand for Lisa.

"Thank you so much, Justin and Tonya, for a lovely evening," Lisa said as she slid over and got up.

"You coming, Tonya?" Brandon commanded more than asked.

"Naw, I am all right. I will see you two later," she said, encouraging the couple with her eyes and tone to leave.

Brandon glared at Justin.

"Don't keep her out too late," he said in a firm tone.

Justin nodded and tipped his hat to the couple. They turned and left, which cued the waitress to bring the bill over to Justin.

"So what are we to do next?" asked Tonya as she put her hand on Justin's knee.

"Go home," he replied a little uncomfortably.

"Okay," she said with a seductive smile, arching her back so her breasts would be brought to his attention.

"No," he said, "not like that." He quickly got up and stuck out his hand.

"No? But why?" she said as she only looked forlornly at his hand.

"You are very tempting, but I don't ever invite someone back to my place on the first date."

"Oh, okay," she said brightly as she grabbed his hand.

"What about the second date?" she asked when she had stood up.

"I don't think there will be a second date."

"What? Why not?" she asked incredulously.

"Your brother doesn't like me," Justin noted as he saw the couple climb into their old truck.

"Screw him, he doesn't like anyone. Besides, he is just pissed off that you took me to an expensive restaurant he couldn't afford."

"It's not just that."

"Oh, I see. It's me."

"Not really. I just didn't get that vibe that we are right for each other."

"Yeah, it seemed like we were forcing the conversation. I guess it is good that you invited Lisa to the table, or it might have been awkward all night."

"Agreed," he said as they left the restaurant and headed toward her car.

Justin pulled the door open for her, and she paused and turned to look at him.

"That doesn't mean we can't have some fun tonight. Or some other night."

"No, I wouldn't do that to you."

"But I want you to do that to me. You are a fine specimen of a man," she said with her seductive smile. "Believe me; I would know what I am getting into."

"I appreciate that, but I am not that kind of a man. I don't think I could have that kind of relationship with you."

"Okay. I wish you luck on finding your soulmate," she said as she got behind the wheel of her car.

"You as well," he said as he shut the door behind her and watched her drive off.

He pulled out his cell phone and searched in his limited contacts for the number he was looking for. He clicked on it and pushed the green phone symbol.

When the voice answered, he quickly explained his situation and then asked the question. "I wish I could, but I cannot tonight. My son is out with his dad, and they will be back in a couple of hours," Wendy replied.

"Two hours is two hours," he replied quickly.

"No, you cannot come here in case they get back early, and your place is too far for me to drive."

"What about a motel?" he suggested.

There was a short pause, and then Wendy replied.

"I'm in."

Chapter

Thirty-Four

Justin drove to Dusty's house, but her Camaro wasn't in the driveway, so he drove to the coffee shop and saw it parked in its usual spot just off to the side of the building. There were lights on inside of the coffee shop, but the Closed sign was clearly displayed.

Lori was standing at the corner of the building, smoking a cigarette and staring at her phone. She wasn't dressed in her normal uniform but rather was wearing jeans, shoes, and a heavy coat. He could tell she was shivering, but she was going to finish that smoke if she froze to death.

"Hello Justin," she said as she smashed out the last little bit and threw the butt in a collector off to the side of the door.

"Lori," Justin answered.

"You are just in time."

"I am?"

"Yep, come on in; we are all waiting on you."

"Really?" he asked, looking a little confused as he followed her through the door.

Inside it was like a construction site. The tables had all been pushed to the side. Boards, tile, and other building materials had been stored on pallets in their place.

"Just in time, cowboy," said Dusty with a smile as she came through a plastic sheet hanging on the wall.

"What's going on?" he asked as he marveled at her new ability to walk through walls.

"Come on; I will show you," she said as she led him behind the plastic sheeting.

Justin walked through the newly cut doorway between the coffee shop and the old thrift store.

"You are expanding now?" he asked her when he finally got it.

"Why not? No time like the present."

"Yeah, but Suzie isn't here."

"No?" asked a worker wearing white bib overalls with a white cap. Her red hair was tied in a ponytail sticking out the back, and Justin instantly recognized that sweet voice.

"Suzie! Hello. What are you doing here?" Justin asked in surprise. He took her beauty in, and her smile made him catch his breath.

"Duh, she came to help expand the restaurant," said April, bringing in an armful of tile.

"I am only here for a couple of days," Suzie commented.

"What about your grandma?"

"She is fine; one of her nieces came to visit for a couple of days, so I decided to head here to help get this kicked off."

"Well, good. How can I help?"

"The bathrooms," April said quickly as she handed him the load of tile.

"Okay, on it."

"Play nice with Brad," April said with a mock innocent smile.

Justin froze in his footsteps.

"He is here?" he asked, looking even more surprised.

"Yeah, he wanted to come and help," she replied with a devilish grin.

Justin felt something in him he could not explain. It was like getting stabbed in the gut and the heart at the same time. Brad in Pennsylvania was definitely going to be different than Brad in Hackamore. Not that Justin imagined him as someone different, but it is easy to dislike someone that you don't know, and his upbringing taught him not to judge anyone before he met them, but he already hated him.

"Did someone say my name?" asked Brad as he came out of the restroom area.

Brad was barely five feet three inches tall and weighed a hefty 260 pounds. Justin sized him up as a guy who had not always been fat. His shoulders were square, and his arms looked like they had been friends with the bench press, albeit not for a while. He wasn't sure whether he felt better or worse about the situation. He knew he was a fine specimen of a man; he had just been told that, but losing to this butterball was not doing any good for his ego.

"Brad, this is Justin," Suzie said slowly as she introduced them.

"Brad, glad to meet you," Justin lied, but he did it well enough no one suspected. Having a slow drawl and having been raised right, he could pull off friendly rather well.

"Likewise," Brad said with his own salesman's smile.

"You need some help in the bathroom, I hear," Justin said, forgetting about the circumstance and concentrating on the task at hand.

"All right, follow me," Brad said reluctantly.

Justin followed Brad into the bathroom, where Brad explained what he was trying to accomplish, and then he and Justin went silently to work. Both men were hard workers and found that although they were at odds, they quickly jumped into the task, helping each other to finish the job.

"Whoa, that was intense," Justin heard April comment as he walked into the bathroom.

Chapter

Thirty-Five

After Justin and Brad had left the room, Dusty turned and glared at April. "What? We were all thinking it, and it was pretty intense," April said with a defensive tone.

"Let's get back to work," Suzie ordered as she went back to painting the walls.

Night turned into late night and then into the wee hours of the morning. The two women and their staff worked diligently in getting the new restaurant painted and decorated, and they hung the new light fixtures as they often glanced toward the back, hoping not to see or hear the two bulls settling their differences.

Sometimes Dusty would hear talking or occasional swear words from the bathroom, but other than the occasion where Justin or Brad would come out to grab more materials, the two kept to themselves in their work area and the others avoided it like the plague—except, of course, for April. She constantly was making trips with drinks, snacks, and small supplies for the men.

"April!" exclaimed Dusty.

"What?" she asked with an innocent tone.

"How much water do you think they can drink?" Dusty asked as she eyed the two fresh bottles in her hands.

"They are working hard in there and need refreshments," April protested.

Dusty froze as she heard a loud thud, and then came swearing and the sound of two men wrestling. The room thickened with panic as all attention was turned to the doors. April dropped one of the bottles in fear as Dusty high-tailed it toward the restroom hallway Suzie was hot on her tracks.

Thirty-Six

"What the hell is going on in here?" Dusty demanded as she burst through the lady's room door.

"Justin, what did you do to him?" Suzie asked fiercely as she went over to Brad.

Brad was sitting up against a wall, holding the back of his head, while Justin sat across from him, rubbing his shoulder.

"Well?" asked Dusty as she put her hands on her hips and stared down at Justin.

"Yes, well?" asked Suzie, glaring at him.

"Stop!" Demanded Brad. "You two need to take a chill pill."

They both turned to Brad.

"I lost my balance when I was up on the stool. Justin saw me going down and tried to catch me. If it hadn't been for him, you might be rushing me off to the hospital right now."

"I always knew he was a hero," April blurted out.

"April, go get some ice and towels, please," Dusty asked, starting to calm down. She turned her attention back to Justin. "That the truth?"

"Yeah, why wouldn't it be?" he asked starting to get up.

"Not easy to catch a fat man, is it?" Brad joked.

The room went silent for a split second, and then everyone started laughing. April returned with Lori and the rest of the staff, bringing towels, ice, and the med kit.

They tended to the two men and talked among themselves as Justin looked at the many faces helping out.

"One thing is for sure," Justin remarked.

"What's that?" asked April curiously.

"These bathrooms are much bigger than the old ones. You could barely fit one person in those other ones."

They all chuckled as they pulled the men to their feet, and all of them headed out to the new dining area, where they pulled up chairs and sat in a misshapen circle.

"I really thought you two had started throwing hands," Dusty remarked.

"Naw, we got our differences sorted out while we were working," Brad told her.

"Yeah, we are okay. I guess we were both a little jealous of each other," Justin added.

"I've always wanted two guys fighting over me," Suzie remarked with a smile, still fussing with the small lump on Brad's head that had formed when he hit it on his way down.

"Some girls have all the luck," Lori remarked as she continued to rub Justin's injured shoulder.

"Having fun?" Dusty asked Lori.

"Just doing my civic duty," replied Lori as she continued to work out a knot.

"Don't bother her; this feels good," Justin replied with his eyes closed.

"I guess I am tired. It's like 5:00 a.m. back home." Brad remarked.

"Yeah, it has been a long day. Thank you everyone for pitching in and helping." Suzie told the group.

"We are still getting paid, right?" asked Lori.

Thirty-Seven

"Hello."

"Come on in, Dusty." Justin told the voice lingering outside the door to his room. She walked in with two drinks. A coffee for her and a water for him.

"How's the shoulder?" she asked as she sat on his neatly made bed.

"A little sore, but fine. It's my body that aches."

"Oh?"

"Yeah, I hit the whole wall when I caught him, my shoulder got tweaked but my body really took the brunt of the whole collision."

"Poor baby," she mocked.

"Yeah, whatever. Shouldn't you be working?"

"Naw, we closed the restaurant for the next few days to finish the remodeling. We are having our grand opening on Thursday; that is when we will reopen."

"Will everything be done by then?"

"Yeah, we are almost done, just a few odds and ends to tie up. The biggest thing we have now is to put in all the new tables and take out all the old things and trash we are not going to be using."

"That sounds like a lot."

"That's why you are going to help," Dusty said matter-of-factly.

"Gee, thanks for volunteering me."

"Wasn't me; it was your mom."

"I am quite certain you had something to do with that," Justin retorted.

"Moi?" Dusty said innocently as she placed her hand on her heart.

"Yes, you and my momma are quite the conspirators when you get together."

"I am sure I have no idea what you are talking about," she said with a huge smile before taking a slow drink of her coffee.

Justin couldn't help but think how sexy she looked as she stared at him over the rim of her coffee cup.

"So tell me about last night. How was your date?"

"Oh, um, it was good," he said with a huge grin.

"You didn't!" she exclaimed.

"What?"

"You got you some."

"Quiet! Momma," Justin said in a hushed command.

"She was leaving when I got here."

"Damn it. Church. I forgot."

"I explained what happened last night and how grateful Suzie and I were for showing up. She was okay with you missing church for helping us out."

"That's awfully Christian of her."

"Enough with the stalling; get on with your sexcapade story."

"Okay."

"Wait, first show me her picture and profile."

Justin shrugged and turned toward his computer and booted it up. Dusty slipped out to use the restroom.

"Whoa, momma," she exclaimed as she walked back into the room and saw Tonya's picture on the monitor. "You did good, cowboy."

"It wasn't like that."

"Sure, sure. I would believe you if it wasn't for that shit-eating grin on your face."

Justin vacated his seat and took up station on his bed. Dusty sat down and studied the profile as though she were fixing to take a last-minute pop quiz.

"Young, beautiful, no filters. She seems genuine. What is wrong with her? Oh my God, did she catfish you?"

"Nope, that is her."

"You got to see her naked, didn't you?"

"Nope."

"No? Your face tells a different story," Dusty said, glaring at him.

Justin took a deep breath and told Dusty every detail about his date, the chaperones, and her offer.

"You turned that down?" she asked incredulously, pointing at the smiling picture on the monitor."

"Yep," he replied defiantly.

"Dude, I have known you a long time, and that face says you got you some last night."

"I did."

"But not with her?"

"Nope."

"Damn it, Justin, quit stalling."

"Wendy."

"Oh. Why Wendy when you could have had her? I mean, she said she didn't exactly expect a relationship from you. This is every man's fantasy. She's smoking hot, young, and she was willing to give it up without a relationship. What's wrong with you, dude?"

"Momma and the promise I made to her."

"Yeah, but what she doesn't know …"

"*I* will know."

"But still, maybe you could trade in Wendy for her. I mean, that would be all right, I am sure."

"Maybe."

"You are probably right. Girls that young will say things they don't mean."

"What do you mean?"

"Like, she has good intentions. She may say she just wants a sexual relationship, but then she may get clingy and try to move the bedroom activities to a full-blown relationship."

"True, and then there is the family," Justin interjected.

"Actually, bringing her brother along wasn't a bad idea. He would be there if any guy got too grabby with her against her will."

"I'm sure he wouldn't agree even if it was with her approval."

"That's true. Guys like that are stupid."

"He was just protecting his sister."

"No, I mean yes, but who protected the girls he slept with from him? I mean, those guys are real assholes; they don't want any dude sexing up their sisters, daughters, friends, or other females in their lives, but they want unrestricted access to the women they are pursuing."

"I guess I never thought of that. Yeah, I am sure he would be trouble."

"Nothing you couldn't handle, sounds like."

"Not the point. Drama is still drama, and I really don't want that."

"Understood. Still, she is smoking hot. She might be worth the trouble."

Chapter

Thirty-Eight

The next morning, after Justin got done with his chores, he made his way to the kitchen.

"How is your dating going?" Doreen asked him as they ate a huge breakfast she had fixed for them both.

"I think I am going to take a break for a while."

"Oh?"

"Yes. It is a whole different world now, and I never knew it was so complicated. Besides, I was volunteered to help Suzie and Dusty get the restaurant ready for their big opening."

"Sounds like that will keep you out of trouble for at least a little while."

"I'm in no trouble, Momma."

"Sounds to me like you have had plenty of opportunity to get into some."

"I really wish you and Dusty could find better things to talk about."

"She just fills me in on the things you don't."

"I tell you things."

"Yes, but not everything."

"She tells you everything?"

"I am sure she does not. She would never fill me in on everything since we don't see eye to eye on some of your extracurricular activities."

"Yeah, well."

"Stop. I don't want to hear your lame excuses. Besides, she did tell me you did turn down opportunities that she felt you should have explored."

"Momma! You two really need to quit nosing into my life so much."

"Good luck with that. We both care about you, and quite honestly this is the most interesting gossip that has come through this town in a long time."

"Momma!" Justin exclaimed.

"Shush. Give an old woman this one simple pleasure."

"I don't know what is worse, the dates or the gossip that follows."

"Oh, quit it. She is just filling me in on things that I am worried about. Besides, I don't have many friends left, and she is good to talk to."

"She is a good friend."

"You should remember that" Doreen said as she started to clear the table.

"Speaking of which, I need to head down there and get busy."

"It is only five-thirty."

"Early start today. We have to get everything ready for when the new tables are delivered."

"Are they going to redo the coffee shop too?"

"No, Suzie and Dusty thought it would be better to leave that part alone. Some people don't like change in this town, and they don't want to upset their older frequent customers. They also thought that it might draw people twice as much."

"Oh? How so?"

"They could come for coffee and breakfast in the old shop and then later for lunch or dinner in the new part. Like going to two different restaurants."

"Sounds smart."

"They are thinkers."

"They care about the community and the people; that is a good quality."

"Agreed. I would have never thought about something simple like that," Justin said thoughtfully.

"If you pay attention to those two, you will learn a lot."

"Yes, Momma," he said as he got up, kissed his momma on the cheek, and brought his plate to the sink.

"Don't worry about the dishes, you need to get to work."

"Thank you for breakfast, and for everything, Momma."

He kissed her again and headed to the front room to put on his boots.

Thirty-Nine

Justin's truck rolled into town quietly crunching the layer of snow that had fallen overnight. He parked it in front of the coffee shop and let it quietly idle as he waited for the rest of the crew to show up. After a few minutes, he checked his phone for the time. It was about fifteen minutes before everyone was supposed to show up, so he decided to give the dating site a quick view.

"I thought you were giving that up for a bit," he asked himself as he checked the messages and activity from the last couple of days. Despite the debate going on in his head, he continued to read the messages and read profiles. His heart really wasn't into it, but he wasn't too eager to discount the nice messages that had been left by women who wanted to chat, meet, or try to get him to send them money because they were facing some kind of crisis.

Scammers, he thought as he went through the various ones that Dusty had showed him were signs of fake users and deleted them.

Something caught his attention in the rearview mirror. It was the headlights from a vehicle creeping down the street, headed right for him. It pulled up next to him, and the driver shut it down, jumped out and opened his passenger door, and jumped in.

"Hello, Suzie," Justin greeted her in surprise.

"Hey. Can I sit here for a minute?"

"Sure."

"I needed to talk to you."

"Where is Brad?"

"He is still sleeping. He has had a headache since the accident. I told him to rest so we could get this big move taken care of today, but this morning he was still in pain, so he won't be joining us today."

"No problem, we can get it. Are you going to take him to the doctor?"

"No, he doesn't like doctors," Suzie said quickly.

"Doesn't he sell medical equipment?"

"Yes."

"Don't you have to deal with doctors in that industry?" Justin asked curiously.

"Why do you think he doesn't like them?" Suzie shot back.

"Point taken."

"Look, I didn't mean to cause an issue. When I knew I had some free time coming up, I told Dusty I would come out here and help get the restaurant set up so we could open it before too long."

"There is no issue. I like helping out; it's not like I have much else going on. The ranch is pretty much down for the winter except for the animals. I finally got everything fixed and maintained for when spring hits," Justin informed her.

"No, I mean between you and Brad."

"There is no issue there either. He did well for himself."

"Thank you, but I don't think there is any long game there."

"What do you mean?"

"I mean he will never move out here," Suzie said quietly.

"So move there."

"No," she said, shaking her head. "I had thought about that, but when I got here, I realized how much I miss this place and all of my friends."

Justin repeated the one line everyone seemed to make about Hackamore. "Everyone wants to leave here growing up, but no one can ever stay away for long."

"That's kind of the town's mantra, isn't it?" Suzie asked.

"I think it's every small town's mantra."

"What is it about small towns?"

"The community and the people, we are all one big happy family."

"I wish Brad could see that."

"Give him time."

There was another flash of light, and Dusty's Camaro was coming in hot. It slid into the spot on the other side of Justin's truck, hitting the pole in front of the sidewalk.

Justin jumped out and looked at the damage.

"It's icy out," Justin scolded her.

"Duh," she replied after she made her way around to the front of the car and examined the newest dent.

"You should slow down a bit," Justin advised.

"It's fine, just gives it more character."

"Any more character and it would be Bugs Bunny," joked Justin.

"I don't—" She paused as she watched Suzie climb out of Justin's truck. She looked in surprise at her and then back at Justin. "What's going on here?"

"Just keeping warm," Suzie remarked as she headed up to open the shop.

"Warm?" she asked Justin with an evil smile.

"We were just talking, Dusty," he said defensively.

"Uh huh. About what?"

"Um …"

"Yeah, exactly." She gave him a hug and headed up the two steps and followed Suzie inside.

Another beam of light hit Justin as he saw Lori driving slowly up to a parking spot. April jumped out of the passenger side and skipped over to Justin and gave him an unexpected hug.

"Hello, April. Lori," he greeted them both.

"Let's get out of this cold," Lori said as she rushed into the restaurant.

"Any luck with Charlie?" Justin asked April.

"How do you know about that?" she asked, sounding surprised.

"This gossip chain works both ways," he told her with a grin.

"No, nothing, and the dance is this Friday night. I don't know what I am going to do."

"I heard you have plenty of offers."

She blushed. "Not plenty—a few."

"What do you think I should do?" April asked, wrapping her arms around herself to fend off the cold.

"Ask him."

"No, I could never. Besides, a lady doesn't ask; she is asked. Look, Justin, there are things you don't understand."

"Okay."

"And him asking me is important to me," April insisted.

"I see."

"You understand, don't you?"

"I think I do. Come on; let's get out of this cold," he said as he gently pushed her toward the door.

"What were you two discussing out there?" Dusty asked as they strode in the door.

"The crappy work hours," Justin said with a grin.

"Agreed, we should file a complaint against the manager," Suzie joked.

"All of you are going to get fired if you don't get busy," Dusty joked back.

"Don't tease me," Justin replied.

"Me either," April chimed in.

"Where do we start?" asked Justin.

The next few hours were spent moving around the tables and other furniture they were going to keep and discarding any trash and items that they were getting rid of. Anytime anything was moved, April would jump in with a mop or towel and cleaning supplies to scrub down any accumulated grime. They worked as a team, getting everything ready for the appliance store truck to show up.

There was a knock on the front door, and everyone excitedly looked toward the door, hoping to see the delivery driver. Justin walked over to the door and opened it. It was not the delivery driver. Instead, there stood a boy that could have been Justin's mirror. Charlie Jr. was wearing boots and Wranglers, and his partially opened coat revealed his blue-and-red plaid shirt. He gave a big grin and a nod to Justin as he walked past him and into the coffee shop.

"What's he doing here?" Suzie asked.

"I have no idea," Dusty remarked. "He usually comes by here in the afternoon to grab something before he goes to work at his dad's shop."

"I called him for help," Justin told them as he moved to the front door to let him in.

"Good morning, Justin," Charlie said with a smile.

"Thank you for coming in to help," Justin told him as he shut and locked the door behind him.

"I think the delivery truck is getting fuel," Charlie told the group.

"It is?" asked Suzie.

"Yes, I saw it over at the truck stop as I drove past; should be here any minute."

"Are we ready?" Asked Lori as she and April came in from the new dining room.

April froze and started fussing with her hair.

"Hello, April," said Charlie with a nervous smile.

"Wha … what are you doing here? We are closed."

"He is here to help unload the truck," Dusty said, beaming at Justin.

"Oh, okay," April replied, smoothing out her clothes.

Right on cue, Justin heard the rumble of a large truck moving its way slowly down the street. He and Charlie ran out and talked to the driver about where he should park. The truck moved into position, and the driver got out with another guy. They opened the back of the truck and then pulled out a ramp.

The truck was filled to the brim with tables and chairs. Suzie's crew started grabbing chairs and hauling them inside while the two delivery guys grabbed a dolly and started getting the tables in position to be hauled inside.

"Be careful," the driver told his helper. "We don't want scratches or dents. Make sure you use the blankets."

"Will do," the helper replied eagerly.

"Just put everything toward the back of the store; we will rearrange them after it is all in," Suzie told the crews.

Over the next hour and a half, they worked diligently to get the entire order off the truck. Dusty had Lori make everyone sandwiches and kept the coffee brewing and the bottled water available for the workers. Justin noticed that Charlie and April were giving each other little smiles every time they looked at each other. He also noticed Suzie giving him the same kind of smile.

"That went quicker than I thought," the driver told everyone as he brought in the last table.

"Can't beat teamwork," Justin told him.

"We do appreciate the help."

"And the food," his helper interjected. "Those were awesome."

"Why thank you," Lori replied.

"Anytime you find yourselves in Hackamore, drop on in," Dusty added.

With that, they bade the delivery crew good-bye. Lori packed two extra sandwiches and gave them some coffee to go and sent them on their way.

"Let's take a break before we get started on putting the new tables in place," Dusty suggested.

"Agreed," said Suzie.

They pulled out one of the larger tables and set it in the middle of the floor; then they each grabbed a chair and pulled up to the table. They sat and chatted for the next thirty minutes, Dusty and Suzie both taking lead on what they wanted the room to look like and where to place the different tables and booths. They assigned each individual certain tasks to help streamline the process.

"Um, I or, um, we have to go to school," April interrupted, looking at the clock.

"That's why I didn't assign you any tasks," Dusty replied.

"Charlie, can I get you to help me with one more thing before you go?" Justin asked him.

"Sure, boss. What do you need me to do?"

"Come on, I need help taking all this trash out to the bins in back."

"Sure, no problem."

"I can help," offered April.

"Naw, we got it," Justin told her with an impish grin.

The guys each grabbed a load of trash, boxes, and the protective foam sheets that were on the tables and headed out back.

Justin threw his load in the recycle bin and then grabbed Charlie's load and threw that in as well. Charlie turned to head back in, but Justin grabbed his shoulder and spun him around.

"Charlie, I need to chat with you a minute," Justin said directly.

"Okay," said Charlie.

"You going to that dance on Friday?"

Charlie shrugged.

"I don't know. Maybe."

"Who you taking?"

"Um, well, no one, I guess," said Charlie, looking at his boots.

"Everyone turn you down?"

Charlie shook his head.

"I haven't asked anyone," Charlie said while kicking the snow.

"Why not?"

"I don't know."

"Are you scared?"

"Um, not really scared."

"I get it. I know the feeling; it's hard to lay your pride and heart out for such a beautiful creature only to have it smashed if she says no," Justin said comfortingly.

"That and I don't know how to ask someone without being stupid."

"Good point. The good thing you've got going for you is that you are a dude."

"What's that got to do with anything?" Charlie asked, sounding surprised.

"Men are dumb and clumsy; women know that, and they appreciate it when a guy is bold enough to ask them out. Believe me; most women will say yes to a dashing young man like yourself. In fact, I would bet there are at least a few that want you to ask them right now."

"You think so?"

"I know so."

"Really? Like whom?"

"Who do you think? Why do you think I asked you here to help today?"

"I thought you needed my help, and I could use the money."

Justin pulled out a hundred-dollar bill and handed it to him.

"Thank you."

"No, thank you. And you need to ask April to the dance—only if you want to."

"I do, but how do I know she will say yes?"

"Does it matter?" Justin asked.

He thought about it for a while, nervously looking around. When the thought finally hit him, he looked back at Justin.

"I guess not. I do like her and would like to go with her to the dance."

"Then ask. Dude, did you see her when you showed up?"

"Well, yes."

"No, did you really see her?"

"What do you mean?"

"When she saw you, she immediately started preening her hair and clothes. She was okay looking like a ship rat around us, but when you showed up, she started to make herself more presentable for you."

"She could have done that for anyone; she works with you guys, so that's different," Charlie stated.

"What about all the times you come in here after school and talk to her?"

"Well, um, she never said she likes me."

"No, dumbass, women aren't going to come out and say that."

"Oh. But she could just be being friendly to a customer."

Justin sighed a long sigh, now realizing what Dusty had been experiencing with him.

"All right, here it is, dude. She has been bitching the last two weeks that you haven't asked her, and now she is getting nervous you won't ask at all."

"She has?"

"Yup and has turned down other offers to go. Waiting on you," Justin informed him.

"She has?"

"Yeah. Don't break that girl's hopes about going with a charming young man."

Charlie stood there looking dumbfounded, and then a smile started to spread across his face. April came out through the door and looked at the duo as they sheepishly returned her stare.

"What?" she asked curiously.

"Charlie here was wondering if you needed a ride to school," Justin said as he bumped Charlie's shoulder.

"I would love a ride to school," April said enthusiastically.

Justin smiled at Charlie, who returned the smile. Charlie walked April over to his pickup and opened the door for her and helped her in.

"What were you two devils talking about?" Dusty asked Justin suspiciously when the couple left.

"Told him to ask her out." Justin answered.

"Did you pay him to ask her out?"

"No, it was for helping us out."

"We can pay him."

"A hundred dollars?"

"You gave him a hundred?" Dusty gasped.

"Sure, why not? He earned it. Besides, I really wanted him to come."

"Sounds like Charlie is lucky to have you as a wingman."

"A good wingman is hard to find. Besides, I learned from the best."

"So what's up with you and Suzie?"

"Suzie?" Justin asked confused.

"Don't pretend like I didn't see her in your truck when I pulled in."

"You mean when you crashed into the post?"

"Shut up and don't avoid the question," Dusty retorted as she looked over at the Camaro, which was still pressed up against the post.

"Nothing. She just was getting warm," Justin said with a smirk.

"Uh huh. Her car doesn't have a heater?"

"She said she wanted to talk."

"About what?"

"Brad."

"Oh really?"

"Yeah, she likes him well enough," Justin said, remembering the short conversation before it was interrupted.

"But?"

"But she doesn't see him moving here."

"So she could move there."

"That's what I told her, but she wants to stay here."

"And she asked you for advice?"

"Not really, I think she just wanted to air it out. Momma does that a lot. I learned from Dad to just to shut up and listen; We don't have to fix everything even if it kills us inside."

"We do like to air out our problems."

"Then why not try to solve it?"

"We just want to get it in the open. I think we want understanding more than a solution."

"Empathy?"

"Exactly."

Chapter

Forty

"So what's up with April and Charlie?" asked Suzie as Dusty and Justin came back inside the restaurant.

"Same ol' same ol'. She still is wanting him to ask her to the dance on Friday," Dusty responded, grabbing a towel and starting to wipe down the tables and chairs that had been set into place.

"So is he going to?" Suzie asked as Justin helped her grab another table and move it to its spot.

"God, if he doesn't, she will be unbearable to work with," commented Lori.

"Justin paid him to ask her," Dusty said with an evil smile.

"You didn't!" Suzie scolded him.

"Damn it, Dusty. I told you it was for helping us," Justin said defensively.

"I know, calm down cowboy. I was just joking around," she replied.

"But you talked to him?" asked Suzie.

"Yeah, I told him that it might be a good idea."

"Wow, you have come a long way, cowboy," Dusty remarked.

They spent the rest of the morning moving everything into place, cleaning, recleaning, setting up the decorations, and placing the new menus and silverware until the place looked spotless and ready for business. The coffee shop hadn't changed much. New light fixtures were added, and all the booths were taken out so the dining area would be completely stocked with tables and chairs.

The restaurant side was all new. They laid a brand-new wood-grained floor and added booths along the wall, while the rest of the area was filled with tables that could accommodate either four or six guests. The walls were decorated in western fashion. Pictures of John Wayne, Clint Eastwood, James Stewart, Sam Elliot, and even Lee Van Cleef were hung around the room, along with bull horns, lassos, and other cowboy paraphernalia, to give the customers a western experience.

"That will about do it," Suzie remarked as she surveyed the entire scene.

"I am so excited," Lori said as she, too, admired their work.

"The whole town is talking about it; I even submitted an article for the local paper," Dusty told them.

"Did they print it?" Suzie asked her.

"I think they will. It comes out Wednesday, so hopefully it will draw a bigger crowd. April has been telling everyone at school."

"It sounds like this is going to be a smashing success," Justin agreed.

They finished up, and then Suzie asked whether some of the staff wanted to open for lunch.

"Sure, I will stay," said Lori quickly.

The cooks and another waitress said they would be happy to continue working. Suzie promised them they would close by two, depending on the traffic; she didn't want to spoil the big grand opening tomorrow.

"Dusty, why don't you take the rest of the day off; you deserve it," Suzie told her manager.

"Sounds good," she said as she went to grab her things.

"You going to be here Thursday, cowboy?" Suzie asked Justin.

"Wouldn't miss it. Momma wants to come as well."

"Good, I look forward to seeing you then," Suzie said, beaming.

Forty-One

Justin pulled his truck into Dusty's driveway the next morning after he completed his chores, showered, and had breakfast with his momma.

He let himself in and sat at his usual spot on the couch. Dusty brought him a water and settled herself in her chair opposite him. There was a smell of bleach, ammonia, and some air freshener attacking his nose, and he noticed her vacuum was sitting quietly near the kitchen. He saw those telltale marks in the carpet that she had just used the vacuum. He slowly surveyed the room, taking note that there wasn't anything out of place and everywhere he could see had been thoroughly cleaned. Thinking back, he remembered that she wasn't always OCD clean, but she did like things neat and organized. He smiled, as he felt proud of her. Even the boxes had been emptied and put away. It looked more like she had been here for years than for a couple of months.

He turned his attention back to her and realized she had been staring off into space this whole time.

"So tell me what's on your mind," Justin said to her as he took a sip of her water.

"I am excited about our grand opening," Dusty remarked as she turned to him.

"No, tell me what's wrong," Justin encouraged her.

"Wrong?" Dusty asked as she now focused on her friend.

"You have been in a mood," Justin pointed out.

"Ugh, it's nothing."

"Bullshit. Tell me."

"All right, I went on a date the other day," Dusty admitted.

"Good for you."

"Yeah, I thought so too."

"What happened?"

"He was nice. He is good looking and was saying the right things."

"What's wrong? Let me guess—he didn't put out?" Justin joked.

"Well, he wanted to."

"You didn't? That's a surprise."

She laughed.

"Shut up! No, I would have, but I think I have reached that point in my life where I want something more than just an FWB."

"FWB?" Justin asked.

"Friend with benefits. Like what you have with Wendy."

"Oh, I see. So you want more than just sex?"

"Yes."

"Did you tell him that?"

"No."

"Then how is he supposed to know? You are the one that is always saying that we men are clueless."

"That is absolutely true. But I didn't want to talk to him about that when we got to his place."

"You were too excited to get naked for him?"

"Well yes, duh. I mean, he was doing everything right."

"So what stopped you? His wife?"

"No, dumbass, he is single—very single," Dusty said pointedly.

"What do you mean?"

"Well, when we got back to his place, it was a mess."

"Okay, is that a problem? I mean, I know what you mean; I like a clean house. But that shouldn't be the only factor in not choosing a man for a relationship."

"See, I have discovered that if a man doesn't take the time to keep his place halfway decent, then what kind of effort is he going to put into me? I am much harder to take care of than a few dishes or even five minutes to make the bed."

"Well, maybe he wasn't expecting you to come back with him."

"Not the point. A man, and really a woman as well, needs to take care of the small things instead of apologizing for the mess he didn't clean up."

"So being dirty means they aren't good in a relationship?"

"There are exceptions, of course, but generally if people can't take five minutes to make their beds, what kind of effort are they going to put into a relationship?"

"I guess I never really thought about it that way."

"Men go to great lengths to see a woman naked. They buy flowers, give gifts, and say romantic things, but once they have us, it seems like that is checked off their list and they go back to being, well, being men—clueless and lazy."

"Lazy?"

"Maybe that is not exactly the right word, but they give up trying because now we don't need as much encouragement to get us in the bed with them. They assume that we don't want or need those little acts of kindness anymore because we are with them or because they won our hearts."

"You learned this from dirty dishes?" Justin asked, looking confused.

"I learned it from dating different guys."

"Really?"

"Yes, the ones that really took care of me and our relationship were the ones that constantly kept up with the small things in their lives. The ones that didn't usually let our relationship fail because they didn't think they needed to try anymore. One guy even had the balls to tell me that one only needs to reel a fish in once."

"Wow."

"That's what I thought when I drove away from his house for the last time."

"Do you think that is what happened with Joleen?" Justin asked.

"Maybe, but I don't think so."

"Why not?"

"Because you make your bed," she joked.

"No, really."

"Because she would have left a long time ago if you hadn't taken care of her."

"I did buy her flowers quite often and spent a lot of time with her."

"Quit worrying about it—water under the bridge."

"But I want to know for next time."

"Justin, sometimes there are no answers for your questions," Dusty pointed out.

"It's frustrating."

"I know, but you aren't the only one."

"You have guys not give you an explanation?"

"I think sometimes a crap explanation is worse than no explanation, especially when a dude cheats on me."

"You have been cheated on?"

"Oh honey, yes, quite a few times; guys are assholes when it comes to getting into another girl's pants."

"That must really suck."

"It hurts worse when the girl looks way worse than you do."

"A guy cheated on you with someone uglier?"

162

"More than one. The worst part is they weren't doing it because they were in love or wanted to date the girl."

"Why then?"

"Another notch on their belt. They were horny. Whatever the bullshit excuse was, they just couldn't turn down sex."

"They could."

"Not Chads. They will cheat on their wives or cheat with someone else's wife, it is a selfish impulse that they do not want to control. They feel that they are some kind of studs. Truth is, most of those guys are awful in bed. They get on, take care of themselves, and then get off."

"Why would you put up with that? Why would women in general stay with a guy that is selfish like that?" Justin asked.

"I told you, we are stupid."

"I find that hard to believe."

"You are right; mostly it's because we believe the lies they tell us," Dusty remarked forlornly.

"Like, they are single?"

"That or that they are getting a divorce, that they love us, or some other bullshit lie that convinces us that we can trust them and get naked for them. Honestly, dating sucks, as you are learning. Once we find someone that we feel comfortable with, it is easy to start overlooking some of the negative things."

"Flags come in different colors; the red ones are the hardest to see. How do you prevent that?"

"The best way I have found is abstinence. Getting to know the guy seems to alleviate a lot of questions or the guy checks out himself. Either way, I know what his intentions were and can save myself some heartache. See, if a guy just wants sex, he will start off slowly, just trying to romance me. The longer I put him off, the more impatient he will become and the more he will start pulling out all the stops. Pretty soon he gets frustrated and starts being demanding."

"Demanding how?"

"Like he is owed sex because he did all of these things for me, and I owe him."

"What would you owe him for?"

"Dinner, drinks, dates, gifts, or anything else he bought for me. Sometimes a guy will even think that since he took the time to spend with me, he should also get rewarded for that. Usually by that time he has already found someone else. He will still stay in touch in case all that time and effort pays off. If he scores, he scores."

"If he doesn't?"

"Doesn't matter to him. Like I said, he has found someone else or is actively looking, if he ever even stopped."

"That's why I hate this," Justin remarked.

"Everybody hates trying to date. I mean, at the beginning when you find someone it is fun and exciting, even exhilarating, but then all the awkward moments turn into fights, and the pressure of getting rid of all those you have been chatting with brings arguments."

"Why wouldn't you want to get rid of those you were talking with?"

"Most people see it as though if they give that up, then if the relationship doesn't work out, they have no plan B."

"Doesn't that sabotage the relationship anyways?"

"What do you mean?"

"I mean if you really want to be with someone, then getting rid of everyone else is a no-brainer." Justin remarked.

"It's not that easy," Dusty said defensively.

"Sure it is."

"What if it doesn't work out?"

"I am not saying you have to delete everyone after the first date, or the third when you are supposed to have sex, but if you and he decide that you want to make a go at it, get rid of everyone else so you can focus on him and the relationship."

"What if he doesn't?"

"Then you need to get rid of him quickly."

Justin watched her as she slowly processed his words.

"You aren't all that dumb after all, cowboy."

"It's not about being smart; it's about using common sense. You cannot focus on two or more people at once. It clouds everything you are trying to accomplish with the one you want to be with."

"But what if it doesn't work out?" asked Dusty again.

"It won't anyway if you try to keep a backup plan."

"Common sense would dictate that keeping a backup plan would cover your ass in case it doesn't work out," Dusty argued.

"It seems people will justify stupidity as common sense to cover their own dumb decisions and justify their actions," Justin replied pointedly.

"Wow, okay. Point taken."

"I am not saying you are stupid, but if you really want a relationship with someone, then go in 100 percent. Give it your all, no looking back, no backup plans. Just dive in headfirst and put your all into it."

"What if it fails?"

"Then it wasn't meant to be besides, at least you will know that you did your part."

"But what if it fails?" Dusty asked again, sounding unconvinced.

"Remember when we lost that football game to Whitefish in high school?"

"Yeah, they won in the last few seconds with a field goal."

"No one gave us a chance to win that ball game. They were undefeated and won the state championship that year."

"I remember; it was heartbreaking."

"It was, but we kept up with them score for score, hit for hit, and never gave them the chance to run away with the game like everyone thought they would."

"I know; I remember that people started showing up at halftime because they wanted to see the rest of the game."

"We played our hearts out and still lost," Justin said with a smile.

"I know. I cried when they kicked that field goal."

"I felt better after that game than even after some of our wins."

"You did? Why?" Dusty asked.

"Because every one of us threw ourselves into that game. Coach always told us to leave it all on the field, and we did."

"But we still lost; how could you feel good about that?"

"Because we didn't look back. We didn't have a plan B. We didn't look toward our next game; nor did we look at our record or theirs. We put *everything into it*."

"But the result—"

"The result," Justin said, "was that we could hold our heads high because we went against a giant and did not let them break us. They beat us, but they did not conquer us. We did our best, and we walked away from that game knowing that we did not give up no matter what the odds."

"You think the same will work in my dating life?"

"Absolutely. You give it your best and leave it all on the field."

"That sounds hard."

"Sure, you are opening yourself open to rejection, cheating, and putting your heart on the line."

"But I don't want someone to break my heart again."

"It gets broken despite all of your attempts to wall it off. It is selfish to believe that you can keep someone you care about at a distance, and it is unfair to them."

"But it hurts when you let someone in, and they break it."

"It hurts the same when you don't let them in, and they break it anyway." Justin pointed out.

"Good point."

"Besides, it takes the same amount of time and effort to fix your heart whether you let them in or not."

"Who are you, Dr. Phil?"

"Who?"

"Never mind, I forgot you don't watch TV. Okay, I get it."

"You keep going like you are going, you will keep getting what you are getting," Justin reminded her.

"So you think I should have trusted that guy and slept with him?"

"No, I think you have a valid point about a guy taking care of the small things. You learned that lesson, so add it to your dating experience rule book."

"Well, you have given me a lot to process."

"I am sorry; I didn't mean to make you think."

"Dumbass," she replied, smiling.

Chapter

Forty-Two

Justin and Dusty took a break from their conversation and started unpacking some of the moving boxes Dusty had carried upstairs. She had mentioned that since the downstairs was now completed, she wanted to focus on getting the upstairs squared away.

First they took the boxes and placed them into the corresponding rooms; then they started unloading and putting the items in their appropriate places. It wasn't hard work, but it was tedious, and all the bending and sorting left Justin feeling a little stiff. After two hours, they finally emptied the last box, and Justin broke it down and brought it out to the street, where he had placed the recycling bin next to the trash bin for pick up the next day.

When he arrived back upstairs, Dusty was in her room, cleaning off some of the dust on her dresser. She turned to him with her hands on her hips.

"I am ready for a nap," Dusty proclaimed.

"Sounds like a winner to me," he replied, wiping some sweat off his forehead with a paper towel.

"Come take one with me," she suggested.

"Wait, what?"

"We will keep our clothes on, dumbass."

"Why?"

"Because we don't want to ruin our relationship, apparently."

"No, I mean why do you want me to take a nap with you?" Justin asked curiously.

"Oh, well, that was embarrassing."

"It shouldn't be I just was wondering why you wanted me to take a nap with you."

"I just am tired of sleeping alone; it would be great just to snuggle up to you while we had a nap. I mean, it's not like we didn't used to do it all the time in high school."

"Usually when that happened, you were a bit more inebriated."

"Well, now I am not. You didn't take advantage of me then, and you probably could have."

"Only if I wanted a black eye."

"I wouldn't have hit you. Well, at least not hard enough to leave a mark."

"I was talking about Momma."

"I love that woman."

"All right; let's do this."

Dusty grabbed a T-shirt and went to use the restroom while Justin slipped off his Wranglers and then realized that he, too, needed to use the facilities, so he headed down and used the one downstairs.

When he got back to Dusty's room, she was under the covers and lying on the left side, facing the wall. Justin pulled back the covers and froze.

"Uh, whoa!" he exclaimed.

"Get over yourself."

"You drawers are awfully revealing," Justin commented at the thong that was barely being covered by her T-shirt.

"It's all I had clean. I've been wearing granny panties all week and haven't had time to do laundry."

"But still."

"Just shut up and get in."

"Are you not wearing a bra?'

"No, I don't sleep in one usually. Just get in and hold me."

"All right," he said hesitantly as he slowly complied.

Before Dusty could thrust her butt into his groin, he quickly slipped a pillow in between them. He lay there in the silence just listening to her breathe.

"Thank you for this." Dusty said as she wiggled a little closer.

"No problem," he said as he put his arm around her.

After the long morning, they had no trouble slipping off to sleep.

Chapter

Forty-Three

Dusty awoke first two hours later. She felt the warmth coming off Justin's body and realized she hadn't slept that well in a long time. She felt safe with him; he wasn't like those guys that were constantly groping her and trying to get her naked.

Speaking of groping, she thought to herself as she looked down at her chest. Justin had grabbed her right boob while he was sleeping. She smiled to herself.

I guess a little groping doesn't hurt; in fact, it feels kind of good, she thought with a smile.

She lay there trying not to move, trying not to breathe, because she knew that if he woke up, he would be embarrassed and then things would get awkward between them. He started to move, and then she heard his breathing change. She closed her eyes and pretended to be asleep.

"Damn it," she heard him whisper as he slowly and carefully moved his hand from her breast and moved it farther down her body till it stopped on her stomach. Dusty smiled. She listened as Justin waited a few minutes and then quietly slipped out of bed, grabbed his jeans, and headed downstairs. She sat up and stretched a long stretch. The front door squeaked as it closed, and a few seconds later she heard his truck fire up and pull away.

Dusty wondered why she had never given him a chance. In high school he was pretty wrapped up in trying to date Suzie, but that never happened. High school Dusty was different from adult Dusty, but not much. She always wanted that charming, handsome, passionate relationship where the man swept her off her feet and took her to exotic places and they did exotic things. Justin just wasn't that kind of man. He was good looking, but his idea of exotic was trying a new fishing hole or traveling over to Wyoming or Idaho—not the kind of extravagance she was looking for in a relationship.

Chapter

Forty-Four

Thursday at 4:00 p.m., Suzie's restaurant, the Chuck Wagon, was starting to show life. The country music played just loudly enough to be heard over the small groups that were sitting around the dining area chattering excitedly about the new place and the delicious-looking items on the menu. Hackamore had never had a steak house before, and everyone Justin had talked to about it were eagerly awaiting it to open. The last time Hackamore had seen this much excitement was when Clint Black's bus had gotten a flat just outside of town.

Justin escorted his mother through the main doors and stopped at the hostess's station, which was occupied by Suzie.

"Justin and Doreen, welcome!" exclaimed Suzie as she greeted them.

"Hello, Suzie," Doreen said with a smile.

"Suzie," said Justin as he tipped his hat.

"Doreen, you look wonderful all dressed up. What is the occasion?" Suzie asked.

"Your grand opening of course," Doreen replied with a smile.

"You got all dressed up for this?" she asked.

"Definitely! This is an important occasion, and I wanted to dress accordingly," Doreen replied as she smoothed out her best Sunday dress.

"Come, let me show you to your table," Suzie said as she grabbed two menus and led them further into the dining room.

Justin and Doreen followed Suzie into the new dining room and were seated near the window in a booth.

"April will be right with you."

"Doesn't she have school today?" Justin asked.

"She does, but she was able to convince her parents and the school that this was important. She also had to convince Dusty and myself it was worth missing."

Doreen jumped in. "She would rather work than go to school?"

"Well, she is going to the dance tomorrow tonight and won't be able to help out, so with a lot of pleading we finally agreed to let her work," Suzie remarked as she used her hip to bump Justin on the arm.

"Justin!" he heard April exclaim as she ran over and hugged him, knocking his hat off.

"Jeez, April," he remarked to the chokehold she put on him.

"Thank you so much!" she said as she kissed him on the cheek and then straightened back up and pulled her notepad out of her pocket.

"For … for what?" Justin stuttered.

"Do all guests get this treatment?" Doreen asked with a smirk at the clearly reddening Justin.

"Justin here convinced Charlie to ask me to the dance."

"I wouldn't think a boy would need much convincing to ask you out," Doreen remarked. "You are awfully pretty and have a great personality, April."

"Thank you, Doreen. He was a little shy, but Justin gave him the confidence to ask."

"Well, that was nice of you," Doreen remarked, beaming.

"It was nothing," Justin said, trying to shrug off the compliment.

"Well, I am very appreciative of you," April replied, beaming.

"You are most certainly welcome," Justin said as he grabbed one of the new menus.

She took their orders and skipped off to the kitchen.

"For someone who cannot seem to find a date, you sure have all the women around here riled up," Doreen said with a smirk before sipping on her coffee.

"I didn't say I had a problem finding a date, I said I couldn't find anyone *to* date," he replied.

"Seems like to me you should turn off that computer and focus on your surroundings."

"What?"

"Don't 'what' me; you know what I am talking about," his mother said, raising one eyebrow. "There are two women that work in this store that you get along with quite nicely."

"Suzie is dating someone, and Dusty … well, Dusty and I are just friends."

"Napping friends apparently."

"Jeez, how do you know about that?"

"I called Dusty right before you got home yesterday. She told me you had helped her unpack, then you two took a nap."

"We had our clothes on, Momma."

"I know. I am not concerned."

Justin eyed her suspiciously, trying to figure out what was going in that woman's head. He knew that she wanted grandkids but had never mentioned it to him; nor had he ever feel pressured to have any for her. He knew she was always rooting for him.

"What are you thinking, Momma?"

"How much I misjudged you."

"What? How?"

"I was so focused on how sad you were being single and didn't realize that you were just hurt about a love lost."

"Well, I was hurt."

"'Was' is the key word here. I see now that you have plenty of female companionship."

"I do have good friends."

"I thought the only way you could be happy was being in a relationship with someone."

The words hit Justin like a freight train. He had never realized that although he missed Joleen and their relationship, he was now happy once again. Their relationship didn't just revolve around sex and spending time together; she had been his friend and companion for such a long time that when she left, he felt truly alone. Now he had time to rebuild a friendship and start new ones—something he would have never done if she hadn't left. He and Dusty had always remained in touch. Even Joleen supported their friendship, but Justin always felt a little awkward when they talked or spent time with or without Joleen, because he didn't want her to feel as if they were more than friends. Dusty also supported his standoffishness when they contacted each other because she knew Justin's heart and his unwavering loyalty to Joleen.

"I do feel a lot better now. I am happy, Momma," he finally said.

"I can see that. I never was single for very long. I dated a bit in high school, but when I asked your father to homecoming, we were never apart after that."

"You asked Benson out to the homecoming dance?" an eavesdropping April asked in astonishment from another table. She turned to her guests, looking a little embarrassed. "I am sorry; I don't know what came over me."

"Its fine," said the woman whose back was to Doreen's in the next booth.

"Go find out what happened. We are going to need a few more minutes to look over the menu," the man encouraged her.

"It seems our conversation isn't a private one. Hello again, April." Doreen commented with an impish smile.

"I am so sorry."

"Its fine," Doreen remarked with a smirk.

"I thought a lady doesn't ask; she waits till she is asked?" April asked curiously.

"Ladies who wait to be asked become old maids with lots of cats."

"Momma!" Justin exclaimed.

"What? It's true." She turned to April. "Don't ever let something you want go unasked for."

"But won't that make me seem desperate?"

"That kind of desperation is called pride. It is okay to humble yourself to ask for what you want. There is nothing wrong with asking a boy to the dance or out to eat or whatever you want from him. Men are cowards when it comes to us beautiful women; they absolutely hate being rejected. That is why many will ask someone uglier, because they think that is more of a sure thing."

"Momma!" Justin scolded.

"Shush, you. This is girl talk, and your opinions are not welcome here."

"So it's okay to ask for what I want?" April inquired.

"Sure it is, you may not always get it, but at least you will know you tried, and that is good enough to hold your head high. It will also give him some clues as to what you want, and he won't always have to ask you."

"Good advice, Momma," Justin interjected.

"Is everything okay over here?" asked Dusty, approaching the table.

"I want a raise," April said to her boss.

"What have you been telling her, Justin?"

Justin shrugged and pointed across the table to an innocently smiling Doreen.

"Well?" asked April impatiently.

"Jeez, okay. We will talk about it later," Dusty replied with a smile. She turned her gaze on Doreen. "I am watching you, lady."

"You should; I can be plenty of trouble."

"Ain't that the truth," Justin added.

Chapter

Forty-Five

Friday night at exactly 11:00 p.m., Justin walked into the closed Chuck Wagon and took a seat at one of the dining room tables, which was also occupied by Suzie and Dusty.

"How did it go today?" Justin asked them. He realized the mistake he made right after he made it. The women were sitting at a table, looking as if they had been the door greeters at a department store on Black Friday.

"We won," Dusty said with a tired grin.

"I think we did good," Added Suzie. "It was busy until about five minutes after nine; then the dance let out and we got slammed."

"You did?" Justin asked.

"Yeah, I mean we are pretty much the only game in town, so it will probably be like that especially after dances, sporting events, and other school activities," Suzie said, stretching.

"Good thing April jumped in," Dusty said.

"I thought she went to the dance?" Justin asked.

"She did, but when she saw we weren't keeping up, she grabbed an apron and started waiting tables, dress and all," Suzie informed him.

"She just left Charlie at the table and started waiting?" Justin asked, looking perplexed.

"No, she put him to work bussing tables and bringing out orders," Suzie replied.

"I don't know what Doreen said to that girl, but she is a changed woman," Dusty added.

"Momma has that effect on people," Justin said as he saw April come out of the kitchen.

April was wearing a beautiful full-length, long-sleeve sapphire-blue dress with white trim. Her blonde hair was tied up in the same fabric as the dress, accompanied with a white bow. She had makeup on that was starting to fade and run because of sweat, and a white apron that covered most of the dress, which read "The Chuck Wagon" in red across the front.

"Justin!" she exclaimed as she ran over to him.

He looked at her bare feet, which he could barely see under her dress.

"Where are your shoes?" he asked her.

"It is too hard to work in them, so I slipped them off."

"Gotcha. Where is Charlie?"

"I made out with him for five minutes and then sent him home."

He stared at her in shock.

"What?" April defiantly asked the group, which also seemed to be in shock.

"You made out with him and sent him home?" Dusty asked, as she was the first one to recover.

"Yeah, he was too slow to make a move, and I needed to help finishing up in here, so I kissed him long and hard; it just lasted for like five minutes."

"You go girl," Suzie said with a smile.

"Welp, I have to get back to work," she said, and she started to go back to the kitchen.

"April, you can go home; we will finish up here," Suzie told her.

"It's okay, my mom told me she would come get me when we are done."

"I can take you," Justin offered.

April nodded and told them she was going to go text her mom with the new plan.

Justin bade the women good night and headed out to his truck and fired it up.

Forty-Six

"That girl has more balls than both of us," Dusty remarked after April waved to them as she headed out the door.

"I wish I would have been as brave as her," Suzie added.

"You are brave. This"—Dusty waved her arm around the restaurant—"takes a lot of guts to pull off."

"I meant with Justin," she replied in a whisper.

"Uh oh," Dusty said starting to connect the dots.

"Yeah, I really wish I would have moved on him."

"What about Brad?"

"With Brad, I am afraid it is more than the distance. I mean, I know I cannot really judge too much, because he dropped everything to come here with me."

"But?" Dusty asked, leaning forward.

"When we started dating, he was so great, doing the right things and saying the things I needed to hear, but lately he has not been spending time with me unless he wants sex. Then it's off to sleep or, usually, its hop out of bed and get on the phone."

"Wow. Hops out of bed and gets on the phone?"

"Yeah, it's horrible. I feel so used sometimes, like, 'Okay, I am done satisfying myself; now I gotta do my other stuff.'"

"I know the feeling, but in a relationship it should be different."

"He used to lie with me and chat. His phone was always on silent during those times. Today when I sneaked home between rushes, I was feeling a little frisky. I was up for a quickie."

"I also know that feeling." Dusty smiled.

"His phone started ringing when we were in the middle of doing it."

"No! He didn't!"

"No, but he almost did."

"No!"

"Yes, and if I hadn't glared at him and said some very unladylike things to him, he probably would have answered it," Suzie said pointedly.

"Wow. I can't even imagine. How did you feel?"

"It totally ruined it for me. We used to be so close and spent a lot of time talking and getting to know each other. Now it's like he just wants someone to have sex with. He doesn't even want to get to know me or even talk. Honestly, after he got up, I spent the next couple of minutes just lying there thinking 'This can't be right.'"

"No, no that is not right at all. Then what happened?"

"He got up and dialed whoever had called him. I lay there for a while, and then I got up and came back here. He didn't even kiss me good-bye; he just waved like I was some old pal."

"Wow, that's terrible," Dusty remarked, thinking about all the times that had happened to her.

"I want to dump him when we get back. I don't, but I do. I just can't decide."

"What's holding you back?"

"I like the attention he does give me, and honestly, I have been awfully horny lately, and I know he is safe—you know, no diseases and no criminal background."

"Those are your parameters for a good relationship?"

"No, but for what I need right now, it's enough," Suzie replied, letting out a sigh.

"You know, Justin wouldn't have gone out with you if you had made the first move," Dusty said after a quiet moment.

"What? Why? Doesn't he like me?"

"Actually the opposite."

"I am confused."

"So is he. It really comes down to him wanting to get some dates out of the way so he can be ready for you."

"He wants to sow some wild oats."

"Not really. He is nervous about messing up with you."

"I thought he had a booty call girl."

"Yeah, but he is only doing it for the sex; he is scared to death to even give that woman a chance. He wanted to get good at dating so he wouldn't make any mistakes with you."

"Dating is all about making mistakes. That is what makes it fun. That and getting to know each other."

"Really?" Dusty asked, looking confused.

"Sure, if I wanted someone perfect, I would have to marry Jesus. But like I said, it's part of the process of getting to know each other."

"Damn, I guess I didn't realize that."

Forty-Seven

Outside the Chuck Wagon, Justin rubbed his hands and kept putting them in front of the vents, hoping his truck would warm up quickly. He spent his time watching Dusty and Suzie chat. They didn't look like they were having a great conversation. At times he saw them look at him, although he couldn't imagine them being able to see him in the darkness and through his windshield that went from frosty to foggy.

"What are they talking about?" Justin asked April when she shut the door and strapped in.

"What? Who?" asked April, looking confused.

He pointed to the table through the window. Both women were waving at them, and she waved back.

"I don't know."

"I thought you were some sort of secret spy when people were talking."

"I was talking to my mom and telling her about tonight, like she can't possibly wait ten minutes till I get home and tell her."

"Well, moms are like that."

"Yeah, but now I am going to have to tell her all over again with my dad present, because he is going to want to know everything."

"Even the kiss?"

"Yeah, he will want to know about that too."

"You are going to tell him about that?"

"I told my mom, so I am sure she told him, and he will be wanting to know."

"Dads are like that. He might not like your answer," Justin pointed out.

"I know; he is very protective of me. He wanted to be a chaperone for the dance, but his schedule wouldn't allow him to be there on time."

"So was the kiss good?"

"No."

"No?" Justin asked, sounding confused, and he put the truck in reverse and pointed it toward the road leading to April's house.

"Well, not at first; I had to tell him how I wanted to be kissed. Then it got better."

"You had to tell him how to kiss?" Justin asked, surprised.

"Apparently he hasn't done much kissing, probably not ever—not like we did."

"And you have done a lot of kissing?"

"Only a couple of times, but they were awful as well."

"And you had to teach them too?"

"No, I didn't say anything."

"Why now?"

"Your momma said to ask for what I want. With those other boys, I wanted to tell them, but I was too afraid they wouldn't like me or would think I was weird."

"You are weird."

She reached across and playfully punched him.

"Well, I may be weird, but at least now I am getting kissed like I wanna be kissed."

Chapter

Forty-Eight

Justin was nearing the intersection to his road from April's house and turned on his right turn signal. There was a bright light coming up the road quickly from that direction, so he decided to slow down before he got to the stop sign in case the oncoming vehicle decided to turn his way or at least let it pass so he wouldn't get caught in an accident if the driver lost control.

The red Camaro zipped past the intersection and continued north.

"Damn it Dusty, slow down!" he yelled at the taillights.

He switched his blinker from right to left, and after he came to a semi moderate stop, he turned his truck to follow the fleeing sports car.

The county had done their job well during the day with the plows and salt. His tires gripped the road solidly, so he allowed himself a little more accelerator. He pulled into Dusty's driveway and noticed her car was already parked and shut off.

He pulled up behind the Camaro and killed his truck. His boots made a crunching sound as they hit the snow.

Something didn't feel right to him, so he paused and listened to the quiet night. A quiet breeze rustled the trees nearby the house, and the sounds of snow freezing made its quiet clicking sound. Other than that, there were no discernable sounds of trouble that he could make out.

He walked up to the steps and then across the porch to the door. It was unlocked, so he stepped inside and pulled off his boots. Dusty was sitting on the couch, cradling a beer in one hand, a wad of tissues in the other.

"Go away," she said without looking up.

"Not a chance," he replied as he walked over to the fridge, grabbed a beer, and then sat in the chair opposite her.

"I'm not in the mood," she informed him, wiping away some tears and then blowing her nose.

"Dang, and I was hoping to get some tonight," he joked.

"Damn it, Justin. Don't try to make me laugh. I am not in the mood."

"What's going on?"

She sat there softly sobbing.

"I am not leaving until we get this sorted out," he said firmly.

"Nothing to sort out," she replied.

"All right, tell me what has a burr under your saddle."

"I am single. I feel so alone and unwanted."

"I am single too, and I feel alone and unwanted," he assured her.

"No, you have a booty call and a few good friends you can talk with."

"This is about sex?"

"No, dumbass."

"Then what, Dusty?"

"I am lonely."

"You have me," Justin said enthusiastically.

"I mean I want someone to date. I want someone to love me. I want to have someone in my life to make feel like I matter. I hate that I cannot find a good guy to settle down with."

"I see."

"It's not fair, why does everyone else get to have someone and I constantly get rejected by guys I want to like me? Or only get chased after by guys that want me for my body?"

"I don't know."

"I am so sick of the only guys that want me trying to get in my pants."

"That is part of a relationship, usually," he said softly.

"I am not saying I won't give myself to someone, but I want more. We spend such a short amount of time having sex in a relationship compared to everything else, and yet that is all they seem to focus on."

"I can see that."

"The problem is that's all they want. Wham, bam, thank you ma'am, and off to the next chick that will put out."

"There are some good ones still out there; you just have to be patient."

"I am so tired of being patient. I haven't always been patient, and when I go too fast, I get hurt. When I go too slow, they leave me."

"I know; I feel the same way."

"What the hell are you talking about? You have Wendy to relieve your sexual frustrations. Then you have Suzie and me to talk things out with. You have it all. What the hell are you bitching about?" Dusty replied in an angry tone.

"Calm down, cowgirl. I want something with sustenance—someone to build a life with."

"So this is all temporary?"

"Yes, of course. I don't want this to be the rest of my life. Well, I take that back; I do want to continue our committee meetings on how to run my life."

She finally cracked a smile. "So you aren't happy?"

"I am happy you are in my life to keep my head straight."

"You are pretty naive," she joked.

"Agreed."

"So what do you want to do now?"

"I think I am going to give up dating right now," Justin said, again trying to convince himself.

"Why?"

"Like you said, I have it all right now."

"But you won't find someone if you have given up."

"True, but I think I want to wait for Suzie now."

"Okay. You think you are ready for that?" Dusty asked as she sat up.

"Sure, I hear she and Brad are having issues."

"Don't be an ass."

"What are you talking about?"

"I am saying she hasn't broken up with him yet."

"That will change," Justin said confidently.

"It might, but I think that when they get back to Pennsylvania she will change her mind."

"What makes you think that?"

"This was their first time together away from where they are used to being."

"That shouldn't make a difference."

"You would be surprised. Besides, Suzie is also lonely and likes to be romanced. Brad does that for her."

"But she said he was a jerk," he commented frustrated.

"Sure, but he had to leave his business on short notice. Plus there was the whole bathroom incident."

"That wasn't my fault."

"I know. We all know. But it is the same with Suzie; we still talk constantly about her restaurant. I am sure she does her part of ignoring him while she is there."

"She never mentioned that."

"She probably doesn't realize it, just as he doesn't realize it when he was doing it to her here."

"So you think she will stay with him?" Justin asked.

"For the short term, yes. We don't know what will happen when she is no longer needed there. When her grandma finally passes, she will need someone to turn to—someone to hold her and let her cry in their arms."

"I hadn't thought of that."

"I guarantee she has. She is planning for it; she looks at the big picture and what she is seeing. When that time comes, no one will be there to comfort her if she is single."

"Damn it!" Justin exclaimed.

"So we need to get you back out dating again."

"I don't know if I can handle too many more bad dates," Justin admitted.

"Just think of them as learning experiences."

"Like falling off a horse?"

"I think you would rather fall off a horse than go out on a date," Dusty joked.

"You ain't lying there."

"I think you should just keep at it."

"All right."

"Want to spend the night here?" she asked, suddenly changing the subject.

"I though you would never ask."

Chapter

Forty-Nine

Saturday afternoon, Justin walked into the Chuck Wagon and saw Dusty and April sitting at a table, both looking exhausted. Dusty was leaning back in her chair with her eyes closed and her arms hanging down, almost touching the floor. April had her hands on her head and her elbows on the table.

"You two look like you just rode out a tornado," Justin commented as he sat next to Dusty, opposite April.

"Pretty much," Dusty replied, not moving and not opening her eyes.

"The first real weekend lunch rush hit us like one," April commented.

Dusty sat up and smoothed out her hair.

"Tell us about your date. You have one tonight, don't you?" Dusty asked.

"Oh yes, please do," April encouraged, sitting up.

"Brittney," Justin told them.

"Brittney is a beautiful name," April commented with her sly smile.

"Is she cute?" asked Dusty.

"Fair enough. I have been taking more time reading profiles and picking out things that the women are writing there that I like."

"So now you've decided that looks aren't everything?" April asked incredulously.

"No, that is still important to me. I mean, I want to be attracted to the woman I might be potentially dating."

"No more hotties with naughty bodies?" April persisted.

"Well, I … um … I,] … well, I have to be attracted to them. I have nothing against women I am not attracted to."

"You just don't want to take them out on dates?"

"Well, no, why would I?"

"What do you think, Dusty?" April asked, turning the conversation to their third wheel.

Dusty seemed to be deep in thought. "Huh? What?" she asked.

"I asked you what you thought about Justin not wanting to date ugly girls?" April asked again.

184

"There are no ugly girls," Justin hurriedly interjected.

"I agree with him; you need to be attracted to whomever you date," she said confidently.

"Thank you," Justin said with a smile.

"But what if the right one for you is ug … um, not attractive?" April pursued.

"Then she isn't the right one for me. Whomever she is, she needs to be attractive to me and have the qualities I want and need in a relationship," Justin informed her.

"Suzie is pretty," April said with an impish grin.

"She sure is, and she is also taken," Justin shot back.

"He is a jerk wagon," April said with a face only a teenage girl could make with distain.

"Where are you taking Brittney?" asked Dusty, getting back to the subject.

"To that place I took, um, that other girl."

"Tonya?" asked Dusty.

"The young super hottie with a naughty body?" April asked humorously.

"Why there?" asked Dusty, trying to ignore April.

"I like the food there. It is a little pricy, but I haven't eaten out this much in my life, and I am starting to enjoy it."

"I wish I had someone to take me out to eat," Dusty remarked forlornly.

"You want to go?" Justin asked her.

"No, dumbass, I am not going to be a third wheel. Talk about a bad date. Bringing your friend that is a girl—yeah, I am sure that will win her heart over."

Justin was shaking his head and looked at April, who got it.

"He's saying he will take you instead," April told her.

"Dumbass," Justin added.

Dusty smiled and blushed.

"No, I have work to do here; besides, this might be the one."

Justin got up and left. He took one look back into the front windows of the diner and then pulled out of his parking spot and pointed his truck northward. As he drove to his next adventure, he thought about Dusty. He liked her as a friend, and sleeping with her had been great, but there was something missing. He knew she would never want to date him, but lately things had changed. Maybe she was growing up and wanted sustenance over fairy tales. Maybe she was changing her mind about him. The problem was that he was starting to change his mind about her. He would rather have her as a friend than as a girlfriend.

Chapter

Fifty

The Pittsburgh International Airport was loud and busy that afternoon. Suzie and Brad had made it out of the plane and headed down the concourse to the baggage area. Suzie was watching the people hustle and bustle while Brad was checking emails on his phone.

"Okay, what's the verdict?" Brad asked Suzie when he had finished, and he slipped his phone back into his pocket.

"Verdict?" she asked confused.

"Don't play coy with me, Suzie. I saw the way you acted toward me when we were in Montana, and the way you looked at that cowboy."

"What are you talking about?"

"You breaking up with me?" Brad asked harshly.

She stood there quietly. The bell started to ring as the belt kicked on and luggage started pouring out of the wall, making its way around to where the passengers were waiting to snatch them up.

"No answer is an answer," he said, looking at her.

She returned his gaze and shook her head.

"No," she replied softly.

"No what?"

"No, I am not breaking up with you." Suzie said pointedly.

"Things changed when we were back there. It was that dude, wasn't it?"

"No, it was you," she shot back.

"Me? What did I do?"

"First you became jealous; then you started ignoring me. I thought you were the one that was going to end it."

"What? Well of course I was going to get a little jealous, and I never ignored you."

"First, you need to trust me, and you have nothing to worry about with Justin. Secondly, you *did* ignore me," Suzie retorted.

"I only ignored you when I was on the phone, and that was only because of my business."

"What about when we were having sex and you reached to answer your phone?"

"Well, that, um … er … We had been trying to close this big contract. I am sorry, I was a jerk for doing that."

"I don't want to be second to your business. I don't want to be second to anything in this relationship."

"I have to make money," he replied slowly.

Suzie saw her suitcase and grabbed it. There was another suitcase and someone's skis that were making it difficult to pull hers off the belt. She turned and looked exasperatedly at Brad, who was looking down the line for his suitcase. Suzie stood up and crossed her arms. Brad and the crowd around them all noticed this. Brad jumped to and ran down the belt after her suitcase and pulled it out of the mess just before it turned the corner to go back behind the wall.

He held it over his head as if it were the Stanley Cup. Suzie couldn't help but smile. He was trying, and she realized that he didn't have quite the tools to or understanding to date her the way she wanted to be dated. She was going to have to use Doreen's wisdom and April's tenacity to make this relationship work. After all, Brad's ex-wife had been completely independent and had more or less used him for sex and tax breaks. There had been no real love or affection in their marriage, and she had never let him do anything for her; nor had she wanted to spend time with him unless they were naked or trying to impress peers or coworkers at parties.

She watched in admiration as he carried her bag, still over his head, back to her.

"You missed your bag," she told him with a smile.

"It will come back around. I can wait on it."

"Can you?" she asked optimistically.

"Are we talking about the luggage?"

"Yes, but also me."

"I can wait. I know this isn't easy for you, and I know you have been thinking about the long game, and it doesn't look pretty. Not for us, anyways." Brad sounded a little concerned.

"What does it look like to you?"

"It looks like we are going to have to figure some things out."

"I don't want to live here," Suzie remarked. "I miss being home."

"I think this discussion should be carried on elsewhere," he said with a smile as he gestured to the growing crowd that had forgotten about their luggage and had taken interest in this juicy drama unfolding before them.

"Agreed," she said as Brad went to grab his bag.

Fifty-One

Justin sat once again at the bench outside of the Italian restaurant. He checked his phone and then noticed a woman smiling and walking toward him.

"Hello, Brittney," Justin said as he saw the petite brunette approach the entrance of the restaurant.

"Hey Justin, nice to finally meet you."

She gave him a quick hug, and they went inside.

The hostess eyed Justin suspiciously, and then even more so his date. She led them back to the exact same table where Justin and Tonya had had their date as if she were telling him, "I remember you and what happened last time you were here."

"This place is so nice," Brittney remarked when they had settled in.

"I do like it a lot," Justin replied.

"That would explain the look."

"What look?"

"You have brought other dates here before, haven't you?" she asked with a knowing smile.

"Well, um … er, yeah, but how did you know?"

"The way the hostess looked at you and then me and then back at you and then rolled her eyes."

"I saw that and felt it was a bit unprofessional," Justin remarked.

"What do you expect? She is, like, sixteen. Besides, in that look she gave me a bit of juicy intel."

"Oh yeah? Like what?"

"Like it might have gone badly for you."

The waitress came and took their drink and appetizer order.

"Well, it didn't go as planned," Justin remarked, picking back up the conversation.

"Do tell!"

Justin explained about his date, the chaperones, and the uncomfortable situation that had happened the last time he had been here.

"No wonder you are unpopular here," Brittney said with a giggle.

"It wasn't me."

"Did you sleep with her?"

"Naw, she wanted to, but I just couldn't."

"You didn't want to sleep with her? Why? Was she ugly?"

"No, not at all."

"It's not like a guy to pass up sex, especially with a cute woman," Brittney remarked slyly.

"True, but there was a lot of drama with that one, and I just wasn't interested in—" His words froze in his mouth as he saw Tonya rise up from the booth adjoining theirs. This whole time, she had been sitting back-to-back with Brittney, listening in on their conversation.

Tonya held nothing back as she laid into Justin, calling him everything in the book. Then she turned to Brittney and lied to her about the way things had unfolded, telling Brittney about how she refused Justin's advances and how he begged for it out in the parking lot. Brittney's eyes kept darting back from the raving lunatic at the end of their table to her date. Justin could tell that no matter what he said, no amount of truth was going to save this situation.

When Tonya had finished her rant, she again warned Brittney about this sex-crazed brute that would ultimately break her heart and maybe even hurt her physically as he had her own brother. Then she turned and walked out the door. Whomever had been sitting with her at the next booth had already gotten up and left during the middle of the rant, so Justin wasn't sure whom she had been with.

"Well, that was exciting." Justin remarked with a smirk.

"I think I am going to go," Brittney said as she gathered up her purse and coat.

"Really?"

"Yeah, that was very uncomfortable and a lot of drama for someone who claims they try and avoid it."

"You can't possibly believe I orchestrated that, do you?" Justin asked incredulously.

"It doesn't matter what I believe; I saw it with my own eyes. That was brutal and quite embarrassing. I don't know who you are, and you might not be like that, but this was an awful first date, and that is all I need to know."

"All right. Want me to walk you to your car?"

"No," she replied as she quickly hurried out and drove away.

The waitress looked apologetically at Justin as he sat in his booth alone.

"Do you want this to go?" she asked as she gestured to the appetizer that had just been laid on his table.

"Heck no, I am going to eat them here. I am also ready to order."

"You are going to stay here after that?"

"Why not?"

"Aren't you embarrassed?"

"Not enough to leave. I am hungry, and you have great food here."

"Well thank you."

"And the service here is amazing."

"Thank you so much; I really appreciate that."

Justin ate his dinner in silence as he contemplated what had just happened. He felt or saw the occasional stare from the guests sitting around him and started to feel uncomfortable, but he wasn't going to let the onlookers have the satisfaction of shaming him for something he had no control over.

Relationships are hard, but dating is a nightmare. There are so many different people that have their own agendas that finding the right person to mesh with your own dreams and goals seems impossible.

He resolved to keep moving forward and not to let the many bad experiences deter him from getting in the way of finding the gem hidden in all the rubble.

Chapter

Fifty-Two

Justin left the Italian restaurant and headed over to Dusty's. He had text her he was coming over and wanted to talk to her.

"You are back early," Dusty commented as Justin walked into her house.

"Yeah, it was a rough one," he replied as he took his boots off.

"All right, I will grab us some beers, but you have to leave soon."

"Why? You got a hot date coming over?"

"I wish. No, I have to open in the morning," she replied, trying to stifle a yawn.

"Oh, gotcha. I can leave, and we can talk about it tomorrow."

"Not on your life. I see that look on your face; I want to hear about this one," Dusty remarked with a smirk.

Dusty gave him a bottle and sat on the couch across from him. She pulled the throw blanket across her lap as she tucked her feet next to her butt and shimmied for a minute until she got everything exactly right.

"Comfy?" Justin asked her with a grin.

"I am so ready for a good crash-and-burn story from you," she said with a smile.

"What? Why?"

"No offence, dude, but you have the best luck in dating. I am looking forward to hearing about some not-so-good experiences."

"What about the catfish lady? That wasn't good luck."

"Yeah, and explain to me how the rest of that day went for you."

Justin smiled sheepishly.

"Exactly. You got laid and set up a revolving door with Wendy for a booty call anytime you want it," Dusty said defiantly.

"It's not exactly like that."

"Yes, it is. It is exactly like that," Dusty retorted.

"All right, I have had some good luck while internet dating."

"Beginner's luck I would say."

"I am still single, though."

"That's because you are being picky. Don't get me wrong; I admire that, but you are having women throw themselves at you, and it just seems unfair."

"I am sure you have a bunch of dudes chasing after you."

"Yes, but they are all Chads. They just want to get in my pants or have me send them nudes. Jeez, I am so sick of dudes that want nothing but sex from me. I just wish they would legalize prostitution to weed out the morons that just want sex and not a relationship."

"Wow."

"What? It's true. The dudes on these dating sites are just there to add notches to their belts because they are losers, and they need sexual gratification to cover up that fact. They don't want to romance a woman because they don't really want a relationship."

"How do they get sex if they don't romance a woman?" Justin asked.

"Well, some of them are just so freaking hot that women want to have sex with them just because they are hot."

"That seems pretty shallow."

"It is, on both sides. They both get to have sex and fulfill a primal urge, but it does nothing for their relationship, if there is even one. On the other hand, many women will have sex with a guy because they want to keep him, or they think he might be looking elsewhere and that if they give their bodies to him, it will make him stay."

"That doesn't work?"

"Hell no, it never works."

"Why?"

"Because if a guy is looking elsewhere, having sex won't stop him from going there if the opportunity presents itself. In fact, it will give him more courage and more of an ego, which seems to drive the other women right to his bed."

"So abstinence is the best policy?"

"Of course it is, but it is so hard."

"Why? I thought it was easy for women to turn down sex."

"No, dumbass, it's not. Women have been hit on by pervy guys ever since we started developing boobs—and unfortunately with some assholes before that."

"What? Really?"

"Yeah, some guys are scumbags. They are always offering ways to see us naked."

"That's horrible!"

"I was fortunate enough that nothing like that ever happened to me—at least not directly."

"So something did happen?" Justin asked, feeling his temperature start to rise.

"It's hard to say."

"No its not; it's easy to say."

"No, you don't understand. Sometimes it's hard to tell whether someone is just being friendly or is being pervy."

"You don't know the difference?"

"It's like this: A guy will give me a hug. There are no real definitions on how long someone should hold you during that hug, or how closely. Sometimes I wondering if he is pressing me so close to him so he can feel my boobs or if he is just that kind of guy. Did a friend or relative rub my back in concern or friendship, or was he trying to get a cheap feel of my bra? It's things like that that women have started having to ask themselves before they tell them to stop or call for help."

"Jeez, I had no idea; I am sorry, Dusty."

"It's why a lot of women are not so eager to jump into bed with anyone, especially with someone who shows them some affection," Dusty pointed out.

"Why, because they think the guy is just a perv?"

"No, it's because we don't want to get used for sex and then just thrown aside. You see, women can have sex just about anytime they want to. They can just go up to a guy or accept a match on a dating site or even a friend request through social media. Then all they have to do is remark that they are open to a sexual encounter and—*boom*—they have tons of offers."

"That easy, huh?"

"Yup. Most guys only care about two things when having sex with a woman."

"What's that?"

"If they have a disease and if they are on birth control."

"Wow."

"Yeah, it can be pretty disgusting. That's why women get very selective on who they do have sex with, because they have so many other options."

"Even if they feel like they are being used?"

"Sometimes women are the users. Sometimes women will have sex with a dude they know that can really ring their bell in the bedroom. Of course, he isn't dating material; nor is he worth the time fretting over. Because of his skill set, he has many women utilizing him as well."

"So, like, a gigolo?"

"No, dumbass, more like a guy we use to give us orgasms without the dating and commitment and putting up with his bullshit."

"I thought women didn't like this kind of relationship."

"Not for the long term, but when we get horny and need a good go-to guy, we use someone we can count on that will get us off."

"You have one of these guys?"

"I had one in Idaho; I think I found one here. Well, not here in town."

"He is okay with this arrangement?"

"For now, I think. He was looking for a friends-with-benefits program, and I thought it might be good to see what he had to offer, and it was pretty good."

"I would think more guys would want to do this."

"Oh, believe me, they all seem to want that kind of deal."

"So why don't more women sign up for that?"

"Two reasons."

"Which are?"

"The first reason is because it is only a short-term deal for women. It is the way to satisfy some needs until they find the one they want to commit to."

"Fair enough. What's the second reason?"

"Because most guys aren't that good in bed. Most of them that want that kind of friendship just want to get laid with no strings attached. In fact, they don't even care if the woman gets off; they usually don't even want to snuggle afterward, and most guys are assholes to you when you give them that arrangement," Dusty said.

"Really?"

"Yeah, so it's best to leave the wannabe Casanovas to prove themselves first before I ever would establish that sort of relationship with a dude. Oh, and that's a great way to tell if they are even any good in bed; if they don't know who Casanova is, it might be a short, unsatisfying night."

"I see."

"Speaking of which, tell me what happened to your date," Dusty said, looking at her clock and returning to the matter at hand.

Justin let out a long sigh and related how Tonya had been there to basically destroy his evening and chased away his date.

"But you still ate there?"

"Yup. It's good food."

"You gonna ever take another date there again?"

"Sure, I don't care what happened there on that night; there will be others."

"What about the hostess?"

"What about her?"

"Aren't you upset that she gave you that snotty look?"

"Heck no, April gives it to me all the time; I am used to it and kind of figured that was on par for girls that age."

"I guess you are right."

"Well, I'd better get going; you do have to open in the morning."

"Yes, I do," she said with a sigh.

"What's wrong? I thought you liked your job."

"I do; it's the going to bed alone that gets me."

"I can stay."

"I would like that," Dusty said as she got up and led him upstairs.

Justin lay in bed next to Dusty, listening to her breathe. He was trying to find that missing link that would change this from friendship to relationship but couldn't find it. He rolled over and smiled. There was no love connection but sleeping next to her was something he was starting to enjoy.

Chapter

Fifty-Three

Dusty pulled into the driveway at the Walker Ranch. He saw Justin walk out of his front door, his arms full of luggage and boxes. He packed the suitcases and gifts into his truck and then loaded up Doreen in the passenger seat. Dusty shut off the Camaro and walked over to the duo.

"What's she doing here?" Justin asked his mother.

"She probably came to see her best friend off," Doreen retorted.

"I just saw you this morning," Justin pointed out.

"I wasn't talking about you," Doreen interrupted with a smile.

"Doreen, you look absolutely stunning. Are you ready to go visit your sister for Thanksgiving?" Dusty asked Doreen, ignoring Justin.

"Well thank you, Dusty. Yes I am," said Doreen sweetly.

"Why are you here?" Justin asked curiously.

"Not to see your dumb ass," Dusty shot back.

"See, I told you," chided Doreen.

"Your mom asked me to come over and check on things while you two are gone," Dusty explained.

"Did she make you a list?" Justin asked.

"Of course I did, Dusty; it's on the fridge," Doreen informed her.

"Thank you. You gonna be okay, Cowboy?" Dusty asked Justin.

"Yeah, why wouldn't I be?"

"Just didn't know if you could survive without the committee meetings," Dusty joked.

"I am not going to be dating anyone in Billings."

"Why not?"

"It's Billings. It's like six hours away."

"So? You know you can change your location on your dating app."

"Really?"

"He's not going to be whoring around while we are visiting relatives," Doreen interrupted.

"Momma!" Justin exclaimed.

"Well, you are not."

"I wasn't going to anyway."

"Yeah, he's taking a break from the dating scene. He has it all figured out," Dusty interjected.

"Oh really?" asked Doreen, surprised.

"I had it figured out," Justin said grimly.

"Want to talk about it?" Dusty asked, now obviously concerned.

"I will when I get back."

"Dude, that is like three weeks from now."

Justin leaned in and kissed Dusty on the forehead. Dusty blushed and smiled at him. He then shut the passenger door and headed to his side of the truck.

"Don't they say,'Always leave them wanting for more?'" Justin remarked with a grin.

"You are an ass." The words came from Doreen, and both Justin and Dusty stood there staring at the older woman in shock. She simply opened her purse and got out some Chapstick and slowly applied it to her lips.

"Daylight is burning, boy. Get the lead out. Dusty, he will talk to you when we get to Martha's." Doreen waved to Dusty and rolled up her window, and Justin put the truck in gear and pointed it southward.

Dusty stood there looking at the smoke that was still hanging in the air as the duo drove off. Her stomach had gotten a knot in it the moment Justin had mentioned he had not had it figured out, but what now? Did something change? Was he not happy again? Did he find someone?

"Damn him," she thought. "He'd better spill the beans when I call him."

Fifty-Four

Dusty was looking at her reflection in the mirror in the women's bathroom at the Chuck Wagon. She had left the Walkers' after Justin and Doreen had left and had come in to work the lunch rush. She adjusted her blouse and smoothed out her skirt. She frowned that the mirror was too high for her to do a full-body check. She made one last close-up of her face to make sure her makeup and lipstick were in order. She grabbed her clothes she changed out of and her purse, and she headed out of the restroom.

"Why are you all dressed up?" April asked Dusty as her friend exited.

"Jeez, Dusty did you change in the bathroom?" asked Lori, who was wiping down a table.

"I have a date, and yes I changed in the bathroom. Anything else, Nosy Nellies?" Dusty answered with a grin.

"Duh! Who is he? Where did you meet him? Is he cute?" asked April.

"Are you going to give him some booty?" Lori added.

"Jeez, now I know how Justin feels. No wonder he calls us 'the committee.'" Dusty commented in remorse. "His name is Billy, on the dating app, and yes, he is very hot," Dusty answered to April's inquiries.

"What about Lori's question?" April prodded.

"Not on the first date," Dusty said pointedly.

"But you were saying the other day you could use a good fu—"

"April!" Dusty exclaimed as she cut the teenager off. "If your momma heard you finish that sentence, she would have both our hides."

"Well, you did," April replied indignantly.

"Look, it's been a while since I have been on a date, and I am kind of nervous. I really appreciate how both of you have stepped up and helped gotten this restaurant running. It really means a lot to me and Suzie. I honestly have been working and helping Justin so much that I forgot about myself. I have been talking to this guy for a couple of weeks and haven't gotten to meet him yet, but I really want to. I don't know if he is the one, and right now I don't care; I just want to go out and have some fun and a good night." She directed her gaze at Lori. "If he says the right things and looks at me the right way, then yes, I will give him more booty than he will know what to do with."

She gave them a big smile as they stood there looking stunned.

"Well, I didn't expect that," Lori commented.

"Go get 'em boss!" April said encouragingly.

"Billy just might be getting himself into more than he can handle," Lori added.

"Yeah, but I bet he will enjoy it," April said with a smirk.

Dusty turned and walked out the door with a little spring in her step.

Chapter

Fifty-Five

"Well?" asked April as she walked into the restaurant after school and saw Dusty. "What? No 'Hi, Dusty?' No 'What's on the schedule for today?'" Dusty retorted.

"Uh huh, I wanna hear about Billy," she shot back with a smile.

Dusty couldn't help but smile; she felt her face reddening and saw April noticed this.

The bell rang on the door as Lori walked through and noticed the duo chatting away. Their faces gave away that something was up.

"Oh, my goodness. Don't you dare talk about your date without me here," Lori scolded them as she hurried to join the committee meeting.

Dusty started from the beginning about how he had contacted her online. He had sent her a funny pickup line that made her smile. She decided to look at his profile, and the more she read, the more she smiled; it was very humorous. Before she realized it, she had read the entire thing. She scrolled back up to the top and started reading it again, trying to pick out the red flags.

"He said he was married and just looking for a hookup because his wife was pregnant," Dusty told them, recalling his profile.

"He is married?" April asked, his eyes widening.

"No, he followed it up by saying he was joking. The whole profile was like that—funny and fun to read—and it made me feel good," Dusty said with a smile.

She told them that she had clicked on him and, the next day, he sent her another humorous text and asked her some questions about herself. Some were standard bucket-list questions, and some were about foods she enjoyed, but one was a bit obscure. He wanted to know what planet she would like to live on if she got kicked off of Earth.

"That's a weird question," April said, scrunching her face.

"It's a great question," Lori replied.

The two women looked at her curiously.

"How?" April asked. "I mean, it's not like it will ever happen. Dusty is too awesome to kick off the planet, and they have no colonies established on any other planet."

"It's not about the question; it's about getting her to think and doing it in a humorous way. He is just trying to connect with her and separate himself from all the other dudes trying to get her attention. I will bet no one has ever asked you that question before."

"Correct, no one ever has; and no matter what happens, I will never forget that one question" Dusty replied.

"Okay, so what planet would you want to live on if you got kicked off of Earth?" April asked her.

"I will have to think about that one," she said as she cocked her head and processed the question.

"I think I would like to live on Mercury," Lori commented.

"Why is that?" April asked curiously.

"Because it's the hottest planet in this system, and I am so done with this cold," she said jokingly.

"I know," Dusty said suddenly as an idea popped into her head.

"Oh yeah?" April asked eagerly.

"Well, if men are supposedly from Mars and women are from Venus, then I choose Mars," she said, laughing and winking.

"Yeah, I think I want to change my choice as well," Lori added among the giggling.

Chapter

Fifty-Six

Billings was cold. Justin had experienced very cold weather in Hackamore, but it was surrounded by mountains. Billings was more or less in the wide open, and the cold, bitter wind never seemed to stop blowing. It chilled him to bone, so when his Aunt Martha came out to where he was cutting firewood, he eagerly took the opportunity to go inside and soak up the warmth of his previous efforts burning in the fireplace in the front room.

He saw the phone receiver lying on its side on a small table next to the couch opposite the fireplace. He grabbed the receiver and the base of the phone and pulled the cord to the other end of the couch so he could sit closer to the fireplace.

***

"I really hate this," Dusty told Justin as they chatted a few nights later.

"Hate talking to me?" he asked in surprise.

"No, dumbass, the fact that I can only talk to you this late at night and we cannot text during the day."

"Aunt Martha lives way out of town, and there are no cell towers here. She also doesn't have Wi-Fi here for me to hook on to with my phone. Besides, since Uncle Art died, she hasn't really taken care of the farm and it has gone to crap."

"How long ago did he die?"

"Umm, about seven years ago."

"Jeez, that's a long time to go without taking care of anything."

"Well, it wasn't nothing. She does some things, and occasionally kids from the church, 4H, or FFA swing by and do some work to help her out."

"I am glad you are there to help," Dusty said sincerely with a hint of jealously.

"This is the last year for her here, though."

"Are they going to put her in a home?"

"Yeah, Momma's," Justin answered quickly.

"She is moving in with your mom?"

"They have been talking about it since we got here."

"How do you feel about that?"

"I'm good; it will keep Momma busy and give her purpose, and someone else to talk to."

"That will mean two Nosy Nellies in your business instead of one."

"Two? I already have five; one more isn't going to change much."

"Oh, right. I forgot about the committee."

"Exactly."

"Speaking of which, I now know how you feel," Dusty said, changing the subject.

"How's that?"

"I had a date."

"You did? How did it go?"

"It was good."

"Why the committee meeting?"

"You know my girls."

"All too well. Did they evaluate every word and action and break it down to a microscopic level?"

Dusty giggled. "Right when I got back from the first date."

"Oh, so you had to face questions impossible to answer."

"Jeez, we were really hard on you, weren't we?"

"Naw, it wasn't bad. You gals actually helped a lot."

"Good. I am glad we weren't difficult," Dusty replied, sounding relieved.

"Whoa there, cowgirl. I didn't say you weren't difficult."

"Oh, so we *were* difficult."

"Dusty, you are always difficult. So what happened?"

"We went out for drinks and did some line dancing."

"Ugh, line dancing. I hate that. It isn't dancing if you ain't touching."

"Who says we didn't touch?" Dusty asked.

"While dancing?"

"Well, no, but there was some touching and maybe a little groping."

"Good for you."

"I like this guy."

"Good. You deserve someone good."

"I didn't say he was good; he's really a Chad," Dusty pointed out.

"Oh? Which kind?"

"The kind that says all the right things and then uses me for sex."

"I am sorry; at least you got some booty."

"I did not. I am going to make him pay for it first. I told him the three-date rule was in effect."

"Which is?" he asked sarcastically.

"You don't have sex till the third date," Dusty reminded him again.

"I see, there are a lot of rules to this dating thing."

"You seemed to have mastered them pretty quickly."

"Anything quickly gained can be quickly lost."

"Uh ho, that doesn't sound good. What happened? Is there trouble in paradise, cowboy?"

"I guess you could say that. Wendy has found herself a steady boyfriend. Suzie is dating that Brad guy, and most of the girls I have been chatting with have disappeared—um … I mean ghosted me. There haven't been a whole lot of new ones to chat with. It seems my luck has run out."

"It's the pendulum."

"Pendulum?"

"Yeah, I noticed that happening to my accounts over the years as well," Dusty informed him. "It seems that I have more guys than I can deal with; then they all go away. It happens to everyone."

"Even pretty girls?"

"Yep, that isn't limited to cowboys or men in general. One day you have what seems like an unlimited catalog, then the well dries up. Don't worry; it will come back. Besides, it's almost Thanksgiving, and people are taking a break from dating to be with family."

"I guess I didn't think about that."

"Don't worry; women will be looking for someone to kiss on New Year's."

"I see. Well, I guess I need to be prepared when I get back home."

"For sure!"

"That will help."

"Quit worrying about it. Besides, Suzie and Brad are having issues. She might be back on the market soon."

"She will want some time to recover, won't she?" Justin asked.

"Maybe, but I would still be ready for a phone call if I were you."

"She will call me when she is ready to date?"

"I think she will be wanting to hear a familiar voice that will also build her self-esteem back when it happens."

"So what's going on with their relationship? I thought they were getting along great till they came to Montana. You said they would go back to normal when they got back east."

Justin was starting to feel conflicted. He wasn't sure whether he wanted to root for the breakup or not. He cared about Suzie but didn't want to wish for her get hurt.

"I did, but it doesn't seem to be going good. I think they got a real eye-opener when they got back here. I think it got too real too fast and the proposition of the future made them think about where they are going to be in a few years."

"You think Suzie is going to want to come back?"

This was encouraging news for him; he would like her to be near, with Brad far away.

"I think she really enjoys working in her restaurant and can't wait to get back so she can serve people in a less dire situation."

"Good, I will wait for her phone call."

Fifty-Seven

Dusty wasn't far off the mark. Suzie sat on her bed with tears in her eyes, staring at the phone. She and Brad had been texting all night since he was busy doing payroll, ordering equipment, and taking care of other administrative duties and couldn't talk. They had been having a good conversation about the future when she asked an important question, and he hadn't responded in the last fifteen minutes. Up till then he had been diligent about keeping the conversation going, but it now seemed as though the whole world had gone quiet, as if the phone company had shut down the entire system. Her phone remained silent in her hand.

She knew he wasn't being bothered by employees or vendors; after all, it was 10:28 p.m.

"Maybe he is getting ready for bed; surely he will answer soon," she thought hopefully.

At 11:11 she made her wish he would at least tell her good night as he always did, but there was no notification on her phone that told her otherwise.

She threw the phone on her bed and put her head in her hands as she sobbed silently.

After a few minutes, she popped her head up and grabbed her phone. She did some quick math in her head as she stared at the time on her phone. With a shaky hand, she pushed her contact button, scrolled down, and then pushed the name she was looking for. She smiled. The window opened a little wider and revealed more choices, and she depressed the green phone symbol.

She held the phone to her ear as she listened for the ring. There was no ringtone, only a friendly voice directing her to leave a message for the number she had dialed.

"Dang it," she said out loud. "Dusty did say he didn't have any service at his aunt's house.

She scrolled through her contacts again and repeated the process for the new name.

"Hello boss," Dusty said with a cheerful tone in her voice.

"I told you, you didn't have to call me that."

"I know, but it's so much fun listening to you squirm when I do," Dusty pointed out.

"Oh, okay."

"What's wrong?" Dusty asked quickly in a more serious tone. It wasn't like Suzie to be so melancholy.

"Who said there was anything wrong?" Suzie replied, trying to hold back her tears.

"Your voice. Now tell me what's up."

"Brad."

"Oh no, I'm so sorry. What happened?"

"Nothing really, we were just texting, and then he stopped when I asked him a question.

"You didn't propose to him, did you?"

Suzie laughed. She knew calling Dusty was the right choice.

"No, nothing like that."

"Well, what did you ask him?"

"I asked if he wanted to move to Montana and open up shop there. I did some research while we were in Hackamore and saw that there was a definite need for his business there. He could do very well with little or no competition."

"What about his business there?"

"He could sell it or franchise it out to one of his employees or to someone else. It wouldn't really take much. He hired well and trained his employees to basically run the business anyway."

"I thought they kept calling him for direction. Especially when he was here."

"I think that was them needing reassurance rather than direction. Like I said, he trained them well, and once they get rolling without him, they will be able to do it without his direct supervision."

"I do remember we had a lot of conversations when you first left," Dusty remarked.

"Now look at you; I barely am needed there anymore. It would work the same here for his company, or he could sell it and wash his hands with the whole thing."

"Who would buy it?"

"He's had a few offers, especially from his competitors; they would love to get in on his area."

"Does he have family there? Maybe that's why he doesn't want to leave."

"No, his parents live in Chicago, and he is an only child."

"So nothing is holding him there?"

"Nothing," Suzie replied, starting to sob again.

"Hey, hey, maybe he just fell asleep or needs time to think about it."

"I don't know if I want him to answer."

"Then why did you ask him?" Dusty asked, sounding confused.

"I guess I wanted him to tell me no so I could get on with my life. I honestly feel like I am stuck in purgatory with him. There is no moving forward until I can go back to Montana, and that will be by myself. I enjoy being with him, and he isn't a bad guy, but there is no future with him."

"What about if you stayed in Pennsylvania?"

"I have thought about that, but when I went back there, well, that is where my heart is. It would be a nightmare and so expensive to start a restaurant here. I just don't think I have it in me to start all over again, especially with the expenses and the competition."

"What are you going to do?"

"I am going to finish here and then move back."

"I, um … well, do you know how long that will be?"

"Talking about my great granny's demise isn't something that scares me anymore. She is ready to go, and we have been talking a lot about it lately. We even joke a little bit about it."

"You joke about it?" Dusty asked incredulously.

"It's just a little thing we do. She says, "I could go any day." I respond with "Don't tease me." It really is a way we break the tension. Her attitude toward death is like it is one last goal she has to complete. She led a great life and has had no regrets about moving on. She wants to be able to sleep without pain and not having to worry about her treatments or constantly taking medications."

"Sounds like she is looking forward to it."

"She is, in her own way. Her pain is getting worse, and her body is slowly starting to resist the medications. She doesn't want to die, per se, but doesn't want to live in pain anymore."

"I can see how death will be a relief to her."

"It will be a relief to all of us who hate to see her suffer."

"Then you will come back?"

"Of course. I am not going to miss the chance to boss you around in person."

Chapter

Fifty-Eight

Justin's patience was wearing thin. He loved his momma and auntie, but they were really pushing the limits. It all started when he was loading up his truck and the trailer he had rented to move the majority of Martha's things to her new home in Hackamore.

Of course, he couldn't load the trailer correctly, and the two wardens made sure he packed and unpacked the trailer at least a dozen times. There was always something they figured was going to get broken and needed to be rewrapped or placed in a better crash-safe area of the trailer. He painstakingly held his tongue while bringing something back in for them to adjust to their liking; then he hauled it back outside to the trailer or truck and carefully loaded it while the two women watched from the bay window, hollering out their commands.

When he had finally finished, he thought that would be the end of it, but no. There was the six-hour drive back home. The women had been fussy about where they sat and were constantly yelling to each other over the sound of the not-so-well-insulated cab of the truck. Then there was the fight over the temperature. Doreen was too hot sitting in the front, while Martha couldn't seem to stop shivering in the back, so he pulled over and helped them change places.

That didn't work, because now the reverse was true. He smiled to himself as he pictured shoving both women into the trailer.

I would probably do that wrong as well, he thought to himself with a smile.

Justin couldn't seem to drive past an exit with a truck stop or gas station without having to stop and let the sisters out to go do their thing. But their thing wasn't just a quick bathroom break; nope, they had to peruse the store and purchase knickknacks, gum, snacks, and, of course, hot coffee.

They were to make sure they included him in their purchases, and he had enough jerky to last the next four years. The time was trying; however, he would much prefer just to make the six hours with only stopping for gas. He was able to text Dusty when they stopped, and she did offer some insight about the two old women.

"This might be their last road trip together, and they want to remember it," she wrote in one text.

Justin thought about that and decided to give them some slack. They continued onward home slowly, even slower because they would always fuss at him anytime his speedometer got anywhere close to the posted speed limit, making the journey even longer.

Their six-hour trek lasted just over ten hours, and Justin was never so happy to see his driveway when he pulled up. He paused as he pulled into the yard, as the snow had come down pretty heavily while they were gone, but his driveway had been plowed by some anonymous Samaritan he was going to have to thank when he found out who it was.

The truck rumbled to a stop, and Justin ran into the house to bump up the heater and start a fire in the fireplace. With those two tasks done, he went out and helped the women into the house and started unloading the trailer.

He was right; the unpacking went a little smoother, convincing the wardens to shower and relax while he unloaded the boxes into the living room. They were a bit doubtful at first, but he promised on the Good Book that he would not start unpacking any boxes until they were ready to supervise.

He heard the Camaro pull into the drive, and soon Dusty was at the door with a box in hand.

"Hello, Dusty," Doreen greeted her cheerfully.

"Hello, Doreen."

"My goodness, is that little Brandy Mann? Girl, you have grown into a fine-looking woman." Martha remarked.

"Why thank you, Martha," Dusty replied as she gave each of the women a hug.

The women chatted for a bit while Justin continued to unload the trailer and truck. He finished up and swept both out, and he then returned the broom to its station on the porch.

"I am so sorry," Dusty told Justin as she gave him a hug.

"For what?" he replied as he savored the embrace of his friend.

"Not helping you unload the truck."

"You actually helped more than you know."

"What? How? I only brought in one box."

"You kept the two gang bosses busy so they wouldn't interrupt me," Justin joked.

"They were pretty hard on you, huh?"

"Jeez, I didn't think you could load a truck, drive, or do everything else as badly as I did."

Dusty grinned and hugged him again.

"Come here, you poor baby. Momma will take care of you," Dusty chided.

"Shut up."

"You really are a good guy."

"Speaking of which, how is your good guy treating you?"

"Tomorrow is the third date," Dusty informed him.

"Oh, well lucky him."

"Ha, don't you mean lucky me?"

"That too."

"I almost slipped up on date number two, which he considers as date number three."

"I don't understand."

"He brought me lunch, and we went over to my place while I ate it."

"That was nice of him."

"Yes it was. I almost gave in, but I told him this didn't count, since I could only be away for an hour and had to get back to work. I am a little concerned about tomorrow, though," Dusty said thoughtfully.

"Why is that?"

"Well, the snow isn't going to let up anytime soon, and it will be difficult getting to Kalispell for our date—and probably worse trying to get back."

"Where does he live?"

"About ten miles north of here. He bought a little farm with some acreage; he travels a lot with his job so he can live anywhere."

"You have the perfect opportunity then."

"What do you mean?"

"Invite him over to your house, fix him a dinner, and then let him have his way with you. Or, better yet, when he shows up, greet him at the door wearing nothing but a smile; he will get the picture."

"Oh my goodness, I don't know if I am that brave," Dusty said, her cheeks reddening.

"Then wear something lacy and see-through."

"I love you so much; thank you. I need to get home to get ready."

Chapter

Fifty-Nine

Justin spent the next day moving things out of the other main-floor room the family had used as an office over the years, since Martha didn't need to be trekking up and down the stairs and could that way be closer to her sister, who was in the master bedroom, also on the main floor.

He had fooled himself into believing that unpacking the boxes and bringing them into Martha's new room would go much smoother than loading them into a trailer. He was really, really wrong, as both sisters had different ideas on how the room should look and where the bed, the dresser, and other furniture should sit. Then there was the question of the power outlets. This being an old house, they had only one in the room, and Justin soon had to move everything back into the living room so the electricians could rewire the room and add two new power outlets to each wall so there would be plenty to choose from.

Justin wrote the check with a smile, covering up a grimace, but he knew that he would eventually inherit the old place so he might as well not gripe about the $2,800 bill the boss electrician handed him.

A few miles away, Dusty was preparing for her night.

She had picked out new bedding and put it carefully on her bed. She knew better than to add a whole bunch of pillows, so she chose two of her fluffiest ones and placed them at the head, side by side.

Then she went down to the kitchen and started the water to boil. Chicken Alfredo wasn't her specialty, but it was too cold to grill, and she wanted to make something that was simple but still tasted good.

After she circled the house for the hundredth time to make sure everything was exactly right, she started lighting candles. The timer went off in the kitchen, alerting her that the water was probably boiling and she needed to add the noodles.

With the noodles in the pot boiling, she focused her attention on the chicken. She had cooked it last night and put it in the fridge to await its next step. She diced it into bite-sized pieces and placed them into a bowl next to the pot of boiling noodles.

When the noodles had finished, she dumped them into the colander in the sink and put the pot back on the stove and started adding the ingredients for the Alfredo sauce. Happy with the taste, she added the chicken and the noodles, turned the stove down to its lowest setting, and then ran upstairs to change.

She held up a very revealing negligee and frowned and then shrugged. She stripped down to nothing and slipped the garment on. It was red and came down to just above her knees. There were some extremely uncomfortable panties that had been included, so she slipped those on as well and returned to her full-length mirror. She spun around, making sure her butt looked good, and then turned back to the mirror and adjusted her boobs to make them stand up even more. There was some more fiddling, and she swore she had to pull material out of her butt crack at least a hundred times. It was as though every time she moved even slightly, it made a run up there.

"If he rips it off with his teeth, it will all be worth it," she reminded herself, retrieving them again.

She continued to spin and twirl and adjust for the next few minutes. She had pondered taking Justin's advice and meeting Billy at the door with nothing on, but she did like being unwrapped and felt that was one more attribute to being a lady. Her palms were starting to sweat as she started to get nervous and have doubts. She had never considered Billy for the long term. He traveled a lot, and his roughneck lifestyle wasn't something she would ever look for in a mate. Not that she was against what he did or who he was, but she felt he would always be on the move and that being on the road made it way too easy for him to cheat or get distracted. His time away would definitely be lonely for her.

So why am I even doing this? she thought as she again adjusted her boobs and did a full-body profile pose to check out her work.

"Is he just going to be my booty call? What if he wants something more? Justin did say that many men were okay with that agreement, but what if Billy is different?"

Her thoughts were interrupted by a knock on the door. She checked the clock and noticed it was a full thirty minutes before Billy was supposed to arrive. She did one last full-body look and headed to the bathroom to freshen up her perfume.

She ran down the stairs and threw open the door with the sexiest grin she could muster. The cold hit her like a freezing punch in the face. Her body instantly was covered with goosebumps, and her nipples hardened to diamonds.

Justin stood there stammering; his face turned redder than the old fire engine in town.

"What the hell are you doing here?" she demanded, running to grab the throw blanket off the couch.

"I, um … er, I …well, damn it Dusty, you asked my momma to bake you a pie for your date tonight; I was just bringing it over."

"Oh my goodness, I am so sorry, Justin; I forgot."

"I can see that."

"Well, I did want your opinion on how I looked, but I knew you would never agree to it."

"You are right about that, but I guess it's too late for that."

"Well?"

"Well, you look good. I gotta go. No way in hell do I want to be caught here with you looking like that," he marched over to her and gave her the pie, kissed her on the forehead, and turned and headed back out the door. "Relax, you are going to do fine!" he said over his shoulder as he hurried down the steps to his truck and drove off.

Dusty couldn't help but have a good laugh at the retreating truck making good time racing down the road back to the Walker Ranch.

Sixty

Dusty sat on her couch, trying to recompose herself. It had been too much of a thrill for her childhood friend to see her almost completely naked. She sat there trying to figure out why the hell she didn't want to date him; he was a good guy, and she did love him. The main reason she had not dated him in the past was that he was too boring and never did anything spectacular with his life, but wasn't that the exact same reason she didn't see Billy for the long term?

Her mental debate was interrupted by a loud knock. She quickly got up and ran to the door in anticipation. She knew it wasn't Justin; he definitely wouldn't be back. But she felt as if she did need a man right now and she was good to go.

The door swung open, and there stood Billy with a dozen roses in hand. He smiled when he saw her, and she smiled back.

"Cold?" he asked her.

Dusty's heart sank; she still was wearing the throw blanket. She shook her head and dropped it to the floor.

Billy paused as he took in the delightful sight before him. Everything wasn't perfect on her as she had planned; sitting in the blanket on the couch had messed everything up. But Billy didn't seem to notice. He stepped in and kissed her hard. Then he grabbed her by the hand and started for the stairs. She let him drag her along. They quickly went up the stairs. Halfway up, Billy stopped and kissed her again, but this time it was softer and longer. He took his time, enjoying exploring her mouth with his tongue. His hands fell to her waist; then his fingers slowly slid down to the hem on her negligee, grabbed it, and pulled it up over her head. Her arms were in the air the moment she felt the garment start to rise.

There was another quick yank on her arm. She had hoped for the Viking warrior treatment, but this was playing out surprisingly well. They hurried into the bedroom, and she helped him quickly undress as he kissed and stroked her body.

They spent the next thirty minutes upstairs, gratifying each other.

The bedroom door swung open, and Billy came down with a T-shirt and boxers on while Dusty followed, having chosen close to the same attire as her beau had.

After dinner and a delicious pie, they made their way back upstairs to the bedroom and spent the rest of the night alternating between lovemaking, talking, laughing, and sleeping.

When Billy left the next morning, Dusty smiled and breathed a sigh of relief. She had needed that for such a long time and living vicariously through Justin's sex life was no longer cutting it.

Her alarm on her phone went off, and she got up and got dressed for work.

Chapter

Sixty-One

Justin brought his cocoa to his lips and slowly drank the piping hot liquid. April brought his breakfast over to him and, instead of just placing it in front of him, sat down and grabbed a fork.

"So tell me what happened," she said as she poked a sausage and started nibbling on the end.

"I went to my aunt Martha's. We spent Thanksgiving there, and then I helped her move back here."

"No, dumbass. With Dusty last night."

"Aren't you supposed to be in school?"

"It's still winter break, besides its Saturday."

"Dusty had a date last night with some dude named Billy, I wasn't allowed to be there during that time," he said sarcastically.

"I heard you had to drop off a pie and got quite the tip for being the delivery boy."

Justin's face started to turn red.

"That sausage is your tip," Justin shot back.

"Uh huh. Tell me, what was she wearing? Was she completely naked?"

"How did you know about that anyway?"

"Dusty told me."

"No she didn't."

"Yeah she did, we were all surprised because she wasn't scheduled to come in till this afternoon," she said as she reached for another sausage, but Justin stabbed her with his fork.

"She came in early. Did her date show up?" April asked, surveying the plate for something else to steal.

"Yeah, but I guess he had to get going, so she decided to come in," Justin replied, shoveling his breakfast into his mouth.

"Ah, speak of the devil," Justin remarked as Dusty approached the booth and shooed April over.

"Let me see if I can guess what you two are discussing," Dusty said, also starting to survey the plate.

The bell on the door rang as Lori hurried into the diner.

"I am sorry I am late," she said as she pushed on Justin so he would move over.

"I am never sitting at a booth again," he dryly remarked.

"We cannot have a committee meeting unless we are all here," April said, eyeing Justin's plate.

"Oh, a committee meeting. Count me in," Lori said as Justin finally relented and gave her his seat.

"Might as well; we are dead this morning," Dusty remarked.

"I know; the roads are terrible. That's why I am late. I couldn't get out of my driveway with all the snow piled up from the plows. Good thing my neighbor saw my dilemma and got his snowblower out and cleared my driveway."

"He is single," Justin said with an impish grin.

"Yeah, and he has money," Dusty added.

"And he is like eighty," Lori rebuffed.

"Still," Justin joked while ribbing her.

"What are we meeting about? Oh, right, Dusty had her date last night," she said, ignoring Justin's attempts to get her riled up.

"Don't forget about her visitor before the date. Kind of a test run if you will," April added, sneaking another sausage off Justin's plate.

"Visitor? What visitor?" Lori asked, grabbing the last sausage off Justin's plate.

Justin groaned, and Dusty and April started giggling.

"What am I missing here?" Lori asked again.

"Cowboy here stopped by before her date to drop off dessert and got a little treat of his own," April said with her impish smile.

They explained the encounter before the encounter, much to Justin's chagrin. Dusty was openly honest with the committee, and the more she talked, the redder Justin got.

She covered from when she went upstairs to change till Justin had left. She didn't stop there and went straight into the date and how it went down. She did, however, skip the part where she pondered on the couch. That was too much to process, she and didn't know how Justin would react. She was getting feelings for him, but she didn't want to confuse him and quite frankly didn't know whether her feelings were real enough to act on them. She felt she might be just living a fantasy, thinking that they might ever be together.

"Sounds like a great night," Lori said when Dusty had finished telling them about her night.

"Are you dating Billy now, or is he one of those friends with benefits?" April asked curiously.

"I don't know. I mean, I do like him, but I was hoping he would have at least stayed for a while this morning. It seemed like he just couldn't wait to leave," Dusty said, taking a fork and stirring Justin's eggs around.

"I bet another romp in the sack wouldn't have hurt, either" commented Lori.

"Yeah, that would have been nice," Dusty agreed.

"Can I get some breakfast over here?" Justin hollered to one of the cooks who had come out from the bathroom and was heading back to the kitchen.

"You just ordered," April said with a mock innocent smile.

The girls had taken turns picking at his eggs, toast, and hash browns until the plate was practically bare.

"I will get you another order," Dusty remarked as the committee broke up.

Chapter

Sixty-Two

April brought out Justin's second breakfast and placed it in front of him.

"Thank you, April."

"You are welcome," she said a little glumly.

"What's up?" he asked, realizing the happy-go-lucky girl wasn't feeling so happy-go-lucky.

She slowly sat down and put her head in her hands.

"I think I am in love," she told him through her impromptu mask.

"That's the worst proclamation of love I have ever heard," he said with a chuckle.

"I mean, I know what I am feeling, but everyone keeps telling me I don't know what love is. They say I am too young and most likely things with Charlie won't work out and he is going to break my heart."

"How can you get your heart broken if you aren't in love?" Justin queried.

April looked up and thought about that.

"I never thought of it that way."

"Way I see it; you are in love, or you aren't."

"How do I know if I am or not?" April asked hopefully.

Justin realized he wasn't going to eat today's breakfast in peace. He didn't mind, because he could tell the teenager was in distress and he wanted to help her; he just didn't know how.

"I have always thought being in love isn't a choice. You cannot fall in or out; those are decisions. Love is something that grows inside of you, inside your heart. It affects every part of your life."

"What do you mean?"

"I guess you could say there are some signs."

"Like that feeling I get when I am around him?"

"Deeper than that. It's that feeling you get even when he is not around."

"Like during the day when I am thinking about him?"

"Yes, but the most important thing you need to remember about being in love …"

"What is that?"

"That person must make you a better person."

"What do you mean? I mean everyone tells me that I must be a better person first; then I will be ready to find that someone."

"That is only partly true, April. You must add value to you and who you are. The problem I see with most relationships, especially with women, is that the guy makes them feel good because they are paying attention to them. He will use flattery and other techniques to win them over so they will fulfill some fantasy or preconceived notions about how women should look or act or be."

"But what if I want to change for him?"

"There is nothing wrong with wanting to please your man and changing things to please him is part of a relationship. He should change things for you as well."

"You just said that he shouldn't ask me to change for him."

"No, I said he should add value to you. If he asks you to do something that takes away from you, then that is where the trouble begins."

"Like getting a boob job?" April asked after some thought.

"Well, um, I guess yes, that would be something that, if he urged you to get it and you weren't wanting to, then yes."

"That would add value to me, wouldn't it?"

"If it is something that you wanted, then yes; but if you are only getting one to make him happy, then it might not be the best move for you."

"How do I know if he is adding value or just being selfish?"

"If he doesn't accept you as you are, then that should be the clue."

"Dating is hard," April said with remorse.

"Yes, dating is hard, but people are harder. In this era of online dating, people are finding out they have many options to choose from, and when they find one thing they don't like about a person, they are quick to jump off the boat and find another boat to jump on. That is why being patient and taking your time is so important. Time reveals a person's true character and will let you know whether he or she is there for the long haul or just trying to get some booty."

"How do I know if Charlie is right for me right now?"

"When you wake up, is he the first thing you think of? How about when you go to bed; is he the last thing on your mind before you fall asleep? Are you excited to tell him first about your day and the highs and lows in it? Do you want to make him happy? Do you look forward to spending time with him? Can you see living with him every day?"

"I do; I love being around him, and I think about him all the time."

"Do you smile when you think about him?"

She couldn't suppress the smile that lit up her face.

"Yes," she replied shyly.

"Sounds like you are in love to me."

"So you don't think I am too young to be in love?"

"Look, April, don't listen to those women back there or anyone else to tell you what to think and feel. I know women of all ages who haven't figured out what real love is. You can tell because they go from boyfriend to boyfriend, in and out of relationships and marriages, thinking that this time they have it figured out, only to realize the guy is not the prince charming of their dreams. There are very few people that have love figured out."

"How will I know? How do I know if Charlie is the right one for me?"

"Honestly?"

"Of course."

"Spend time with him and save sex for when the time is right."

"Uh-oh."

"You already had sex with him?"

"Well, I … um, we fooled around the other day."

She looked at Justin and saw him shake his head. She then turned around to see Dusty giving them a curious look, and then Dusty shrugged and went back into her office.

"How did that go?" Justin asked, looking back at the teenager.

"I liked it. It felt really good. I liked making him happy."

"Of course it did. Sharing your body with someone is not only exhilarating; it feels wonderful."

"I don't think I am ready to go all the way, though," April said.

"That's fair enough."

"But I really want to take that next step," she said slowly.

"What is the next step?"

"I want to be intimate with him. Like, really intimate."

"Sex is the result of intimacy, not the pursuit of it," Justin said carefully.

"Whoa, dude, that was deep."

"It's the truth."

"No, I mean that was *really* deep."

"April, you have to understand that sex is only a small part of the relationship. There will be times when you cannot have sex or don't want to. He is going to have to want to be

223

with you during those times. If he is only spending time with you so he can see you naked, then you are with the wrong guy."

"So I shouldn't have sex with him?"

"You should do what you want to, but my advice is to only do it when the timing is right. Remember to practice safe sex, and you should probably wait."

"Like, after the third date?"

"No, that is dumb. Do it when you both agree the time is right."

"He thinks that time is right now."

"Of course he does. Guys think the time is always right for sex."

"But I want to wait."

"All right, so the time is not right. Remember: your body is a gift only you can give to whomever you choose, whenever you choose. You should try to hold out till you are eighteen or, better yet, have moved into your own place."

"Why is that?"

"Because once you have it, you are going to want to do it all the time. I am sure your parents are going to object to that. It will make your life complicated even if they don't find out."

"But doesn't that mean I don't love him?"

"Of course not. It means you want to reach intimacy with him."

"And that isn't caused by sex, but it causes sex."

"Exactly. Feel better?"

"Yes, much better. Thank you, Cowboy," she told him as she got up and kissed his cheek while she slipped another sausage off his plate before skipping to the kitchen.

Justin finished his breakfast and sat there drinking his cocoa and contemplating his own nightmare he called his dating life. Dusty came over and cleared his table, and he then brought over a saucer that held one of the biggest cinnamon rolls Justin had ever seen.

"Whoa, that thing is enormous," he remarked as he marveled at the pastry.

"It was Marco's idea."

"Who is Marco?"

"One of the new cooks we hired. He is pretty awesome, and he has been suggesting new items to our menu since we are now a full-fledged restaurant."

"Well, it looks good for sure."

"I have been wanting one but couldn't eat a whole one by myself."

"Really?"

"Shut up. Anyways, did April tell you about her debauchery?" Dusty asked, picking at the roll.

"Yep. Well, sort of. She didn't go into much detail."

"What did you tell her?"

"That is between us. How are you doing?"

"Eh, Billy wasn't quite the romantic I was hoping for."

"So a no-go?"

"Oh, I am going to use him for sex for sure. He is good while he lasts for the five minutes."

Justin spit out his cocoa.

"Dumbass," Dusty said while she wiped up the mess.

"Sorry, but that was funny."

"Don't get me wrong, he is rather good in the sack. He does things to get me off. But once he gets off, he is not much for conversation or even snuggling."

"No romance though? Not even on the dates?"

"Oh, he was the perfect gentleman, but the rest of it is average at best. He doesn't want to talk or cuddle, and I am thinking he doesn't want to have an official relationship with me—just his booty call when he isn't working."

"How often is that?"

"Usually for a week every three to five weeks he comes home."

"And you are okay with that?"

"Sure, for now. I mean, getting laid once a month is better than nothing, and I don't have to worry about him cheating. I think it will work out for now."

"Well, good for you."

"What about you?"

"Joleen called me the other day."

Dusty looked shocked. She leaned back and crossed her arms. Justin could tell she was visibly upset by the scowl on his friend's face.

"What did that bit—" she stopped before she finished the word bitch.

"She called me when we were at Auntie Martha's," Justin continued.

"What? How did she know you were there?"

"She didn't. Auntie Martha had always liked her, and they often talked on the phone when we were married."

"So she felt like it was okay to continue that relationship after what she did?" Dusty asked harshly.

"I don't think they talk a lot anymore. She was just calling her to wish her a Happy Thanksgiving. Then she said she had been informed that I was there and wanted to know if it was okay to chat with me."

"And you agreed?"

"Yup."

"Dumbass."

"Maybe."

"Well? What happened?"

"We talked."

"About?" Dusty looked as if she was getting irritated at him. He figured this was because he was making her wait or not giving her all the information she wanted.

"At first it was just catching up," he continued.

"Then?"

"Then we talked about what happened between us."

"Did she tell you why she left?"

"Nope, and I didn't ask."

"Why not?"

"Because I am over it. No use digging up the past and reliving that pain."

"Did she want you back?"

"That hardheaded woman would never admit to that. She did talk about her dating a couple of different guys. Seems she is finding the same guys you are."

"She dated some of the guys I dated?"

"No. Well, I don't know that; she has just been running into a bunch of Chads that are romancing her until they get into her pants. Then, when they get tired of her or find someone else, they fly the coop."

"Serves her right."

"I got the impression she wanted to try again, but every time it came up, I steered the conversation elsewhere."

"Good for you."

"I think that made her want me more."

"Women do seem to want what they cannot have."

"It was a good chat, but I now know that I am over her, and I don't even want her back."

Dusty looked stunned. She fiddled with her roll and then broke off a piece and ate it.

"Good for you. So what will you do now?" she asked after she finished off her bite and drank some milk to wash it down.

"I don't know at this point. Wendy is dating; there aren't really any good prospects right now, and, well, I don't know."

"I think Suzie and Brad are going to be done soon."

"Really? It's really hard for me to keep up with where she is at with that guy."

"Me too, but Suzie is starting to see the writing on the wall. I talked to her, and she said she doesn't want to give the restaurant up and misses being here running it."

"Do you think I should call her?" Justin asked hopefully.

"I think you should man up and tell her how you feel."

"I don't want to be the reason they break up."

"You won't be. That ship has already sailed. They are just dragging this out."

"Why would they do that?"

"Because they are comfortable with each other, and probably because they are horny. No one likes a breakup."

"I can attest to that."

"It's more than that. Your situation was different. In this situation, they were both lonely and looking for companionship. They found each other and decided to give it a go. More than likely, they didn't talk much about the future or what their plans were and jumped right into bed. If they had taken time to get to know each other, they might not have even dated."

"I agree; that's what April and I were talking about."

"Her and her puppy love?"

"Momma and Daddy met when she was fifteen. It seemed to work out for them just fine," Justin informed her.

"But she is too young to know—"

"Know what?" Justin said, cutting her off. "Know what true love is? Do you?"

"Good point," admitted Dusty.

"What should I do about Suzie?"

"Call her. That would be a start."

"What do I tell her?"

"Tell her how you feel. Didn't you tell me to put it all on the line?"

"I sure did," he said thoughtfully.

Chapter

Sixty-Three

Two weeks later, Justin pulled his truck to a stop outside the Walkers' house, which he had grown up in, and looked at it as he reminisced about his childhood and growing up there. *Things sure have changed a lot over the last fifteen years. Heck, over the last year.* He remembered just a few months ago, when he had walked up the stairs and sat on the rocking chair by the door and cried until his mother came out and comforted him. It was then that she had offered him to use his old room until he got his feet under him.

From then on, his life had taken a direction he had not expected nor wanted at the time, but now he was glad it had. There was something he had to do, and now was the time to do it.

He slowly got out and pulled off his hat and wiped the sweat from his forehead. He was about to do something bold and spontaneous that he had been secretly planning for a while now and was glad to see things were falling into place.

He had started the ball rolling last Saturday when he called Mrs. Charlotte, the farm's accountant, an old family friend. She had been reluctant to talk about finances and the direction of the farm without Doreen present. It wasn't that Justin was doing anything wrong, as he surely had the authority to do so, but Doreen was a firecracker and was adamant about being involved in every aspect of the ranch's business. Justin assured her that he was only checking on a few things, but she resisted. Exasperated, he relented and laid out his plans to the retired schoolteacher-turned-accountant of his upcoming daring adventure.

Mrs. Charlotte was thrilled about the plan and eagerly went to work crunching numbers and helping Justin with a part of his plan he couldn't have done by himself. He wasn't dumb and understood numbers, but he had to make sure that his own calculations were correct and that this part of his grand scheme was feasible under the worst of circumstances.

Two hours later, Mrs. Charlotte called to confirm that the numbers looked good. The worst could happen, and everything would be okay. He hung up the phone with a smile. Then he dialed another number he wasn't positive was still good, but the voice answered and assured him he was talking to Rico. Little Ricky, as he preferred to be called, answered with his thick Hispanic accent. Justin inquired about his plans for the upcoming spring and his long-term plans. Little Ricky enthusiastically agreed that he and his two helpers would be more than up to the task.

Justin always liked the trio; they were hardworking and more than capable hands they had hired to help Justin run the farm when Benson could no longer keep up. After his death, Justin and Doreen had agreed to keep them on every year during the busier times and lay them off when the work got slow. Justin had just negotiated their employment to a year-round position to make sure the ranch would always be looked after.

"Check and check," Justin said to himself as he went down his list he had scribbled on his reliable old notebook.

He knew he was going to have to eventually tell Dusty about his plans, but that blabbermouth was going to have to wait like everyone else. He was apprehensive about Mrs. Charlotte letting the cat out of the bag before the time was right, but that was a risk he had to take. This whole week she had kept her word, and no one was the wiser.

Justin saw the curtains in the kitchen move as two faces appeared, staring out at him. He smiled and waved.

"Here goes nothing," he said to himself.

The steps creaked as he slowly walked up them and entered the house. He paused as he sat in the chair next to the door and pulled off his boots and then slipped out of his jacket and hung it on the coat rack.

The breath he took felt like his last as he tried to calm the butterflies in his stomach. He was getting to the end of his checklist. Everything had fallen into place better than he had expected, but this checkmark was the pivotal point in whether his plan would move forward or be derailed.

The two women were sitting at the table. Doreen was doing a crossword puzzle while Martha was struggling with her Sudoku.

"Hi, Momma, Auntie Martha," he said with his best smile.

"Justin," Auntie Martha said without looking up.

"How was breakfast?" Doreen asked, looking up from her puzzle.

"We need to talk," he replied, figuring to dismiss the small talk and beating around the bush. Doreen would have called him out in a minute on his bull if he had tried to sweeten the blow. Besides, she wanted everything straight, and he could tell by the look in her eyes she knew something was up.

"I need to go make my bed," Martha said as she started to get up.

"No, it's okay, Auntie; you can stay," Justin assured her.

"You are going to listen in anyway," Doreen said with a smirk, never taking her worried eyes off her son.

Justin sat down and pulled out the folded-up papers from his breast pocket, laid them carefully on the table, and used his hands to carefully straighten out the creases. He then took another long, deep, breath.

The kitchen was deathly quiet; only the old clock could be heard ticking as it counted off the seconds. The two women were staring at him hard and folded their hands as they waited patiently on the next words to come out of his mouth.

Justin carefully read over the first page and then dived into a speech he had been rehearsing for over a week now. His words were succinct and well thought out. His numbers, which Mrs. Charlotte had given him, were explained thoroughly, and he was sure to add they had been checked by the accountant.

It took him close to an hour to lay out his intentions and the ramifications of the journey he was about to undertake.

"Well?" he asked when he was finished.

"Do it!" Martha exclaimed.

Doreen got up and wiped a tear out of her eye.

"Of course we support you! I am glad you have finally manned up and found your purpose in life."

"It's about damn time," Martha added.

"Thank you, Momma."

Chapter

Sixty-Four

Suzie wrote down the numbers on her pad next to her great-grandma's bed with all of her vitals on it.

"Do we have to do this every day?" her grandmother moaned.

"Three times, doctor's orders. Besides, I have to do all the work; you just have to lie there," Suzie joked.

"How about for noontime I take the readings and you lie here and get poked and prodded," she joked back.

The doorbell rang, and they both looked at each other curiously.

"Don't look at me," Grandma said, shrugging. "You are the one that has a suitor and an addiction to online ordering."

"Brad and I are over, and I haven't ordered anything lately."

"Does he know it's over?"

"Well, I did tell him that I needed space."

"That never works, you need to tell him to leave you alone."

"I know, I know," Suzie said solemnly.

The doorbell rang again.

"Well, it's not a package; they only ring once and then run away," Suzie said as she laid the pad on her grandma's lap so she could read the numbers.

Suzie made her way to the front door, feeling apprehensive; she didn't want to see Brad or talk to him right now. She paused as she put her hand on the doorknob.

Maybe if I don't answer, he will go away, she thought to herself.

The bell rang again.

"Suzie!" Grandma yelled from her bed.

Suzie pulled open the door and stood in shock.

Before her stood not Brad, but a tall, lanky cowboy with flowers in one hand and a suitcase in the other.

"Justin? What are you …?" she stammered.

Before she could finish, Justin dropped the suitcase, grabbed her waist, and pulled her to him. He kissed her hard and long. Suzie, a bit surprised, went rigid but then melted into him, put her arms around his neck, and kissed him back eagerly.

"Wow," she said when they stopped.

"Suzie, I have wanted you ever since I met you. I know this is spontaneous, but I don't want to lose you, and I could not bear living one more minute without knowing how I felt about you."

"This is so sudden. I don't know what to say. What about Doreen and your farm?"

"I have that all worked out. I just wanted to be close to you."

"What are you going to do?"

"Well, if you want to try this, I am going to get a job here. I have plenty of money to last for a while. I can get an apartment here, and we can …" He stopped short as Suzie saw him staring at something behind her.

Suzie whirled around and saw her grandma wearing a nightgown and a hairnet, and carrying the largest, oldest shotgun she had ever seen. Grandma was struggling to bring the gun up to level.

"Grandma!" Suzie exclaimed.

"Who is that?" The grandma asked as she finally got the gun level with Justin's belt.

"I am Justin, ma'am," he said nervously.

"Grandma!" Suzie cried again. "Put that down."

"I was just trying to scare off that damn Brad. Besides, it isn't even loaded," she said, putting the gun down by her chair.

"Well, it worked; I don't see that damn Brad anywhere," Justin joked.

"What exactly is going on here? I thought you were in Montana," Grandma said as she pointed her bony finger at Justin.

"Well, I, um … I came to check up on Suzie," Justin replied slowly.

"It's so nice to finally meet you, sir." Grandma said as she extended her hand. "I've heard so much about you."

Justin took the woman's hand and shook it gingerly.

"I hope it was all good stuff," Justin remarked.

"I am glad you are here; Suzie needs a real man in her life. From what I heard, you fit the bill."

"Grandma!" Suzie scolded.

"Suzie, make up the guest room for our handsome cowboy."

"That's okay, I am going to get a hotel room till I can find somewhere to stay."

"Posh." It was Grandma's turn to scold. "Besides, you will be sleeping in Suzie's bed before long anyway."

"Grandma!" Suzie exclaimed again.

Grandma waved her hand at Suzie and pulled Justin inside and led him back to her third bedroom. Suzie stood there dumbfounded with a giant smile on her face.

Sixty-Five

Two days later, Justin was helping Grandma with the dishes when he heard his phone ring. He dried his hands and saw "Dusty" on the screen. He smiled, picked it up, and pressed the green button to answer; he then held the phone to his ear.

"You are an ass!" Dusty told Justin.

"What, no 'Hi, hello, how're things going?'" Justin asked.

"Hi, hello, how're things going … You're still an ass!" Dusty shot back.

"Why, because I didn't tell you I was leaving?"

"Exactly. I would have kept your secret," Dusty insisted.

"Listen, blabbermouth, one thing you cannot do is keep a secret. You are too transparent."

"Still, you should have said something."

"You talk to Suzie every day; she would have suspected something."

"That doesn't mean I would have told her," she insisted again.

"Dusty, we both know how you are."

"I know, I just wanted to know. So how is it going so far?"

"Great. Actually really great. Even Grandma is on board."

"Really?"

"Yeah, she insisted I move in with them right away."

"Really? You go, Cowboy."

"I am excited about the future."

"I bet you are. Well, sounds like my job of wingman paid off."

"More than you know. Dusty, I really appreciate what you did for me and what you taught me, even though it didn't turn out the way we expected. I will always be grateful."

"I guess my work here is finished," Dusty said, and she clicked off.

Suzie walked in and gave Justin a kiss on the cheek.

"Was that Dusty?" Suzie asked as Justin clicked off the phone.

"Yep."

"How is she?"

"Jealous."

Suzie smiled and stretched up to give Justin a kiss. He gently pushed her back.

"What's that all about?" she asked, sounding surprised and confused.

Justin leaned over and put his shoulder into her waist and lifted quickly. She let out a delighted yelp.

"Ever had the Viking warrior treatment?" he asked as he hurriedly took her to his room.

"I am, well, um … no," she said breathlessly, hanging upside down.

He set her down in front of the bed and then ripped her shirt open. The buttons flew off, and then he quickly started kissing her.

They undressed each other as quickly as their awkward hands would let them. When they were completely naked, Justin threw her on the bed and then joined her.

Thirty minutes later, they both lay there side by side, breathing hard, holding hands, and smiling uncontrollably.

"Was it worth it?" Suzie asked.

Justin thought about their journey from high school to now. He thought about the life lessons he had learned, and the things Dusty had taught him. He hoped he would never have to go through that again, but if he did, he knew he would need a wingman.

"You were always worth it," he replied, and then he kissed her long and hard.

Printed in the United States
by Baker & Taylor Publisher Services